HAIR RAISER

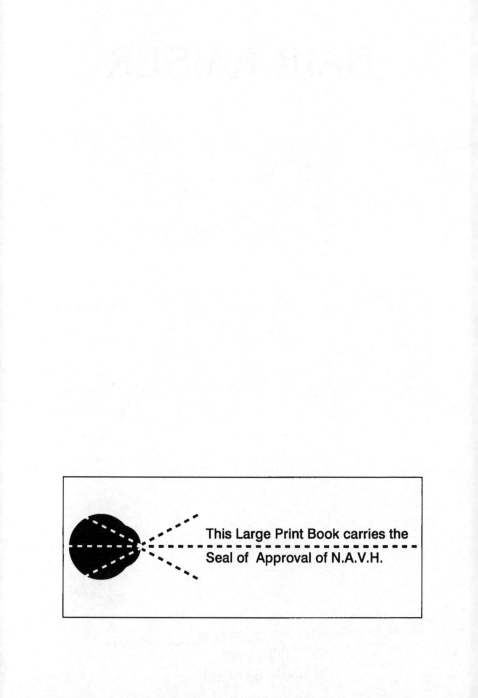

This Large Print Book carries the
Seal of Approval of N.A.V.H.

HAIR RAISER

A Bad Hair Day Mystery

Nancy J. Cohen

Thorndike Press • Waterville, Maine

Published in 2003 by arrangement with Kensington Books, an imprint of Kensington Publishing Corp.

Thorndike Press® Large Print Paperback.

The tree indicium is a trademark of Thorndike Press.

The text of this Large Print edition is unabridged.
Other aspects of the book may vary from the original edition.

Set in 16 pt. Plantin by Liana M. Walker.

Printed in the United States on permanent paper.

Library of Congress Control Number: 2003111456
ISBN 0-7862-6045-9 (lg. print : sc : alk. paper)

To my husband, Richard, and my children, Paul and Sara: Your love, patience, and support have given me the confidence and determination to achieve my dreams. May you find happiness, peace, and success in your future.

As the Founder/CEO of NAVH, the only national health agency solely devoted to those who, although not totally blind, have an eye disease which could lead to serious visual impairment, I am pleased to recognize Thorndike Press* as one of the leading publishers in the large print field.

Founded in 1954 in San Francisco to prepare large print textbooks for partially seeing children, NAVH became the pioneer and standard setting agency in the preparation of large type.

Today, those publishers who meet our standards carry the prestigious "Seal of Approval" indicating high quality large print. We are delighted that Thorndike Press is one of the publishers whose titles meet these standards. We are also pleased to recognize the significant contribution Thorndike Press is making in this important and growing field.

Lorraine H. Marchi, L.H.D.
Founder/CEO
NAVH

* Thorndike Press encompasses the following imprints: Thorndike, Wheeler, Walker and Large Pr int Press.

Acknowledgments

My gratitude to the following for their valuable input:

Captain Joseph Bush, Plantation Police Department; Rabbi Jonathan S. Kaplan; and James Miller, DDS.

Special thanks to my agent, Linda Hyatt, and to my editor, Karen Thomas, for making this mystery series a reality and for bringing my story from manuscript to printed page.

1

"You must treat her like a lover. Stroke her tenderly, undress her, and zen unleash your desire when you devour her. I guarantee you will be satisfied."

Chef Pierre Chevalier fixed his class of fifteen wanna-be cooks with a stern glare. Holding up an unblemished banana, he waved it in the air like a giant phallic symbol. "Observe ze proper technique. To make Bananas Foster, first begin by peeling ze skin with a gentle hand to avoid bruising."

With infinite care, he pared one piece after another as though stripping off his lover's garments. His gaze deepened as he stared longingly at the naked fruit glistening in his hand. "You see? Look at ze velvety smoothness of zis shaft. Ze moist tip and firm inner core remind you of something, no?" A chuckle rumbled from his throat. "Zis we can put in ze mouth, too, but only after it is properly prepared."

Marla watched his movements, amazed that such a stout man with a round face could be so sexy. Perhaps that accounted for the popularity of Pierre's culinary classes. "Never mind the innuendos, I'm gaining five pounds just by sitting here," she commented to her friend Tally Riggs beside her.

The chef finished slicing the banana into a bowl. Several more fruits met the same fate before Pierre melted a chunk of butter in a skillet. He added the banana slices, sprinkling cinnamon on top until a delicious fragrance filled the air.

Tally's blue eyes twinkled. "I could never get brown sugar to melt that way without scorching the pan."

"Wait until he adds the rum. Did you ever think food could inspire such passion? No wonder people flock to his restaurant. Pierre will be a big draw at Taste of the World."

"Ken and I bought tickets already. He feels it's important to support Ocean Guard's fund-raiser. You know how he gets a kick out of joining their beach cleanups." Tally laughed. "It makes me think Ken is a beachcomber at heart. Your cousin is hosting the affair at her estate again, isn't she?"

"Yeah, and she's getting nervous. We have less than two months to get everything ready. I can't believe I let her con me into working as chef liaison for the event. At least I've met most of the major participants, including Pierre."

As Marla watched, he removed the skillet from the heat. His fingers flew through the practiced motions of warming a measure of rum gently in a separate saucepan. "Zis is le *grand finale,* ze moment of ecstasy," he cooed, pursing his lips in an air kiss. "All zat foreplay was just building up to zis eruption of heat. You are hungry, no?"

"Yeah, but not for what you have in mind," Marla muttered. Lifting the smaller pot, he poured liquor over the bubbling bananas. A sugary fragrance wafted into her nostrils, making her stomach growl. Nine o'clock on Wednesday evening, and she hadn't eaten dinner yet. Everyone was waiting to sample the dishes after Pierre finished his demos. *Let's wrap it up, pal,* she thought, folding her packet of recipes and stuffing them in her purse.

Pierre's tall white toque bobbed on his head as he lit a match and tilted it toward the warmed rum in the skillet. The flame had barely touched the liquid when an explosion rocked the room, sending a wall of

11

fire shooting into the air. *"Mon Dieu!"* Pierre cried, tumbling backward to disappear behind the roaring flames.

"Quick! Everyone out!" shouted his assistant, grabbing a fire extinguisher mounted on a wall unit.

Marla hustled away with the others, hovering in an anteroom of the restaurant while someone called for help on a cell phone.

Smoke billowed from the classroom, forcing her and the others to fall back. As time ticked by, sirens wailed in the distance, becoming progressively louder. Coughing and choking, the chef surged from the doorway, leaning heavily on his assistant. His face, reddened and dry, appeared as though it might blister. He cradled his hands against his chest, and she could see that his forearms had been singed. Rushing forward to come to his aid, she halted when his wild-eyed gaze captured her.

"Forget my taking part in Taste of the World. I should have listened to ze warning. Now see what has happened!" His voice cracked, and he ended in a fit of wheezing coughs.

"You should've listened to what?" Marla stared in confusion until the smell of burning plastic coming from the classroom reached her lungs. Gasping for a breath of fresh air, she staggered toward the exit. Outside, fire engines screeched to a stop at the curb. Within seconds, uniformed firefighters charged into the restaurant. Several of them headed for the classroom, from which smoke swirled in acrid increments.

"Tell me what you meant," she called desperately as the chef was positioned on a stretcher by paramedics. Herded outside with her classmates, she followed him to the rescue truck.

A raspy breath rattled in his chest as he shook a finger at her. "You'll see, Miss Shore. Ocean Guard is cursed. You had better quit working for zem before something happens to you."

"What's he talking about?" Tally said, trailing after her.

"I have no idea." Marla's opportunity to question him evaporated when the police took charge and began interviewing witnesses. "Come on, let's get out of here," she urged when they were free to depart. Leading the way, Marla strode along the cracked sidewalk toward the parking lot in the rear. Dimly lit streetlamps cast flickering shadows into the surrounding foliage. Pierre's restaurant, Chez Moi, held a venerable place in downtown Fort Lauderdale behind Las Olas Boulevard. Established five years ago, it drew in a young crowd with its trendy menu and lack of early-bird specials. Marla sniffed gratefully at the sweet scent from a Hong Kong orchid tree, eager to clear her nose of the pungent smell of smoke.

"I hope Pierre will be okay," she said, when they were heading west to Palm Haven in her white Toyota Camry. "Thank goodness no one else was hurt." Her appetite had dissipated with the smoke, even though neither of them had eaten anything substantial since lunch. "Want to stop for a quick meal?" she offered halfheartedly.

Tally pushed back a strand of wavy blond hair and gave her an apologetic glance. "I'd better go home, or Ken will wonder what's happened to me. Rats, I was really looking forward to tasting that food. Can you believe the rum was that volatile?"

Marla shook her head, eyes focused on the road. "Something else must have been added to the liquor. It wouldn't normally react that way. Didn't you hear what Pierre said about a warning? Bless my bones, I'm really getting concerned."

"I didn't quite catch your conversation."

"He said he should've heeded the warning, and if I didn't withdraw from helping Ocean Guard, I'd be sorry. This isn't the first incident. I'm beginning to wonder if someone is sabotaging my efforts."

Tally raised a penciled eyebrow. "What is it you haven't been telling me, Marla?"

Marla swallowed guiltily. She usually told her best friend everything, but she'd discounted each problem as being separate. Now she began to get a glimmer that these weren't random acts at all. "Including Pierre, three of the chefs have resigned from Taste of the World. Three of the Big Ten. This can't be mere coincidence. Someone is out to get me."

A black sedan shot in front of her car, and she jammed on the brakes. Tally grabbed hold of her seat cushion. "You, or Ocean Guard?" she squeaked.

"Well, not me really." Marla's racing heart calmed as she changed lanes and sped away from the erratic driver. "Although I don't see why anyone would be out to get Ocean Guard either. I'll have to talk to Cynthia about this."

"You've been seeing your cousin a lot more than me lately."

It wasn't like Tally to sound petulant. Marla glanced at her, feeling a twinge of remorse. Maybe she had become neglectful since she began working on this project. Her grip tightened on the steering wheel. "Sorry, but ever since Cynthia roped me into working with her, I haven't had any spare time. As if I don't have enough to do working in my salon all day!"

Tally's face softened. "If I recall, you were happy to accept Cynthia's offer since you had to cut back your hours in the salon after your hands were injured. It's not as if she forced you into taking the job. It gave you a chance to recover from your struggle with Bertha Kravitz's killer."

"Yeah, but now I'm back to a full work week. I should've just signed up for Cynthia's volunteer committee instead of agreeing to be coordinator for the chefs. Anyway, Jonathan Doherty from The Backyard Bistro and Emilio Gastroni resigned. Jon's place had a fire break out two weeks ago, and Emilio got a citation for hiring illegal immigrants."

Tally looked out a side window while they passed the Salvation Army thrift store and crossed an overpass for I-95. When they reached an unsavory section of deserted storefronts, she turned her face back toward Marla.

"So why do you think something is wrong? Taste of the World is such a popular event."

"I wish I knew. It's just a gut feeling. But even you have to admit that three instances must be more than coincidence." Hadn't her instincts in the past proved reliable? Witness the two new staff members in her salon. She hadn't been willing to believe anyone close to her would do her harm, but she'd learned differently. Now she was more attuned to listening to her inner voice.

"Cynthia has been in charge of the fundraiser each year because the gala event is held at her estate," she explained. "I've gotten the impression that this year is especially significant, but I'm not sure why. I'll have to let Cynthia know what's been happening. So far I've been able to get substitutes for the two chefs who've resigned, but if this keeps on, we'll run into trouble. It's nearly time for us to send out press releases regarding the program."

"Why don't you consult Detective Vail for his opinion?"

"This isn't a homicide case, so I doubt Dalton would be interested. Anyway, I don't see him so often."

Tally snorted. "I thought he came around rather regularly."

"The man stops in for a haircut every month." She caught Tally's look. "All right, I've grabbed a bite to eat with him a few times. What's the *megillah* in that? We're just friends."

"Lieutenant Vail is not the sort of man for casual friendships." Tally flicked a polished fingernail at a speck of dust on her loosely styled pantsuit. Marla admired the silky material, which shimmered in tints of gold and red. Her own black skirt and forest green sweater seemed bland in comparison, but earth tones suited her bobbed brown hair and matching eyes.

She didn't answer Tally at once, her mind focused on passing through an intersection and continuing west. Derelict street corners and older homes in need of maintenance gave way to lushly landscaped shopping centers and upscale residences. Was this symbolic of her relationship to Dalton? Had she graduated from a prime murder suspect in his view, after Bertha Kravitz's killer was found, to a personal friend? It was hard to tell where she stood on his list, not that Marla was sure how she felt about him herself. She liked the enigmatic detective, but feared their attraction to each other might fall apart if they got closer. The old adage, familiarity breeds contempt, rang in her mind. Hadn't she worshiped Stanley, her hateful ex-spouse, until married life exposed his controlling nature? Why ruin a

18

good thing with the widowed detective by getting more involved? At thirty-four years old, she was happy with her life.

Tally snickered, her dark crimson lips turning up. "You don't have to say anything else, Marla. I know you like him. Why don't you get his opinion about the chefs?"

"I'll see," she said in a noncommittal tone. "First I'm going to pay some of them a visit. I'd like to know if anyone else has been issued a warning."

She'd only been to Dmitri Sarvik's restaurant once, and that was to introduce herself as chef coordinator for Taste of the World. Marla decided to start with him since it had been a while since she'd contacted the Greek restaurant owner. Maybe he'd have some new developments to report. Actually, it was strange that she hadn't heard from him lately. This was November, meaning soon they'd get into the holiday crunch. She needed everything to be finalized by Thanksgiving since the big event was scheduled for December 18. So little time, too much to do.

Greek food was okay by her standards, but it wasn't one of her favorites. Nicole enjoyed it, though, so Marla decided to invite her fellow stylist along. She'd noticed Nicole entering the storeroom during a break in their busy Saturday afternoon schedule. As soon as she was free, Marla strode toward the room at the rear of the salon. Preparing for her next customer, she selected a tube of color from a shelf lined with supplies and took it to a sink.

"Hey, Nicole, can I treat you to dinner tonight?" she asked, pouring two ounces of developer into a plastic applicator bottle, then adding an equal amount from the tube.

"What, don't you have a hot date later?" The dark-skinned stylist grinned, glancing up from the mystery novel she'd been reading. She wore a white, collared shirt under a beige vest with khaki pants. The outfit added to her sleek look, augmented by ebony hair pulled into a high ponytail; a tall, lithe figure; and a graceful columned neck.

"Nope, not this evening." Marla shook the bottle to blend its contents, then squeezed out a few drops to make sure the tip was clean. She spared a moment to glimpse the title of Nicole's latest addiction. Her friend was a book junkie, devouring mysteries and medical thrillers. Marla suspected she was a frustrated medical student who couldn't stand the sight of real blood. "So tell me, what is *Off the Cuff* about?"

Nicole's coffee eyes twinkled. "It's about

a patient strangled by a sphygmomanometer, otherwise known as a blood pressure device. Naturally one of the doctors is a prime suspect in the story, but I think it's the respiratory therapy man."

"Oh. So are you free tonight? I didn't make any plans. Ralph is busy, Dalton went out of town, and I thought tonight would be a good time to visit some of the chefs on my list."

"Why don't you ask Arnie? He'd jump at the chance to escort you anywhere."

Marla rolled her eyes. The owner of Bagel Busters persisted in asking her out despite her kind refusals. Although she was fond of Arnie, and found the widowed father of two rather attractive, she had no desire to get involved with him in any way other than friendship.

"Dmitri's place is Greek. I know how much you like moussaka. Want to go or not?"

"Heck, I suppose. Besides, Eddie promised to take his aunt to Jai Alai tonight, and I hate that game. So sure, I'll go."

Dmitri insisted on giving them a tour of the kitchen when Marla mentioned to the waiter that she needed to speak to him. She and Nicole finished their Greek salads before following the man toward the rear of the restaurant where several cooks sweated over a smoky grill. Hickory smoke rose rich and pungent in the air, and the smell of cooking onions stung her eyes. Dmitri strode out of a rear doorway through which she could just spot prep workers chopping and dicing vegetables.

"Marla Shore!" Dmitri cried, widening his arms to embrace her in a bear hug. She caught a whiff of garlic as his large torso crushed her slender frame. "You honor me by your visit."

When he released her, Marla studied him with a grin. A walrus black mustache drooped over his upper lip. His florid face beamed with a welcoming smile reflected in the warmth of his obsidian eyes. "This is my friend Nicole," she said. "I wanted to ask you how things were going regarding Taste of the World."

"Ah, yes. I was just reviewing my menu the other day. It should work out well as long as my suppliers come through. Did you receive the copy I sent you?"

She nodded, stepping out of the way while a waiter rushed past carrying a breadbasket filled with fragrant rolls. "So, uh, does this mean you still can participate in Taste of the World?"

Dmitri threw her a look of puzzlement. "Of course, why would I not? I am flattered to have been invited."

"That's great. Well, let me know if you need anything." Obviously, he hadn't received any threats. Marla wasn't about to clue him in regarding the warning Pierre had mentioned. Thank God Dmitri was unaffected. Now who should she check on next?

"Let's go have dessert over at the Seafood Emporium," Marla suggested after she and Nicole had both finished a generous portion of moussaka. When their attentive waiter approached holding out a platter with a delectable array of sweets, she shook her head, declining the temptation of a syrupy slice of baklava. "We're not far from the other restaurant, so we might as well stop in there to talk to Max. He's next on my list."

"Hey, girl, I'm going to get fat going out with you!" Nicole complained.

Marla pretended to scrutinize her friend's narrow waistline. "I don't think so, pal. You're one of those disgusting people who never gain weight."

Max was preparing a sauce to go with grilled trout when they entered his kitchen. "Hey, gals," the tall blond young man said while he whisked cream into a boiling mixture of dry white wine, balsamic vinegar, and minced shallots. When the cream had blended in, he added diced tomatoes. Marla recognized the ingredients from her gourmet cooking days when she was married to Stan. Now she had little time to cook, let alone follow recipes.

"This is Nicole. We stopped in for some dessert," Marla explained. "I just wanted to confirm your arrangements for Taste of the World."

Max cut a chunk of butter into the sauce, his wrist rotating with rapid, deft movements. "Everything is fine." A curl of hair fell forward onto his forehead as he bent over to sniff the aroma emanating from the pan.

"You haven't heard from anyone else about the event?"

"Nope. Been too busy." He cast a furtive glance about the room. "You ladies got to excuse me, but I don't have time to chat. We're a cook short tonight, and I've got to do some of my own prep work. Y'all go on out and enjoy your dessert."

He stalked away from them, ostensibly to get some ingredients to add to his dish, but Marla had the distinct impression they were being dismissed. Was he being less talkative than usual because others were in the room?

Maybe she'd corner him another time when they could be alone.

After dropping Nicole off at home, she decided to make one more stop before turning in for the night. Saturday was too good an opportunity to miss since all the chefs were at work. Robbie from the Cajun Cookpot hadn't responded to her latest inquiry. It was worth driving to Davie to ask why he hadn't contacted her.

Too stuffed to order any more meals, she skirted the front door and headed for an employee entrance down a side alley. As she approached, the smell of garbage overwhelmed her. An open trash bin stood outside the kitchen door, its contents loaded beyond the rim. Insects buzzed around, flying in and out the open door to the kitchen from where the sounds of banging pots and pans reached her ears. *Yuck*, Marla thought. *I wonder what else is crawling around inside there.*

Squaring her shoulders, Marla marched inside. A mixture of tantalizing aromas met her nostrils, and she sniffed in a spicy scent that made her eyes water. Several workers looked up, their swarthy faces startled. She braced herself to meet Robbie, who was bound to be displeased by her actions.

"What the hell are you doing here?" he

thundered when he caught sight of her. He was stirring the contents of a giant pot, his thick neck veins bulging, biceps straining under his soiled white jacket. Dipping a spoon into the pot, he raised it to his lips and slurped the hot, steamy liquid. Grimacing, he grabbed a fistful of cayenne pepper that he tossed into the pot, stirring vigorously as he regarded Marla with a glower.

She smiled with a bravado she didn't feel, uneasy at the looks she was getting from his employees. "I'm wondering why you didn't return my form about Taste of the World. Have you selected your menu items? It's getting near time when we have to send out new press releases."

"Get me some more tomatoes, will ya?" he hollered to an assistant. The man glanced up but didn't respond. "Whatsamatta, you no speaky English? Grab me a bunch of those red tomatoes," he shouted as though the guy were deaf. "Christ, this help ain't worth shit." He got up and grabbed the items himself. Reaching for a long knife, he began slicing the plump tomatoes on a wooden cutting board.

"Well? What about the form?" Marla said, tapping her foot impatiently. Frustration made her breath come short, or maybe it was the lack of air-conditioning. A fan blew moist air around the kitchen, but it didn't do much to pull in a breeze from the alley. The garbage-scented breeze, she remembered, wrinkling her nose. Her sweater stuck to her back, and she longed for a refreshing shower.

"I'll get to it one of these days." Robbie spied a roach scurrying away on the counter and he leapt at it, knife blade slashing through the air. After he'd reduced the creature to pieces, he brushed the remains onto the floor and continued slicing the tomatoes.

Marla stifled an impulse to gag. Her eyes fixed on the pot of bubbling stew, circled by a duo of buzzing insects. "Maybe you should take your time. I might want to mention these conditions to the restaurant inspectors."

Straightening his back, Robbie glared at her. "You do and you're dead."

If your restaurant weren't so popular, pal, I'd take you off my list right now. Dirty scumbag. Maybe she'd eliminate him anyway. He was never in a pleasant mood and ran his kitchen like a sewer. She'd have to be careful how she justified herself to Ocean Guard's board of directors, though. Robbie wasn't the type of person you wanted to cross.

"Time for you to leave," he ordered.

"But —"

He brandished his knife, stalking toward her with a menacing light in his eyes. "Get out!"

Marla stumbled into the alley just as he slammed the door after her. It didn't even shut properly; the warped wood prevented closure. Her limbs trembling, she recovered her wits enough to scramble to her car. *Just like that roach scampering away, and it had ended up getting diced to death.*

2

"*Schmo,* you should have spoken to Pierre's assistant. Instead, you're talking to your dog."

Sunday morning found Marla sauntering down the street with Spooks on a leash. Her mental wheels were still spinning about Pierre's mishap. If she hadn't been so afraid other celebrity chefs might cancel out, she would've remembered to follow through on that incident in his class.

She paused while the poodle did his thing on a neighbor's lawn. Living in a townhouse community, she paid her homeowner's fees for communal services like everyone else. Those services included lawn maintenance. Let the grass cutters worry about where they stepped, she thought with a sardonic grin. The grass glistened with dew, and Spooks had just been groomed, so she urged him onward when he finished his business.

"If someone added a stronger substance to the bottle of rum, who had better access than Pierre's aide?" she asked Spooks, continuing around a corner. "I wonder if anyone was smart enough to take that bottle to a lab for testing. Now that the chef is out of the hospital, I should ask him about it. At least his restaurant had minimal damage from the explosion. Regardless of the cause, we've lost a well-known chef from our roster. Do you think I can find a replacement at this late date for the fund-raiser, Spooks?"

She gazed at his uplifted face. "Actually, anyone in that class would've had the opportunity to alter the contents while we were introducing ourselves and stuffing down cheese and crackers. Do I really want to question so many people, including Pierre and his assistant?"

Spooks cocked his head, as though to query her sanity. Maybe she was just having last-minute jitters about the whole affair. After all, time was running out with six weeks to go for Taste of the World. Finding out what had caused that explosion was not her responsibility.

Her glance skittered across the street, where she noticed a blue sedan creeping along, almost as though keeping pace with her stride. It must have come up from behind. A man sat in the driver's seat, facing away from her. His dark-haired head was tilted as though he was looking in the side view mirror. As she passed, the battered condition of his vehicle became evident. It wasn't the sort of car normally found in the neighborhood.

The hairs on her nape rose, and she tugged on the poodle's leash. "Move it, Spooks," she hissed. Quickening her pace, she chugged along until her racing heart caused her to slow down. Good, she'd turned a corner, and the blue sedan was gone. Her house was just around the next bend. Feeling foolish, she halted while Spooks sniffed around a fire hydrant, then lifted his leg. Barking sounded from inside a nearby house, but it was noise from an idling engine that brought her head up. Oh God, there it was again! Was she being totally paranoid, or what? Without waiting to see if Spooks had finished, she yanked him forward and speed-walked the rest of the way home. Her fingers trembled as she inserted the key into her front door lock.

"Remind me to get the alarm connected," she said to Spooks, unhooking his leash once they were inside. Bending over to stroke his soft cream-colored hair, she debated whom to call first. Detective Vail? *He's out of town, you dolt.* Tally? No, best to leave her friend alone on Sunday morning. Tally and her husband liked to sleep late, and Marla didn't want to worry them. Besides, she might be just imagining things. She'd stick to her original plan and call Cynthia. Was eight o'clock too early? Probably, she decided, glancing at her watch. She could use the time to grab a bite to eat. Daring to peek outside, she noticed that the blue sedan was gone. Maybe the guy had been looking for someone's address.

After downing a glass of fresh-squeezed orange juice and a bagel with cream cheese and chives, she took a quick shower and threw on a pair of jeans. For November, the weather was still warm, so she chose a short-sleeved ribbed sweater in rust. Tally would snicker at her choice. As owner of Dressed To Kill boutique, Tally urged Marla to jazz up her style. But Marla felt the proper image was important to project. Her staff expected her to set an example, and she preferred the classic look to Tally's flamboyant fashion. She felt women would rather have a hair-dresser who outfitted herself conservatively than someone dolled up like an oversexed teen. *If you take care with your clothes, you'll take care with my hair.* She figured that's what her clients believed.

After an hour spent on the computer catching up on bookkeeping for her salon, she decided to check the web site for Taste of the World. Babs Winrow, a member of Ocean Guard's board of directors and a client of Marla's, had graciously created the site. A business executive, she had her office staff maintain it. Marla thought it was eye-catching with colorful graphics and up-to-date information, but her gaze widened as she scanned the latest news. Pierre Chevalier's name had been dropped from the list of participating chefs. How the devil did Babs know this when Marla hadn't told anyone? An instant later, the answer popped into her mind. Pierre must have spread the word himself. Or had he? Her heart sinking, she phoned Cynthia.

"Did you know Pierre pulled out of Taste of the World?" she said as soon as her cousin's voice answered.

"Marla, is that you? I'll have to call you right back."

"No wait. I need to see you today."

"Not possible. Hold on." A clunking sound followed, then Cynthia's distant voice shouting, "Annie, don't you dare meet that boy at the beach. He's taking advantage of you. Dammit, give me the car keys!"

Muffled noises followed, and then Cynthia's voice boomed into the phone: "I can't believe this girl. She's driving me crazy. Marla, don't forget the board meeting tomorrow. We'll talk there." *Click.* She'd hung up.

Drat. Marla placed the receiver down, wondering what was going on between Cynthia and her daughter, Annie. She supposed she'd find out soon enough. Cynthia had asked her to attend the Monday meeting even though she wasn't on Ocean Guard's board of directors, and Marla was eager to give her report as chef liaison. Maybe she was being silly to be alarmed by the recent spate of incidents affecting their chefs, but she'd be interested to assess the others' reactions. At the very least, she'd make it a point to find out who had wiped Pierre's name off the slate of participants.

"I changed the information in the Web site," Babs Winrow confessed at the meeting the next day. Marla was seated along with eight board members in an elegantly appointed conference room on the top floor of a bank building in downtown Fort Lauderdale. "There was a message on my answering machine giving me the news. I didn't recognize the voice."

Babs was a savvy businesswoman, married without children, who traveled frequently and gave generous gratuities. She wore her blond hair in a short wavy style that was appropriate for her forty-some years. "What did the message say?" Marla asked, her gaze admiring Babs's finely cut black Armani suit.

The woman's clear hazel eyes met hers. "Just that Pierre had withdrawn from Taste of the World. I called him to confirm it. I've never heard him so disgruntled. He muttered something about an accident at his restaurant."

"I'm not so sure it was an accident." Relating the details, Marla glanced at her cousin for reassurance. Cynthia appeared distracted, her gaze distant. She hadn't said much so far.

"Poor lady, you must have been upset," crooned Digby Raines, seated on Marla's right. The politician settled his hand soothingly over hers and gave her a smarmy smile while his heavy-lidded blue gaze roamed over her dressy pantsuit. With his white hair and even teeth, he could've been called distinguished, but Marla thought his expression more suitable to charming snakes than convincing voters.

She smiled sweetly, swatting away his

hand. "I'm more upset by the idea that someone might be trying to sabotage Taste of the World. Why else would so many of our chefs be having mishaps?"

"If you ask me, I think you're overreacting," sniffed Dr. Russ Taylor, straightening his striped tie. "Maybe this job is too much for you to handle."

Not a hair on his gray-streaked head was out of place, Marla noticed idly. Even his suit was perfectly creased. She wondered how he could maintain his fastidious manner in the operating room. "Excuse me, but I think I've been doing a damn good job. I got chefs to replace the others who dropped out, and I'll find someone to take over for Pierre. Now tell me, is this year's event more significant than others for some reason?"

Benjamin Kline, the attorney with wiry black hair, spoke in a gravelly voice. "We need the proceeds from Taste of the World to secure the transfer of property to Ocean Guard."

Marla frowned. "What do you mean?"

Steepling his hands, Ben leaned forward. "I'm amazed your cousin didn't brief you on our situation. Bordering Cynthia's estate is a mangrove preserve being managed under a trust created by our benefactor,

Popeye Boodles, who died five years ago."

"Shut up, Ben," snarled Stefano Barletti. The gray-haired funeral director's piercing gaze emanated hostility, but he wasn't the only one whose tension permeated the room. As soon as the attorney had begun to speak, Marla could feel malevolent vibrations prickle the back of her neck. It felt as though someone had raised the temperature in the room several degrees.

"Why, we all know about this. No reason not to tell her." Ben grinned wickedly. "Under the terms of the trust, Ocean Guard will receive full ownership of the property next year, but only if it's been maintained as an unpolluted nature preserve. The other stipulation is that Ocean Guard must contribute twenty thousand dollars a year to a certain political lobby. If either condition isn't met, the property and any remaining funds revert to the bachelor's heir in January."

"So Ocean Guard has been raising at least twenty thousand dollars from Taste of the World each year?"

"You got it. Explain it to her, David."

David Newberg was the board member in charge of Ocean Guard's finances. She'd been mildly surprised to meet the man because he didn't fit her image of a staid accountant. His easygoing manner was reflected in a set of twinkling blue eyes, friendly grin, and relaxed posture. Unlike his stiff associates, his attire included a colorful tie with dancing fish. She'd liked him on sight, and instinctively knew he'd present an honest opinion.

"We sell one hundred fifty tickets at two hundred dollars each," he said in a pleasantly resonant voice. "That comes out to thirty thousand. It doesn't leave us much after the contribution, but the rest pays for flyers, postage, and other operating expenses. Ocean Guard doesn't maintain an office, so it's no big deal."

"Who inherits the property if the quota isn't achieved?" She directed her inquiry to the attorney.

"Client privilege. I'm not at liberty to say," Ben replied.

"You use that excuse for everything," Cynthia snapped.

"Yeah, and then you turn around and stab your clients in the back," muttered Digby, clicking a ballpoint pen.

"Only those who have gotten their shoes dirty." Ben's weasely gaze surveyed the room's occupants. "And most of you better keep those shoes in the closet where they belong."

Digby's lip curled. "I wouldn't talk if I were you."

"Right on. We all know who not to trust in this room." Dr. Taylor's voice dripped with disdain as his cool gaze flitted from the politician to the lawyer.

Ben and Digby exchanged glances, then Digby's brows furrowed. "You'd better watch what you say, doc."

"Why? Is Ben going to sue me?" He laughed, a harshly resonant sound that sent a chill down her spine.

Instinctively, Marla didn't like him. Dr. Taylor didn't seem to regard anyone else with the same value he placed on himself. She had no use for people who viewed themselves as royalty; in her opinion, respect was something you earned by kindness and civility.

"Ben only takes cases that thrust him in the limelight. Or at least, that's where he puts forth his best efforts." Cynthia glared at the attorney, her blue eyes glittering like ice chips.

What a bunch of clowns. Marla exchanged glances with David, whose lips quivered as though he were suppressing a grin. The side of her mouth quirked in acknowledgment. At least she wasn't the only one in the room ducking the darts.

Actually, Darren Shapiro, vice president for the bank where they were meeting, hadn't said a word. Her gaze flickered over his respectable suit and solemn demeanor. The guy's hair was suspiciously dark for a man in his late forties. No wedding ring, either. Did that mean he was on the prowl? If so, he was a lot more subtle than Digby Raines.

"What do you think, Mr. Shapiro? Shouldn't we be concerned about the incidents with the chefs?" she asked him.

Darren gave her a diffident smile. "Not necessarily. I'm more concerned about the discord in this room. We have a lot to accomplish in the next few weeks, and you're all bickering like a bunch of women."

"Is that a gender bias I detect?" snapped Babs, looking annoyed. "I say let's review programming so we can get on to publicity."

"You're all just running scared." Ben smirked, drumming his fingers on the table. "You're afraid we won't make the quota. That's why everyone is so uptight. How many tickets have sold?"

"Fifty-four," said Dr. Taylor, in charge of ticket sales. "But it's only been a few weeks since Darren sent out the invitations. We need more ads in the entertainment sector."

Digby shifted in his seat. "I'll send out a

new press release, unless Ben wants to take over publicity. He's got media coverage again for his latest trial."

"Jealous, are you? How's the campaign going?" said Ben, snickering. "I heard your rival is ahead in the polls."

"No thanks to you." Digby clicked his pen on and off.

"Stop it, you two." Babs's eyes flashed fire. "Cynthia, what about decorations?"

"I've got a handle on that. We're going with the cruise theme, and I've got a fabulous raffle planned to go along with it. Stefano, are the flower arrangements finalized?"

"Of course. Are we getting reimbursed for our expenses? I've run up quite a phone bill already." Stefano drilled each member with his somber gaze. Thick, winged eyebrows and slightly bulging eyes gave him a zombielike appearance, as though he were startled to be alive.

"Why should you care? Your rich uncle left you enough," chimed in Ben. "So, Marla, who ya gonna get to replace Pierre?"

"We need two replacements. Robbie from the Cajun Cookpot is uncooperative, so I've decided to scratch him from the list. Does anyone have any suggestions?"

"You might try Alex Sheffield from the

Riverboat," drawled Dr. Taylor, surveying her with a disinterested air. "He participated a while back. I don't recall what made him drop out." He drank a sip of water as though unconcerned.

"Okay, that's one chef. Who else?"

"Hey, I just thought of someone." Ben pulled an envelope from an inner pocket and scribbled on it. "Here's how you spell the guy's name."

The envelope exchanged hands until reaching Marla. She turned it over. On the back was scrawled *Mustafa Ishmail from the Medina.* "Greek?" she queried. "We already have a Greek chef for Taste of the World."

"It's a Moroccan place. Go there sometime. You'll like it."

"How about if everyone calls in a report to Cynthia by Friday?" suggested Babs. "She'll determine when our next meeting should take place. Digby, don't forget those press releases need to go out right away."

"Yeah, if you have any spare time from the campaign trail," Ben sneered.

"Look who's talking. I can think of a few things that would get you in the news, and I don't mean favorably."

Ben's face flushed, and he shot to his feet. "I don't need to hear this. You people do your job, I'll do mine." He stalked from the room.

Gratefully, Marla rose to leave. She'd never been to a meeting where people showed such animosity. Hopefully, she wouldn't have to attend any more planning sessions. From here on, she'd report to Cynthia directly, and her cousin could pass along anything of import to her fellow board members.

Stuffing Ben's envelope into her purse, she hastened after Cynthia, who'd already left the room. Just outside the door to the conference room, her cousin gestured her aside. "Marla, when can you come over to my house? I need to talk to you, but this isn't a good place." Her gaze skittered toward the elevator, where the others congregated.

"Care to stop off somewhere now for lunch?"

"Sorry, I've got to run to an affair at the country club." Cynthia patted her beehive hairdo like a mother bird fluttering around her babes.

God, I must get that woman to change her hairstyle. "I can drop in one night this week after work," she offered.

"I need you to come over when it's daylight."

"Well, then I can't come until Sunday," she said, curiosity overwhelming her. "What's the matter, Cynthia? It's something else besides the fund-raiser, isn't it?"

Cynthia chewed her lower lip. "Uh-huh."

"So tell me."

"Not now. Come for afternoon tea on Sunday, around two o'clock. Good luck with the chefs in the meantime."

Frustrated by her conversation with Cynthia, Marla decided to stop off at her mother's condo. Possibly Ma knew what was going on with her cousin. A lot of restaurants were closed Mondays anyway, so she might as well forget about finding any new participants for the fund-raiser until later in the week.

The delicious aroma of roasting meat mingled with smells of cinnamon and nutmeg as Marla approached her mother's apartment. Rapping on the door, she waited patiently until it swung open to reveal Anita's smiling face.

"Marla! You're just in time for lunch. Do you want some of this brisket and noodle kugel I'm making for tonight? The Steinbergs and Rosenthals are coming for dinner."

Marla stepped inside the brightly lit kitchen, glad her mother was having friends for dinner. Since her husband's death several years ago, Anita had made a busy social life for herself. She still got together with other married couples but had made new friends among the widows in her development.

"No, thanks. I'll have a sandwich, though." She watched her mother's white-haired figure bustling about the kitchen. Nothing made a Jewish mother happier than to feed her children. Marla always accepted something whether or not she was hungry because she knew it pleased her mother to watch her eat.

"I met Cynthia this morning," she said, dropping into a kitchen chair beside a small, round table. Her gaze lifted to the ceiling, where an ominous dark blob showed above one of the plastic ceiling panels displaying cove lighting. Probably a dead palmetto bug. Maybe it was related to the one in Robbie's place. Shuddering, Marla continued, "She seemed upset about something."

"Oh, really? I haven't spoken to her lately, but I know she's been having problems with Annie."

"I guess that could be what's bothering her, but why would she want to talk to me about it? She wants me to come over her house on Sunday."

45

"Where did you see her today?"

"We went to a board meeting for Ocean Guard. Taste of the World has lost a few chefs."

"I'm sure things will turn out fine with the two of you working on it. Is tuna okay?" Anita asked, rummaging in her refrigerator for a loaf of bread. In south Florida, you kept perishables at cooler temperatures unless you liked to eat mold. "Did Cynthia say what time she wants us for Thanksgiving? Last year was too late at five o'clock. Your brother likes to get home earlier to put the kids to sleep."

"She didn't mention Thanksgiving, but I'll ask her about it when I see her again."

Her mother whipped up the sandwich and placed it on the table along with a can of Diet Coke. "Here, is this enough for you to eat? I can give you something else to go with it."

"This is good, thanks." Ma must have had her nails done recently, Marla noted, glimpsing her polished red fingertips.

"Cynthia must know some rich bachelors she could introduce to you," Anita said in a casual tone.

"I'm not interested." Marla popped the lid on the soda can.

"Don't tell me you're still seeing that detective."

"What if I am? That's my business." She chomped into her sandwich, scooping up a dribble of mayonnaise with her finger.

"He's the wrong type of man for you. Listen to me, Marla, that guy will bring you nothing but *tsuris*." Anita sank into the opposite seat, jabbing her finger in the air for emphasis. "Cops make lousy husbands. They're never home, or they end up dead. Why get involved with someone like him when Cynthia can fix you up with a nice Jewish lawyer or doctor?"

Marla choked on a morsel of food. "Stan was a rich Jewish lawyer, remember? Talk about a wrong match. He was domineering, possessive, and egotistical. Now the bastard won't leave me alone. He keeps bugging me to sell that piece of rental property we own together. I told you how he tried to get the landlord to cancel my lease on the salon. Our divorce was the best thing that happened to me."

She gulped down a large swallow of Diet Coke. "Besides, Dalton and I are just friends. He's got a daughter, so I don't want to get more serious about him even though he's interested."

Anita rolled her eyes. "When are you going to get over your hangup about children? Tammy's death happened nearly fifteen years ago. You can't blame yourself for that incident your entire life."

"If I'd been a better baby-sitter, Tammy wouldn't have drowned in that pool. I can't be responsible for a child again, least of all my own. I couldn't stand the pain if anything bad happened. So you don't need to worry about me and Dalton."

Oh no? Then why is it every time you see him, your heart races like you've run a marathon? She bit into her sandwich, chomping heartily. Lately, he'd been too busy to pop in on her unexpectedly. She found herself missing his gruff voice and keen-eyed gaze and wondered when she'd see him next. Barring his need for a haircut, only another murder might bring him in again. *Be careful what you wish for,* she warned herself.

3

She was in the middle of doing a coloring when Detective Vail strode through the front door of her salon as though he owned the place. From the set of his wide shoulders and the steely glint in his gray eyes, Marla could tell he meant business. She swallowed at the determined expression on his face. His bushy eyebrows, a salt-and-pepper shade to match his hair, were drawn together in a scowl as he marched forward, jaw resolute as he regarded her. His presence had an immediate effect on her heart rate. He looked as impressive in that suit as any commander in uniform, she thought, unable to temper her reaction. Hoping he couldn't detect her loss of equilibrium, she willed an expression of surprised interest on her features.

"Hi, Dalton, what's up?" she said, smiling brightly. Waiting for his response, she applied the coloring solution to her client's graying hair, working it into the roots. Her fingers moved automatically, which was a blessing considering how her mind discarded all sense of reason when Dalton was around.

"We need to talk." He ignored the heads turned in their direction. After the episode with Bertha Kravitz, most of her staff recognized him on sight and so did many of her patrons.

"Uh, I'm a little busy right now." She glanced nervously at Nicole, who was doing a haircut at the next station. Nicole's cocoa eyes blinked back a reassuring message.

"It's important." His mouth tightened. "I'll wait until you're done."

Lord save me, now what? She squeezed out the last drops of coloring solution from the plastic bottle in her hand, peeled off a stained latex glove, and set the timer for twenty minutes. "You can relax for a while," she told her client. "When your timer goes off, Giorgio can finish you. Is that all right?" she called to the darkly handsome Italian who was sweeping the floor. They were short an assistant and were forced to share chores.

"Okay by me." Giorgio grinned, a flash of white teeth against his tanned skin.

"Is he available?" hissed her client, an attractive widow.

"Nope. The guy's adorable, but he's gay."

"Oh. Tell me, Marla, what should I do about shampoos at home to keep this color from fading?"

"Use a shampoo formulated for color-treated hair. They're more gentle and less drying than other shampoos. If you use a blow-dryer, pick a lower setting. Too much heat will speed up the loss of color. Same goes for water: not too hot. Be careful with a curling iron so you don't scorch the ends. And stay out of the sun; that's the worst."

Aware that Dalton was waiting for her, she gestured to him.

"Let's go to Bagel Busters. I'll buy you a cup of coffee." They could talk out of earshot of her staff there, as long as she kept Arnie at bay. The manly owner persisted in asking her out even though she'd told him their friendship meant more to her. Ma would approve of him, a little voice whispered in her head. But it was Lieutenant Dalton Vail who steamed her blood, not nice-guy-next-door Arnie.

"Have you spoken to your cousin Cynthia since yesterday?" Vail said when they were seated at a table in the deli a few doors down the shopping strip from her salon.

Alarm frissoned down her spine. "Why? Has something happened to her?" The grim look on his face spelled bad news. "Oh no, it's her daughter Annie, isn't it?"

"They're all right. I understand you were with your cousin at a board meeting for Ocean Guard."

"Yes, that's true." She didn't see where this was leading.

"Ben Kline was found dead last night."

Marla's jaw dropped open. Dead? She'd seen the lawyer just yesterday. She turned her stunned gaze on Arnie Hartman, who chose that moment to interrupt.

"Hey, Marla." His dark, gleaming eyes soaked in her companion, and he gave a grudging nod. Vail had questioned him following Bertha's death at her salon. "What can I get for you?"

"Ruth already took our order, thanks," Marla informed him.

Her jumbled nerves must've been evident, because he placed a comforting hand on her shoulder. "What's wrong, *shayna maidel?*"

Her heart warmed at the endearment. "Somebody I know has just been murdered. That is why you're on the case, isn't it?" she queried Vail.

"Marla's not in trouble again, is she?" Arnie demanded, his tone fiercely protective.

52

Vail smiled although the warmth didn't quite reach his eyes. "Not at this time. I just need information. Now if you'll excuse us . . ." He let his voice trail off purposefully.

"Sure. Marla, if you need anything, just holler." Arnie's mustache quivered as he gave her an encouraging grin.

"Thanks, pal, but I can handle it." Her attention reverted to the somber-eyed detective. "So how was he killed?"

"Bludgeoned to death in his office. That much was in the news this morning. I'm surprised you didn't hear about it."

"I was running late, and I had to take Spooks for a walk. I didn't turn on the TV." She hung her head, the attorney's image popping into her mind: his wiry black hair, cunning eyes, and sneering mouth. God, she'd only just met the guy. "What an awful way to die," she commented.

Vail's mouth curved down. "Is there any good way?"

"No, but having your life ended by someone else is horrible. Can't say that I'm surprised. Ben seemed to get a rise out of aggravating everyone, but that's no reason for murder." Their beverages arrived, and Marla paused to take a sip of aromatic coffee. The hot brew tasted strong, so she added a spoonful of sugar and some cream. *With the amount of caffeine that I ingest every day, I could be a catalyst for rocket fuel.*

"Would you care to elaborate?"

She could sense his impatience by the way he gripped his mug. "The members of the board were tossing barbs back and forth like a bunch of bratty schoolchildren. Cynthia has her work cut out for her coordinating this bunch."

"You're in charge of the chefs, aren't you?"

"Tell me about it. You know how I got roped into the job." She put her mug down and turned her hands palm up. Thankfully, her injuries hadn't left any scars. "I figured I'd go nuts while my hands were healing. Helping Cynthia seemed a good idea at the time. I like what Ocean Guard stands for and want to support their aims. But if I had met those shysters before, I wouldn't have been so eager to volunteer. Now the chefs are turning out to be more trouble than they're worth."

"Explain."

That's what I like about you, pal. You're a man of few words. She related the problems she'd been having with the chefs. "What do you think Pierre meant about a warning and Ocean Guard being cursed?"

His intense, penetrating gaze skewered her like shish kebab. "I'm not sure. I need to hear more about the board members."

"Don't tell me you suspect someone from Ocean Guard murdered Ben?" she scoffed. "He probably had loads of enemies. His practice included criminal defense, and he's been in the news more often than our local politicians."

"We're considering all angles."

"Family?" She examined his ruggedly contoured face, hoping for a telltale reaction, but his features remained as impassive as stone.

"His wife divorced him, moved to California six years ago, and remarried."

"Business associates? Former clients? Current cases?"

A small smile played about his lips. Her eyes inadvertently dropped to his chiseled mouth, and her thoughts strayed in a more imaginative direction. *Bless my bones, if he isn't damned attractive when he's in a stern mood.*

"As I said, I'm looking into different possibilities."

"So I guess you want my impressions of yesterday's meeting." Vail nodded, withdrawing a notebook.

Well, maybe if she shared info with him,

he'd be more forthcoming. "Babs Winrow, a client of mine, is chairperson. She kept trying to get everyone back on track. Digby Raines is running for mayor. Word has it he's got much higher ambitions. He has aspirations where women are concerned, too, if you know what I mean. Dr. Taylor has a superiority complex. Darren Shapiro is a quiet sort, the respectable banker type you'd expect. Stefano Barletti has scary eyes. They bulge out in his grim face, making him look like a walking corpse. But then, he is an undertaker."

"What else?" He scribbled while she repeated the gist of their conversation. When her story finished, he plowed stiff fingers through his hair. *He needs a cut soon,* she observed, the prospect giving her a vicarious thrill. She liked feeling the soft texture of his wavy hair.

"You haven't been around for a while," she remarked.

"I've been busy." He stuffed the notebook back in a pocket. "But I've been meaning to ask you . . . Brianna wants to see *Rent* which is playing at Broward Center next weekend. I bought three tickets for Saturday night. I realize it's short notice, but if you don't have any plans yet, wanna go?" A hopeful expression sprang into his eyes as he regarded her expectantly.

Marla's lips parted. This was the first time he'd asked her to do anything involving his daughter. Mixed feelings assailed her. Did this mean he was getting more serious? She met his earnest gaze and smiled.

"Okay, that sounds nice. I'll look forward to it." In the meantime, she'd see what Cynthia had to say. No doubt her cousin would be upset about Ben's demise. Considering the board of directors' animosity toward him, she wondered if anyone else among the group would be distressed by the news. This latest tragedy meant another jinx on their fund-raiser. She hoped Cynthia would provide reassurance that all was well event-wise.

Marla enjoyed the drive past the main gate into her cousin's oceanfront estate. Framed by a row of malaleuca trees with their papery bark, the packed-earth road wound through grounds as close to a jungle as you could get in this part of south Florida. She slowed the car so she could enjoy the tangle of thick-trunked mahogany trees, sable palms, seagrapes, and gumbo limbos. Among the spreading branches, she caught sight of a spider monkey chewing on a green rose apple. Her eyes narrowed as she peered at the foliage. Cynthia claimed raccoons hid among the palmetto fronds and philodendrons, but Marla had never spotted any. Not that she'd been here that often. Her cousin usually invited their extended family over for Passover. This year, Cynthia and Bruce were doing Thanksgiving instead.

She pulled around a circular driveway in front of the mansion and put the gear into park. Shutting off the ignition, she threw her keys into her purse and emerged into the bright sunshine. She was a little early, fifteen minutes to be exact, but she'd been chomping at the bit all morning to get there. Cynthia had told her to come at two o'clock, but it didn't matter if she arrived sooner. Bruce, a real-estate developer, was abroad on one of his business trips, so she and her cousin could enjoy a private chat.

Her gaze swept approvingly over the Spanish architecture of the main house. The original buildings were constructed by Bruce's great-grandfather who bought the land in the late 1800s. Successive descendants had put their own stamp upon the property, so that now it was fully modernized. The red barrel tile roof complemented the sand color of the house's stucco exterior.

Hot pink and tangerine bougainvillea climbed walls shaded by spreading ficus trees. Built around a central courtyard, the bottom floor had windows protected by green awnings. Ironwork on the second-story balcony balustrades came from New Orleans.

When Cynthia opened the door to usher her inside, Marla felt she was entering a museum. Niches held whimsical wood sculptures of brightly painted animals, African masks, and New Guinea artifacts. Standing on a brick path, she overlooked a central garden framing a stone fountain where clear water cascaded into a blue-tiled pool. Welcome to the lifestyle of the rich but not-so-famous.

Marla turned to her cousin, remembering the distress in her tone at their last meeting. Was there trouble brewing in Paradise?

She'd always felt Cynthia had everything: a wealthy husband, beautiful home, attractive children, and a leisurely life. Was it any wonder she felt so distant from this world? Not that she'd want it for herself. She'd had the chance with her marriage to Stan, a rich attorney. He'd wanted a woman he could control. Thankfully, Marla had regained her self-esteem in time to escape his domineering clutches. She needed to be useful, to make a difference. And being a hairstylist was a calling she'd found impossible to resist once she struck out on her own.

Still, she wished she could look as svelte as Cynthia. Her cousin appeared sophisticated in an ankle-length flowered gown with her bleached blond hair teased atop her head. Feeling underdressed in comparison, Marla smoothed down the khaki pants she wore with a white silk blouse and vest.

"You're looking cool and comfortable," Cynthia said, a warm smile on her face. Crinkles appeared beside her cornflower blue eyes, the only lines in an otherwise wrinkle-free visage. For a woman in her forties, Cynthia maintained herself well. "I had a table set up on the back porch. We can talk there before my guest arrives."

"What guest?" Marla thought *she* was the guest. Who else was her cousin expecting?

"Oh, someone who wants to get to know you. He won't be here until later, and we've got a lot to discuss. Did you hear about Ben? I'm so upset."

"Yeah, I was shocked to hear the news." She peered curiously at her cousin. "How does his absence affect your plans?" Trailing Cynthia, she entered the house past a bamboo-paneled bar and exited through a screen door to the back.

"He'd arranged for a jazz band," Cynthia said, leading the way to a clothed table elegantly set for three with English bone china, sterling silver, and a Baccarat vase of fresh peach roses. "I've got the information, so we should be okay."

Marla wasn't particularly hungry, having eaten lunch an hour earlier, but she took a seat and crossed her legs while waiting for Cynthia to be settled opposite her. "Do you have any theories about who might have killed him?" Thankfully, his demise wasn't putting any crimp in their fund-raiser.

Cynthia leaned forward, her gaze darkening. "I'm beginning to believe what you said about a jinx."

Marla's interest peaked. "Huh?"

"I got a call from Max at the Seafood Emporium. A number of his regular patrons became sick this week, presumably from eating tainted fish at his restaurant. The place has been closed down temporarily while an investigation ensues. Max pulled out of Taste of the World."

Marla felt the color drain from her face. "Why didn't he call me? I just saw him last weekend."

Cynthia grimaced. "Probably was afraid of your reaction, so he called me instead. What's the difference? He thinks someone in his kitchen staff substituted contaminated seafood."

Like someone on Pierre's staff added an explosive substance to the rum bottle? Now it would be even more difficult to find chefs willing to participate in Taste of the World. Was rumor going around that the event was cursed?

She focused on her cousin's troubled countenance. "If this is a conspiracy against Ocean Guard's fund-raiser, who do you think is behind it?"

"Not Ben, he's dead."

Footsteps sounded behind them, and Cynthia fell silent, plastering a polite expression on her face.

"Would you like tea served now, madam?" asked the butler, suited rather formally for a warm afternoon, Marla thought.

Cynthia's clear blue eyes locked on hers. "We'll wait until my gentleman friend arrives. Marla wants to see the beach first. Right, darling?"

Getting the hint, Marla sprang to her feet. "Oh, sure." At last they'd be alone to exchange confidences. Eager to hear what Cynthia had to say, she tossed her purse onto the chair before joining her cousin along a gravel-strewn path leading toward the lagoon. Its murky surface made her shudder. Unprotected bodies of water were hazardous to small children. She'd become even more nervous when Thanksgiving approached. Her young niece and nephew needed close watching, and Cynthia's house had a pool as well as the lagoon. But those worries weren't warranted right now. Other priorities took hold of her mind, and she quickened her pace.

A spicy scent tickled her nostrils as she descended ancient steps hewn from coral and headed for the plank bridge ahead. Lilies floated on the water, disturbed by darting schools of fish. On the opposite bank, acres of forest stretched east to the shoreline. Adjacent to the estate on the south side was the natural habitat preserved under Popeye Boodles's trust.

"Cynthia, tell me again how you and Bruce ended up living next to the preserve. I'm still fuzzy about the details." She watched her footing as the path skirted a lofty fig tree.

Her cousin's gaze narrowed. "Let me see, Bruce's great-grandfather and his friend, Angus Fairweather, were on a trip to Florida in 1898 when their boat blew ashore during a storm. They liked the territory here so much that they bought over three miles of land along the coast for less than one dollar per acre."

Cynthia brushed a strand of blond hair off her face, flushed from the heat. In the dappled light of the woods, worry lines on her face became pronounced. Marla noticed with concern that once her cousin relaxed, she appeared more tired and less carefree. Her chin sagged, and the corners of her mouth drooped. Perhaps not everything was golden in the land of the rich, Marla thought with startled realization. For the first time, she wondered if Cynthia's normally disdainful attitude was genuine. Could it be a cover-up for feelings more profound? She sensed Cynthia's concerns went deeper than problems with a fundraiser.

"Go on," she encouraged.

"Angus passed his portion to his daughter, who bequeathed it to her son, Popeye Boodles. Popeye never had any children."

Marla tripped on a root on the gravelly path and stumbled forward. Regaining her balance, she continued onward, her shoes crunching on dead leaves, twigs, and brown pine needles. "Popeye founded Ocean Guard, right?"

Cynthia nodded, gesturing at the surrounding trees.

"He loved the sea and used his fortune to promote conservation. Except for building a boardwalk, he never developed the land. Popeye remained in contact with Bruce's family, who built our house on the adjacent property. Bruce became caretaker for the preserve sort of by heredity, if you get my meaning."

Black ironwood trees mingled with mangroves as they neared a slough. Marla caught sight of a green heron sitting on a log. Something stung her arm, and she swatted it away. Mosquitoes. Annoying pests. They were supposed to be gone by November, but the cool air from up north hadn't swept in yet. At least it wasn't as humid now as in the summer, or this place would be a steamy jungle. Dense vegetation blocked the sunlight as they proceeded farther into the woods.

"Who did you say inherits Popeye's territory if Ocean Guard fails to meet its commitments?" she asked.

"I don't know. Whoever established the trust would have that information."

"Meaning the attorney who drew up the agreement?"

They both halted at the same time. Marla

knew her face must have registered the wild direction of her thoughts.

"N-No," stuttered Cynthia. "You can't believe —"

"That Ben Kline was murdered because his firm's name is on that trust agreement? I'd say it's a distinct possibility."

4

Cynthia's eyes grew round in her pale face. "Wait until you see what I have to show you. Follow me."

As they neared the shore, the tangle of mangroves thickened into a gnarled web of roots reaching from thin tree trunks down to a layer of muck inches deep. The tide was out because the mud was moist rather than flowing with seawater. By the coastline, rippling waves lapped onto sand littered with dried coconut husks and dead seagrape leaves. Air roots hung off overhead branches like giant spider legs. Except for faint sounds of scurrying creatures, Marla felt they were very much alone. She breathed in the smell of brine mingled with the rich odor of humus. It was a heady mixture, this primal combination of earth and sea. No wonder Popeye had wanted to keep this area in its pristine natural state. Much of the coastline had been lost to splashy hotels and boxy condominiums. Other than state parks, it was rare to find undisturbed habitats by the beach. Too bad Ben Kline's murder sullied her reason for being there.

Not until Cynthia led her a few paces along the boardwalk did she notice the desecration. "What's this?" she croaked, her eyes widening. Bile rose in her throat as recognition dawned. "Lord save me, those look like empty syringes. Oh, how gross." The corners of her mouth turned down as she surveyed dirty gauze pads, used needles, test tubes, and broken specimen containers strewn among the cigar-shaped seedpods on the ground.

Cynthia gave a grunt of disgust. "I couldn't believe it myself when I saw this for the first time last week. I figured the stuff might wash back out to sea on the tide, but it's gotten worse." Her voice lowered. "Even a smidgen of pollution invalidates Ocean Guard's chance to gain the property."

Marla turned an astonished gaze on her cousin. "What do you mean?"

"The preserve is supposed to be maintained in its natural state to meet the terms of the trust. Now that we're coming down to the mark as far as timing goes, everything seems to be going wrong." Cynthia's eyes darkened to indigo, and her jaw clenched. "I think you're right, Marla. Someone intends to make sure Ocean Guard fails. I'll bet whatever happened to Pierre with that explosion wasn't an accident."

No kidding. "Don't forget Max. They're not the only chefs who have withdrawn from Taste of the World in the last few weeks. I'm afraid ticket sales will be down if any more celebrity chefs cancel out."

"In that case, Ocean Guard won't make its monetary quota to fulfill the requirements of the trust, and we'll still lose."

"Maybe you're jumping to conclusions," Marla said, squinting at the debris. "It could be washing ashore from somewhere else."

Cynthia's face folded into a worried frown. "I doubt it. There hasn't been any trash on our estate. See how the tide is out now? Whoever is doing this must have come through last night. My guess is the scum brought a small boat in via the slough and dumped the stuff where it wouldn't wash back out." She referred to a waterway leading to the coastline. "High tide would help carry the contaminants further inland."

Marla stared at a land crab crawling from its burrow in the muck, realizing the extent of damage that might result from one individual's malicious acts. Mangroves harbored many forms of life and were necessary to south Florida's environment. Their tangle of arching prop roots trapped organic debris which, when decayed, built up the soil and prevented erosion. Without this protection, the fragile balance of ecology would be disrupted and habitats destroyed. While Marla didn't consider herself a nature person, she appreciated the benefits of her surroundings. *How dare someone defile such beauty!*

She scratched at a bug bite on her forearm, anger heating her blood, which undoubtedly made her more tasty to the insects. *Getting riled won't solve anything,* she told herself. But it sure as hell made her want to know who'd done this. The sight of a soiled bandage turned her stomach, and she reversed direction on the boardwalk to march back toward Cynthia's terrain.

"Let's think about it rationally," she said, suppressing her rage. "Assuming these events are due to sabotage, someone close to Ocean Guard has to be involved. Who else is familiar with the terms of the trust?"

Cynthia fell into step beside her. "The board of directors. My husband Bruce, because he's caretaker for the mangrove preserve. The trustee, Morton Riley. And whoever inherits the property if Ocean Guard loses out."

"I suppose you'd count the lawyer who drew up the trust agreement," Marla added thoughtfully.

"We'll have to get this mess cleaned up before Riley comes for his next inspection," Cynthia muttered half to herself.

"When is that?"

She grimaced. "Usually in January after Ocean Guard makes its contribution. Bruce will know what to do. I'd better come out here more often to see if any more junk gets dumped." A shudder wracked her well-proportioned frame. "Medical waste. I can't think of anything worse."

Their eyes met and locked. "Dr. Russ Taylor," hissed Marla, remembering the surgeon on the board of directors.

"For all we know, he could be Popeye's heir."

"*He?* Excuse me, but is that gender bias I detect?" Marla smiled, but there was no mirth present in her expression. "The beneficiary could be female, but you've got a point. What better way to keep tabs on Ocean Guard's status than to volunteer for the board of directors?"

It didn't seem feasible that a prominent surgeon such as Dr. Taylor would stoop to carting off his own medical waste, but greed was a great motivator. Hadn't she learned that you couldn't trust anyone? Her own staff members had betrayed her, and yet she persisted in believing in an individual's worth. If she didn't subscribe to that precept, her soul would've been destroyed years ago subsequent to Tammy's tragic death. Without faith in her own innate goodness, she couldn't have survived. Tally said past mistakes drove her to prove herself worthy and to expunge her guilt. Well, maybe that wasn't such a bad thing. Building a reputation from blood and tears to where she stood today hadn't been easy, but she was stronger because of it. Having risen from the ashes, who was she to judge anyone else?

Dalton Vail wouldn't agree with her. He saw everything in black-and-white, guilty or not guilty. In his mind, you were a suspect until proven innocent. Marla couldn't accept his negative view of the world. Better to have faith in mankind's nature than to consign everyone to the devil. Perhaps Dr. Russ Taylor was involved in dumping medical waste on Popeye Boodles' property. But that was only one possibility, and until Marla learned more, she wouldn't blame him.

"Hurry, Marla. My other guest should

have arrived by now," Cynthia urged, gesturing.

"Who's coming?"

"Oh, you'll see."

"Isn't there something else you want to talk to me about? I got the impression that Taste of the World wasn't the only thing on your mind."

"It's Annie," Cynthia replied, sighing. "I don't know why I thought you could help."

Neither did Marla. While she didn't have kids of her own, she was accustomed to hearing clients talk about their offspring. Maybe Cynthia realized she'd be a good listener.

Her cousin developed a pinched look on her face as they approached the house. *Too bad she won't let me fix her hair,* Marla thought absently. Those harsh facial lines would be softened by a more natural cut.

"So what's the problem?"

Cynthia hesitated. "It's this boy she's been dating. He's totally wrong for her, but she can't see it."

"Wrong in what way?" They approached the bridge arching across the lagoon, and Marla slowed her pace. She wanted to hear what Cynthia had to say before they reached the house. Maybe it was simply a matter of class differences. Wealthy folks were always on the lookout for gold diggers.

Cynthia cast a worried glance in her direction. "It's nothing I can put my finger on. Shark dresses decently, shaves, and doesn't have any weird body piercings, but sometimes he looks at Annie as though she's fish bait waiting to be swallowed."

"Shark?"

Cynthia smirked. "Cute nickname, huh?"

Goes along with your own kids, cuz. Annie's full name was Anemone and her brother, off in college, was Kelp. Cynthia and Bruce had always been enamored of the sea.

Cynthia spied a figure seated at their table on the patio and waved. "Fabulous, he's here. Marla, you remember David Newberg, the accountant for Ocean Guard? He was pleased to meet you the other day and phoned me afterward to get your number. I came up with the idea of inviting him to join us today."

Gee, thanks. She remembered the attractive man from the board meeting who didn't participate in all the backstabbing, and an unanticipated thrill coursed through her. His interest was a pleasant surprise, not that she was looking for a relationship.

Her cousin winked. "By the way, David is thirty-five, single, and looking for a wife."

Marla detected a smug tone in her

cousin's voice and instantly grew suspicious. Had Ma been putting a bug in her relative's ear about fixing Marla up with eligible men? She wouldn't put it past her dear mother.

David stood as they approached. His tall, lean frame fit superbly into a cream-colored summer suit. The light fabric contrasted sharply with a vibrant tie of aqua and crimson. Steady cobalt eyes regarded her closely as she neared the shaded porch. His tanned face split into a grin when she stepped up to him and extended her hand.

"Hi, David," she said, smiling. Her gaze swept over fawn-colored hair that brushed his forehead in a casual style.

His eyes glimmered as he took her hand. "I'm pleased to see you again. You look prettier than I remember."

Yeah, right. I look great when I'm sweaty. Pulling her hand free, she turned to the table. "Forgive me, but I'm dying of thirst." Confusion gripped her for an instant. Hadn't she left her purse on the seat? It was slung by its strap on a chair arm. *I must be dehydrated if I'm losing it.* Sinking onto her seat, she took a few noisy gulps of iced tea before regarding David with a wary eye. "I assume you heard about Ben."

"Yeah, I couldn't believe it. We'd just seen him that day."

"What an awful tragedy."

"The bastard brought it on himself." David's eyes blazed for a moment before he seated himself. "I mean, he did his best to antagonize people. You saw for yourself how he behaved at that meeting. Speaking of which, did you ever contact that chef he recommended?"

"Not yet, but I'll get to it this week. I haven't even looked at Ben's note with the guy's name." She'd stuck the envelope in a drawer at the salon so she wouldn't lose it, figuring there was time enough to thank Ben for the referral. Now the attorney was dead, and her thanks would go unheard.

"Let's talk about more pleasant things," Cynthia cut in, an annoyed frown on her face. She rang a crystal bell, and the butler appeared with a platter of crustless sandwiches.

"Tell me about your work," David said, giving a disarming grin. His teeth were so white she wondered if he bleached them. "You must meet lots of fascinating people. How many hours do you spend at the salon? What are your days off?"

Glad to talk about a familiar topic, Marla rattled on about her job. Half her mind listened to birds twittering and sensed the gentle breeze upon her arms. David's battery of questions held her attention, and she described details that brought a smile to his lips and laugh creases around his eyes.

"You've really got some tales to tell," he said, his tone filled with admiration. "It must be tough to take care of all the bookkeeping and maintain your own client list. That takes a huge amount of skill."

"I like working with people. That's all it boils down to, when you think about it." His high regard filled her with satisfaction. Not all men gave successful women the respect they deserved.

"Well, if you ever need an accountant, I'm available." His mouth quirked at the double meaning.

"I'll keep that in mind," Marla murmured. She cast a glance at her cousin who munched on a chicken salad sandwich, pretending disinterest. Becoming aware of her hunger, Marla began eating. As though on cue, the butler reappeared with a plate of cookies.

A door slammed, and Annie bounded onto the patio. She was followed by a young man wearing an angry scowl on his swarthy face. "Hey, Marla," Annie called, grinning. She wore a spandex top that looked as though it would split if her bosom jutted any farther. Below her bared navel, cutoff jean shorts showed trim thighs and a hint of lace panties. Long shapely legs ended in a pair of scuffed sandals, navy-painted toenails peeking out.

Marla's eyes were drawn to the three earrings shining from her ear, then to the brassy highlights reflecting sunlight on frizzy blond hair. *You could use a good toner, honey.* "How's it going?" she responded, keeping her thoughts to herself.

"Okay. This is Shark," Annie introduced her friend. In contrast to Annie's teen rebellion fashion statement, Shark wore a polo shirt tucked into a pair of black jeans. The sneakers on his feet looked brand-new, and even his Coach leather belt still had a sheen. His light brown hair was cut so short, he might as well have shaved his head. *At least he doesn't wear any flashy jewelry,* Marla thought, wondering why some men insisted on looking like pirates.

"Mom, you didn't fill up the gas tank again," Annie said, planting her hands on ample hips. "How do you expect me to go anywhere when you don't give me enough money?"

Cynthia stiffened. "You've used up your allowance for this week."

"So? I had to spend money on food. You should reimburse me for lunch."

"You should ask your friend to pay for his half."

"Leave him outta this. All my other friends get money when they need it. You just wanna be mean. I need to get gas."

"Tough luck. Guess you'll have to stay home."

"We're meeting some guys over at Hooters. Give me a break, will ya?"

Cynthia's scornful gaze turned on Shark. "Why don't you let him drive?"

"His air-conditioning doesn't work. We'd swelter in his car."

"Of course, if he had a job, he could afford to get things fixed," Cynthia sneered.

"I'm trying to save up for repairs," the youth cut in, "but I had to spend my last bucks on new tires."

Cynthia gripped her napkin in her lap. "How unfortunate that your car breaks down whenever you need a ride somewhere."

"It's not that way, ma'am. I know what you think, but I really like Annie. I'd help out if I could."

Sure you would. Marla had met his type before. No wonder Cynthia disapproved. As slick as hair conditioner, he'd have an excuse for why he couldn't contribute whatever the situation. In his mid-twenties, he should be working toward a career, but it appeared as though the only job he was applying for was a gigolo. As though to prove his point, he put his arm around Annie and gave her a possessive squeeze. Marla caught a glimpse of an expensive watch and narrowed her gaze. The boy got money from somewhere. She wondered if Cynthia had traced his background and resolved to query her cousin when they were alone. In the meantime, she exchanged amused glances with David who was wisely remaining out of the conversation.

"I've got to go," Marla said after the teens stomped off to scrounge up another ride. Too many chores demanded her attention, and playing tea party wouldn't get them done.

"Can I call you later?" David asked, rising. "I'd like to see you again."

"That would be nice. I'm always willing to have a good time. Cynthia, can you please walk me to the door?"

As soon as they were alone, she pounced upon her cousin. "I agree with you about Shark. There's something unsavory about him but it's hard to pinpoint. Do you know anything about his family?"

Cynthia stopped at the inner courtyard where a snowy egret was grazing. "I haven't wanted to go so far as to hire an investigator. If Annie found out —"

"Do it." She clutched Cynthia's elbow. "Better to make your daughter angry than to have her saddled with a miscreant." *Bless my bones, I'm starting to sound like Dalton Vail.*

"What about the mess in the mangrove preserve?" Cynthia wailed. "Too many things are going wrong at once."

"Tell Bruce to clean it up."

Her cousin's face clouded with anxiety. "First your chefs quit, then Ben is killed, and now this. I've got all I can handle with Annie." A speculative gleam entered Cynthia's eyes. "Whoever is sabotaging Ocean Guard has to be an insider. Since you're not a board member, you could interview everyone to get an unbiased perspective."

"Sure," she agreed without thinking, flattered at Cynthia's faith in her.

Cynthia's voice lowered. "Be careful, Marla. You know what happened to Ben."

"Don't remind me." Her mouth tightened. "In the meantime, maybe Bruce can dig up the name of Popeye's beneficiary. If necessary, have him ask the trustee without

81

alerting the guy to our problems. The medical waste bothers me. It seems incredible that whoever is polluting the preserve might also be Ben's murderer."

"I can think of a lot of people who'd jump for joy at Ben's demise," Cynthia drawled.

Her cynical tone brought Marla's head up sharply. "Oh? What did you have against him?"

"You don't want to know." Her closed expression said, *Don't ask me, either.*

Marla hadn't known Cynthia and Ben had any association other than Ocean Guard. Her heart sank. She didn't want to add Cynthia to her list of suspects. True, the attorney must have made enemies from his newsworthy cases, but it was too coincidental that he should be murdered now. A gut feeling told her his death was directly related to Ocean Guard's mandate, which would eliminate her cousin from the list. Cynthia was as devoted to the organization's goals as was her husband. But if Ben's murder had nothing to do with their fundraiser, her theory about the pollution being related would fly out the door. Then what? They needed time, dammit, but the clock was running out.

"By the way, when should we arrive for Thanksgiving?" Marla asked.

"Come at three o'clock. Last year at Julia's, your brother had to leave before dessert because his kids were getting sleepy. We can start earlier."

"You know how I worry when Rebecca and Jacob are here." Marla paused. "You don't have any fence around your pool, not to mention that lagoon. Need I remind you drowning is the number one cause of death among children four years old and younger in Florida? Home pools are the most common place where drownings occur. If either child slips away when our attention is diverted, that child could drown so easily."

"You say that every year, Marla. I'm not going to put up a pool enclosure for the few times when Michael and Charlene come over with their family. We never had a problem with our kids."

"All it takes is one mistake." Marla's voice choked; she spoke from personal experience. "It breaks my heart when I read the newspapers during the summer, because nearly every week has a report about some child drowning."

"This isn't summer, remember? It'll probably be cool by Thanksgiving. Besides, if you're watching them, Rebecca and Jacob will have nothing to worry about." Cynthia opened the front door, standing aside for her to pass. Her tone was clearly one of dismissal.

Too bad we couldn't get the mandatory pool fence law passed, Marla thought, reflecting on her activities with the child drowning-prevention coalition. She wouldn't give up because curious children always found a way to get near a pool.

"Will Corbin be coming to Thanksgiving dinner? We haven't seen your brother in a while," she said to Cynthia.

Cynthia blinked. "He'll be out of town."

"What's he doing these days, anyway?" Cynthia rarely talked about him, and he almost never came to family functions.

"You might say he's tied up in a new job. Now, Marla, I've left David sitting back there all by himself. If you'll pardon me, I need to attend to my guest. I'll rely on you to find out what you can about Ben's death. Ask that cop friend of yours, and check into which one of our board members might be involved."

Like you, cuz? Her cousin was hiding something about her relationship with Ben Kline. Marla might not like the dirt she dug up, but her sense of outrage compelled her to investigate.

She exited into the warm afternoon. At least Shark and Annie hadn't blocked her

84

car. Parked in front of the garage was a battered blue Chevy, presumably Shark's vehicle. Seeing it gave her a sense of unease that she shrugged off. Too many other things on her mind. Hastening into her Toyota, she turned the ignition and changed gears.

Priority number one was to find out who was dumping medical waste, and Dr. Russ Taylor headed the list. First thing next morning, she'd make an appointment to visit the eminent surgeon. Now she only had to decide which faux medical emergency should afflict her.

5

Monday morning brought a dreary start to the day. Dark gray clouds lumbered across the sky, bringing the smell of rain and a chill wind, heralding the first cold front of the season. Marla bundled herself into a sweater before taking Spooks out for his walk. It was too early to call Dr. Taylor's office, and she doubted she'd get an appointment for today anyway. You had to be dying in order to be penciled in on a doctor's busy schedule, and even then you were likely to be referred to the closest emergency room. That is, if you could get through the automated telephone answering system to a real person.

"Busy schedule today, Spooks," she told the dog, as they marched briskly through the neighborhood. "You've got to see the vet for your vaccinations, then I'm going to the dentist for a cleaning. Oh, joy. At least you get knocked out when your teeth get cleaned." Food shopping was next on her list. It was her policy to boycott the super-market when she was hungry, so after a dental appointment should be perfect timing to avoid temptation. Later, she'd contact new chefs for Taste of the World and set up interviews with Ocean Guard's board members.

"A busy person is a happy person, right?" she added breezily. Her cheeks cold from the wind, she rounded the corner toward her town house and halted, yanking abruptly on the leash. Idling in front of her place was a blue Chevy Lumina. As soon as she veered into sight, it spun off like a scared squirrel.

Her mind instantly made the connection between this vehicle and the one she'd seen parked in front of Cynthia's garage. That one had looked awfully familiar. Was it because she'd seen the same car when taking Spooks out the other day? Nah, there were plenty of beat-up blue sedans in town. It was merely a coincidence that Shark had the same model. Paranoia was an understate-ment if she thought he was following her, es-pecially since she'd just met the guy at Cynthia's house.

Her neighbor emerged lugging a sack of garbage to put by the curb. It crossed her mind that he might have seen the vehicle cruising by before. Perhaps she should put her neighbors on the alert. If someone was keeping tabs on her movements, extra insurance in terms of neighborly observation would be useful.

Of course, she shouldn't ignore the possibility that dear old Stan had hired someone to annoy her. Her ex-spouse should know that tactic wouldn't work. She'd never sell her portion of their jointly owned property, no matter what nasty tricks he tried. Maybe she should call up his newest trophy wife and sound her out. Kimberly would be happy to brag about Stan.

"Hey, Moss," she called to her elderly neighbor. "How are you doing? If you've got a minute, I need to talk to you about something."

"Sure thing, mate," Moss said in a gravelly voice. Plopping down his bag, he trotted over, a spry character for a man in his seventies. His wife, Emma, hadn't aged as well. Moss was the one who ran errands and took charge of their household. A former carpenter, he enjoyed sea cruises and planned trips to different ports of call. Sporting a naval cap and wiry white beard, he reminded Marla of a ship's captain. His leathery face crinkled with pleasure as he neared her.

"I'm wondering about that blue car that was just in front of my town house," she said, getting straight to the point. "Have you seen it around here before?"

"Can't say that I have. Why?" His brow wrinkled in puzzlement.

Marla waved a hand in the air as though unconcerned. "Oh, it looked out of place in the neighborhood, that's all."

"Any reason why you're wondering about it being in front of *your* house? You do seem to have a knack for attracting trouble. What undertow is pulling you in deeper this time, mate?"

The old codger was too perceptive. Shrugging, she cocked her head. "I'm involved in a fund-raiser, and someone doesn't want our event to be a success. One of our board members was murdered last week."

"Go on." He gaped at her. "You could ask our new neighbor if he knows anything about that car. You met him yet?"

"No, who's that?"

"Name's Goat." Moss pointed three doors down. "Come on, I'll introduce you." On the way, he pulled a paper from his pocket. "I've been saving this to show you."

"What is it, your latest limerick? Let me

see." With a smile on her lips, she read his latest verse:

Computers, calculators, and gizmos galore;
Makes your head spin,
    your eyes red and sore;
These inventions are supposed to make
    life easy;
But they just turn my stomach queasy;
Please don't give me any more!

"I like it," she said, chuckling. Recently, Moss had entered the computer age so he could make travel arrangements on-line, but he was constantly calling her with questions. She handed him back the poem, glad he was still writing in spite of a spate of rejections.

Knocking on the new neighbor's door evoked a strange response. From inside, Marla heard a series of barks that sounded more human than canine. The door swung open, and on the threshold stood a man wearing a sheepskin vest over a Hawaiian shirt, shorts that showed off bony knees, and lamb's wool slippers. A fur hat with a tail capped his head. Wild dark eyes peered at them.

"Ba-a-a," was his greeting. "Who are you?"

In the background, Marla heard faint high-pitched sounds undulating like whale calls. Moss introduced them, then she brought up the matter of the car.

"Not mine, dude. Hey, wanna come in and see my cattle-prod collection?"

"Not today, thanks. Moss, let's go." Grabbing the old man's elbow, she turned away and stumbled down the steps. When she heard the door close behind them, she muttered, "Where did he come from — the zoo?"

Moss grinned, revealing a row of uneven crowned teeth. "Works as a dog groomer. You'd better keep a close eye on your pooch."

"Dear Lord." Marla shuddered at the thought of her precious pet in that man's clutches. "Speaking of dogs, I've got to take Spooks for his shots. How is Emma doing today?" His wife had spent the afternoon at Macy's yesterday, then complained about her legs aching.

"She's well enough to meet her bridge group for lunch."

"Say hello for me, will you? And Moss" — she touched his arm — "if you see that blue car again, let me know."

Walking into the vet's office always produced a maelstrom of smells and sounds. As a chorus of barking and high-pitched yelps assaulted her ears, Marla approached the front desk. A friendly golden retriever leapt at her, bouncing into her leg. She jumped back, tugging Spooks away on his leash. Animals were such close analogies to humans, she thought, keeping a wary eye on the large dog. Golden's overeagerness to greet new arrivals reminded her of car salesmen who wait in parking lots slobbering as prospective customers drive by. If you actually stop, they hound you to make a sale. Worse is the owner who allows the obnoxious behavior, like this guy who let his pet's leash trail on the floor.

Careful to keep Spooks from the larger animal's path, she gave their names to the receptionist. Sniffing, she wrinkled her nose. A strong pet odor tainted the air. Doubtless, the staff members were immune, just as she was used to the chemical scents from her salon.

Eager to complete her business, she was glad when a uniformed tech arrived to lead them into an examining room. Scooping Spooks into her arms, she cuddled his trembling body.

"Poor baby," she murmured. "This won't take long. You'll be okay." Her fingers stroked his soft coat of creamy hair while she examined the tan-and-gray squares designed in geometric swirls on the linoleum floor. Looking as though it had seen better days, the linoleum continued halfway up the walls. Splash guard against pet accidents, she presumed.

Resigned to a long wait, she sank onto a built-in bench against the wall. Its Formica surface was as cold and hard as the examining table in the center of the room. Her gaze roamed to the wall hangings, a color diagram displaying the anatomy of a canine eye and a notice about rabies vaccinations. Spooks, held in her arms, quivered as though he knew what was coming.

A folding door that led to the staff area in the rear creaked open, and a white-coated doctor emerged. Since it was a group practice, Marla never knew which veterinarian she'd be assigned. A perky redhead who appeared young enough to be a recent college graduate washed her hands at a sink unit and then turned to face them.

"How are we this morning?" the doctor asked brightly.

We are anxious to be out of here, Marla felt like saying. Why did medical personnel always insist on using that royal pronoun? Annoyed by doctors who didn't address her

93

directly, she'd developed her own theory about their rationale. Perhaps it helped them maintain distance from their patients. After all, they were taught in medical school not to get emotionally involved. Inquiring about how *you* are feeling might imply that they really cared.

"Spooks is a little nervous," Marla understated, lifting him onto the examining table.

"Well, this won't take long." The vet turned away to prepare a couple of syringes. Marla's gaze fell upon a rectangular red plastic container on the counter. It had a transparent cover and a sticker with the international biohazard waste symbol.

"What goes into that box?" she asked the veterinarian, her interest aroused. Maybe she could learn something about medical waste while she was here.

The doctor called an assistant to hold Spooks while she performed her examination and administered the injections. "That's the sharps container. It's for needles and syringes. We also have one in surgery for disposable instruments."

Marla cringed as the first shot hit home and Spooks whimpered. "I see. And what happens to that box?"

The doctor frowned. "Why do you want to know?"

She shrugged. "Just curious. I've seen them in doctor's offices, but I never figured a vet would need them, too."

The woman smiled. "We follow very strict government guidelines. There are separate bins for other waste products. You know, bloody drapes and gauzes, body tissues. Of course, animal carcasses go to the pet cemetery to be cremated. We follow the owner's wishes in that regard."

"So what happens when the containers are filled?"

"They get picked up, but I'm not sure by whom. Dr. Evans would have that information, and he's not here today." The vet finished her exam and handed Spooks back to Marla. "He's in top shape, Miss Shore. Y'all have a good day now."

Marla exited in a thoughtful mood, depositing Spooks at home and going about her errands until her dental appointment. Sure enough, sitting on the counter at the dentist's treatment room was another one of the red plastic containers. This one was cylindrical in shape with a clear round top. It had a sticker on its side with the standard biohazard symbol. Also in the room was a tall bin with the same markings.

"What do you put in there?" Marla mumbled in the middle of rinsing her mouth.

The cup never seemed to hold enough water. She flipped the handle and a thin stream flowed into the small paper receptacle. A second rinse washed out the coppery taste of blood. Leaning back in the chair, she wiped her chin with the bib tied to her chest.

The dental hygienist, a talkative blond who wore a plastic face guard and latex gloves, resumed scraping tartar from Marla's teeth. "That one is the sharps container." The girl pointed to the cylindrical tub. "Needles, explorer tips, things like that go inside. The biohazardous waste bin is for gauzes, bibs, cotton, other items soiled with blood, and sometimes teeth. It gets emptied once a month into a larger red bag in the back."

Marla made a garbled attempt to ask another question, but the girl placed a saliva ejector in her mouth, making communication impossible. She had to wait for the next break in their routine when the girl switched to a tooth-polishing phase using a slow-speed handpiece instrument. As soon as she was ordered to rinse again, Marla barked out her next inquiry.

"Who picks up the bags and sharps containers?"

"There's a driver who comes by each

month. You can ask Dr. Stiller. He'd know more about it."

Marla fell silent so the girl could finish her job. By the time they were done, her teeth felt clean and polished, and she felt guilty craving a cup of coffee. Caffeine wasn't the best thing for your enamel, but she was never one to refuse any of its liquid forms. Coffee, tea, hot chocolate, and cola were her favorite drinks. So she'd get her teeth bleached someday. The price was worth it; she would never give up her daily stimulant. At least she wasn't a chocoholic like Tally. Even with the cream and sugar she put in her coffee, the calories wouldn't add up as much as a few Godivas.

Marla waited for the dentist to give her a clean bill of health before diving into her next query. "Can you tell me who is responsible for picking up your biomedical waste each month?" she asked, glad to be free of the bib around her neck. She sat up in the chair, swinging her legs over its edge.

Dr. Stiller regarded her with his luminous blue eyes. He had an almost mischievous appearance with short reddish brown hair, freckles, and a perennially boyish expression. Young looking for his forty-some years, his even features added to his allure. The man always asked about her life and work as though he really cared, and she appreciated his interest since it was so rare among any kind of medical personnel.

"There's a company called UFO Medical Waste Systems." He grinned, flashing a set of teeth so perfect they might have been carved from ivory.

"UFO? Do they send the stuff into space?"

He laughed, his eyes sparkling merrily. *Too bad he's married,* Marla thought for the umpteenth time.

"I think it stands for United Freight Operations," he said, sobering. "And no, they don't dispose of the waste in space. They incinerate it. We get the same registered transporter every month. He gives us a yellow sheet that's a biohazardous waste manifest. The bags are registered in my name, so they can be tracked." He accompanied her to the front desk where she waited for the bill.

"How much is the fee you pay to this company, if you don't mind my asking?"

"It's not much, maybe twenty dollars a month." His face lit with curiosity. "Why this sudden interest?"

"You know I do volunteer work for Ocean Guard. There's been some medical waste washed up on the beach, and we're trying to track the source." That sounded like a plausible excuse, and it was half-true. She just didn't mention which beach.

"If you find the labeled red bags, they're registered under the generator's name. Otherwise, it might be difficult to find out where it came from." He scratched his jaw. "I can give you a copy of the regulations if that would help."

"Sure, thanks." Her wheels of thought turned rapidly. "What about an oral surgeon's office? Wouldn't they produce more waste, meaning their fees would be higher?" Maybe someone was dumping medical waste illegally to avoid paying high fees to the disposal company. In that case, the mangrove preserve would merely serve as a convenient dump.

"Betty," Dr. Stiller said to the receptionist who'd just handed Marla her bill, "why don't you call over to Dr. Marconi's and ask them about pickup. Marla, I've got to go. Good luck with your inquiries." Waving, he hastened off and disappeared inside another treatment room.

Betty had an answer within several minutes, which allowed Marla time to write out her check. "UFO Medical Waste Systems picks up at their office once a week. But their fee isn't that much more than ours. Here's a copy of the Waste Acceptance Protocol," she said, handing Marla a set of stapled papers. "Say, can I ask you a question? My hair is awfully wilted lately. What can I do to make it look better?"

Marla glanced at Betty's straight cut. "Try using a good conditioner. That will give you more body. Layering could add more lift and so would taking an inch off the bottom." She grinned. "Stop in at the salon, and I'll work my magic on you."

Still smiling, she emerged outdoors into a blustery wind, thinking about what she'd learned. Medical waste. Who among Ocean Guard's board members had regular access to such products? Dr. Russ Taylor, that's who. The surgeon could be dumping the stuff illegally to save money. That would be logical only if he was suffering financial difficulty and the savings would be substantial. At least it was an alternative to being paranoid and believing Popeye's heir was sabotaging everything.

At home, she phoned Dr. Taylor's office, but she wasn't able to get an appointment until the following week, even though she claimed to have a painful injury. That put a crimp in her plans. How else would she determine the fees paid by a busy surgeon's office to the disposal company? The other option to consider was whether his practice was in trouble, and she knew who to call on that one. Her friend, Lance Pearson, was a computer guru who'd helped her out before. Now if she could only think of a way to request his assistance without having to view his web sites in return.

"Hey, Marla. What's up?" he answered in a raspy voice, as though he hadn't gotten much sleep.

"I need your expertise, pal," Marla replied, picturing his pasty complexion and owlish eyes. The guy ran a consultant business from his home and rarely went outdoors unless he was out of town on a job. "Is there any way for you to check into a doctor's practice to see how he's doing financially? I'm investigating something for Ocean Guard, and this information would really help."

He chuckled. "I read the papers, sweetie. You mixed up with that lawyer who got murdered? Seems to me I heard Ocean Guard's name mentioned."

She let out a resigned sigh. "You're right. He was one of the board members for the organization. So is Dr. Russ Taylor, the surgeon I need you to check out for me."

"So what's the scoop? You think the doc killed the attorney? Ha-ha. Maybe the lawyer got him on a malpractice suit and the doc had to pay."

Hmm. Marla hadn't thought of that one. "Interesting point. Will you be able to do this for me?" Dirt was one thing Lance was good at digging up.

"Sure thing, luv. I'll get back to you. Meanwhile, you can look forward to seeing some cool new web sites I've discovered. I still remember the last time you were over here." His voice deepened. "We had a good time, didn't we?"

Maybe you did, pal. Marla rolled her eyes heavenward. Lance was okay, but he kept trying to put the move on her. "I'll be holding my breath until I hear from you," she crooned.

"Wooie! I'm getting to work on this right away! See ya." *Click.* The receiver went dead.

Now what? Lance was on the trail of Dr. Taylor, and she'd be visiting his office next week. Time to turn her attention elsewhere. Marla placed the phone in its cradle and sat staring at the wall clock in her study. Shaped like a nautical ship's wheel, the brass time-piece rang bells on the hour. Stan had bought it on their honeymoon, and she'd taken perverse delight in claiming it after their divorce, along with other possessions they'd chosen together. Being selfish didn't enter into the equation; their mementoes meant more to her than to Stan. After their struggle over the divorce terms, she'd insisted on keeping those items she felt were rightfully hers.

Louse. She didn't want to think about him.

Maybe she should try calling around to different restaurants to see if she could coax any of the prospective chefs on her list into joining Taste of the World. Not all of the restaurants could be closed on Mondays.

She was reaching for the receiver when Spooks leapt off his favorite seat, barking madly. As he raced for the front door, Marla trailed after him. He threw his small body at the entrance as though he could force it open by mere willpower. Usually he exhibited this reaction when the mailman walked by, but Marla had already retrieved her letters from the box outside. Something whacked against the door, producing a furious assault by her pet. A car engine roared away, but Spooks continued his loud protest.

"Quiet. Move off now," she snapped, peering through the peep hole. No one was visible, so she unlocked the door and swung it wide. A scrunched brown paper bag lay on the doormat, stained with a moist blotch. She stared at the bag, unsure what to do. Unfortunately, whoever had delivered it had driven off, and she'd missed seeing the car. Regardless, caution made her wary. It seemed a good response when the blotch widened and turned a pinkish hue.

Marla backed off, afraid to touch the thing. Her palms sweaty, she shut the door and headed for the telephone.

She didn't even have to look up the number. Previous episodes had etched it in her mind.

"Dalton?" she said when the detective's gruff voice answered. "Can you come over to my house? I need you."

6

"You don't want to know what's in here," Dalton Vail said after peeking inside the brown paper bag. He'd taken it onto her lawn since it was seeping fluid, and because she hadn't been particularly eager to bring it in the house.

Fixated on the coal black highlights in his hair, Marla reluctantly turned her attention to the object that had been cast on her front doorstep. "Tell me."

"I've heard of dead chickens, and sometimes pigeons, but this here sure as hell looks like one of those damned ducks you see waddling around the neighborhood."

Marla clapped a hand over her mouth. "You mean it's —"

"Beheaded, actually." Grimacing, he rose from his crouched position clutching the bag with his fingertips. "Where can I dispose of this? It's going to stink."

"There's a garbage bin by the clubhouse.

Wait, don't you need it as evidence?" she called as he loped off.

"Evidence for what? Could have been anybody throwing it at your doorstep," he yelled back.

Hands on her hips, she glared at his retreating back. "I don't for one minute believe this was a prank," she muttered. "Maybe Moss and Emma saw something, or that guy Goat. I'm not just going to stand here, pal."

No one answered next door at Moss's house, so she trudged down the street to Goat's place. *He must be home,* she thought, her ears tuning into the sounds of jungle drumbeats and parrots squawking. Pounding loudly on his door, she stepped back when it was suddenly flung wide. An apparition stood there, a tall figure wrapped in furs with antlers on its head. It took Marla a moment to ascertain that this was Goat whose face was covered in black grease and dotted with feathers.

"Hey, babe." His eyes brightened as he recognized her. "You're just in time for the ceremony."

"What's that?" She tilted sideways, attempting to glimpse inside his house to see if those bird sounds were real. Probably not, she figured, recalling the whale cries from before. His taste in sound tracks was certainly distinctive, and that was putting it mildly.

"Come on in and join me in welcoming the spirits. The leopard is in ascendancy. His appetite must be appeased."

How, by feeding him a feathered friend? "Uh, do you have many pets in there?"

"Lots." He stroked a scraggly beard, regarding her with a sly expression. "I could show you Junior. He's way cool, although I removed his fangs."

"Ha-ha. What is he, a vampire?" Marla's throat tightened. This guy was one egg short in the henhouse.

"Nah, Junior is my best snake."

"No, thanks. I just wanted to know if you saw anything unusual out here in the past hour, like somebody driving by and throwing a package on my front doorstep."

"Sorry, babe." He jiggled his body. "Didn't see no car." The drumbeat accelerated, and he began gyrations that dipped his antlers perilously low over his forehead. *"Ugamaka, ugamaka, chugga, chugga, ush!"* he chanted. "One bird in the heather, one in the bush! Grab it, twist it, until it goes *squoosh!"*

"Oh, I've got to go. Here comes my friend," Marla said, gratefully spotting Vail hustling in her direction. "Thanks, Goat. Have fun with your ceremony. Maybe you can show me your menagerie some other time." Yeah, right. Like she'd need to have marbles in her head to enter his abode without protection.

Apparently, Vail guessed what she'd been up to. "Learn anything new?" he said, his face flushed.

"Not really. How about coming inside for a cold drink?"

"Sounds great, but I've got to get back to the station." Patting her shoulder, he smiled reassuringly. "Don't worry about this, Marla. Probably was some delinquents getting their kicks."

A flurry of trouble settled in her stomach. "Or?"

His expression clouded. "Or, it smells like voodoo, and I don't mean literally. Could be someone wishing you harm."

She'd heard of *santeria* rituals involving animal sacrifice. In most cases, chickens were used and not ducks. "Then it could be anyone who doesn't like me," she replied, mentally running down the short list. Stan, her ex-husband. Carolyn Sutton, a rival beauty salon operator with whom she'd had a run-in fairly recently. And then there was the heir to Popeye Boodles's estate, possibly willing to stop anyone who got in the way of his or her inheritance. As liaison to the chefs, Marla imagined she scored high on the hit list.

"Anything new on the case with Ben Kline?" she asked, curious to know if the attorney's death could be attributed to his position on Ocean Guard's board of directors.

"Nothing I'm at liberty to say."

Her gaze cast downward. The man's professionalism went too deep for him to confide in her, but knowing the reason didn't lessen her disappointment. "Are we still on for Saturday night?" she asked, keeping her tone neutral.

"Sure, I was going to call you. The show starts at eight o'clock. How about if we go out to eat first?"

"Sounds great." As long as his twelve-year-old daughter didn't mind an evening out with her elders. Not that her dad was so ancient. He looked damned good for a man of forty-two.

His expression darkened. "Marla, I'm only going to say this once. Be careful around those board of directors people. If you get any more warnings, assuming this dead duck was one, let me know immediately."

She shuffled her feet, wondering what he

wasn't telling her. "I'll look forward to Saturday," she said. Maybe by then, she'd have something more definitive to pass on to him.

None of the chefs she hoped to contact were available on Monday, so she put off the rest of her phone calls until the next day. Because Tuesdays were always slow in the afternoon, she should have time to take a break and complete her tasks.

Easier said than done. Marla was checking the appointment book at the front desk when Babs Winrow walked in the door. She looked harried, with her normally coiffed hair in disarray and papers sticking from her handbag, which she was trying to stuff back inside. Her face flushed, she appeared warm in her camel blazer and short black skirt.

"Marla, I know you're busy, but you've got to fit me in. I'm going out of town today, and my hair's a mess. I can't wait for my appointment next week."

Marla gazed into Babs's frantic hazel eyes and her mouth curved upward. Here was a perfect opportunity to interview one of Ocean Guard's board members without any of the others being present. "You're lucky you came in just now," she said. "I've got a

110

half hour before my next client, and I was going to use the time to work on our problem with the chefs. But I can do that later. Why don't you go ahead and get washed?"

"Marla," Nicole hissed from the next station while Marla waited at her chair, "isn't that the lady from your volunteer group?"

"Yeah," Marla tossed back. "She's chairman of the board. You can bet we've got lots to discuss."

Ten minutes later, Babs seated herself in the chair.

"So how are things, Marla?"

"Okay. How's Walter?" Babs's husband kept busy with his golf buddies during her business trips.

"Oh, he's great. You know, shuffles to the office all day then spends the evening in front of the television. I keep trying to get him interested in computers, but he could care less. Thank goodness he's into golf or the man would drive me nuts." She laughed, crinkle lines evident around her expertly made-up eyes.

"Come on, you two have fun together."

"That's true. We eat out a lot and go to art shows and concerts on weekends."

"I'm going to see *Rent* this Saturday night."

Babs grimaced. "Lord, I hope you bring your earplugs."

"Why, is it loud?"

"It's like going to a rock music concert, but the kids love that type of music, and the story appeals to them."

Oh, joy. Brianna should be in kid heaven then. Marla hoped it would be a meaningful experience for her and Dalton.

Lifting several strands of damp blond hair, Marla felt their texture. Slinky smooth from the conditioner, and not too many split ends. "You want the usual?" she asked. Babs rarely deviated from her preferred style, a short flattering bob.

"Naturally. You know, Marla, I'm so upset."

"Oh? Why is that?" Marla hesitated to turn on the blow-dryer in order to hear more clearly.

Babs stared at her from the mirror. "Ben Kline is dead. I just can't believe he's gone."

"Tell me about it. I was shocked when I heard the news."

"Not that it was such a surprise, considering what a lowlife he was. I mean, Ben possessed secrets that could harm a lot of people, in addition to taking on criminal defense cases that no one else wanted just so he could get media attention."

Marla switched on the blow-dryer, leaning forward as she applied her brush to the wet strands. "Aren't lawyers supposed to possess secrets? It's called client privilege." A frown creased her forehead. "Didn't Ben mention that term during our board meeting?"

Babs raised an eyebrow. "So he did. We were talking about the heir to Mr. Boodles's property."

"So if Ben claimed client privilege, that means —"

"He knew who would inherit if Ocean Guard defaults on its obligations."

"Could Ben's signature be on the trust agreement then?"

"No, the trust was drawn up years ago, but Ben had joined a group practice. They drew up the original document for Popeye, who was their client. After the group split up, Ben became his legal representative and maintained possession of his papers."

"Which might still be in his office." Wheels of thought spun in her head. "Do you think the heir doesn't want his identity known? And that's why Ben was murdered?"

Her client's mouth dropped open. "Marla, really!"

Marla switched her position to work on

113

the other side of Babs's hair. It was good that she was adept at lipreading over the sounds of a dryer because she didn't want to miss anything Babs said. "It's possible that one of Ocean Guard's board members is the heir to Popeye Boodles's estate. How else could someone be thwarting us using inside information?"

Babs's expression clouded. "I'd considered that angle, but Ben's death might have had nothing to do with Ocean Guard. At least not in the sense that you mean. Certainly some of our members were not too happy about Ben sitting on the board."

"Why is that?" Marla schooled her features into a look of mild interest, not wishing to show her eagerness for juicy gossip. Given the right situation, almost anyone could be coaxed into ratting on their associates. It was one of the baser qualities of human nature, but it sure led to some wild stories.

Babs tilted her head, and Marla danced around to complete the section of hair she was working on. "You'll never believe what I heard about Digby. He was involved in some kind of sex scandal that only came to light because Ben Kline exposed him. The whole thing was covered up, and most people don't remember it today, but Digby still bears a grudge. This happened about eight years ago. Now Ben is dead just when Digby is running for mayor. I'm sure he wouldn't want this old laundry hung out on the eve of election. He probably jumped for joy when he heard about Ben's death."

"Or he caused it himself out of revenge and fear of discovery," Marla muttered, examining her handiwork. Babs's hair had a nice sheen now that it was dry. "What about Dr. Taylor?" she asked, thinking about the polluted mangrove preserve. So far Cynthia hadn't informed anyone else on the board about their newest problem, planning to let her husband deal with a cleanup.

Babs raised her hands heavenward. "I love that man. He really helped me when my shoulder went out. His specialty is sports injuries, which is a popular field today. I don't begrudge him his Rolex watch or his Lexus, either. He's a skilled surgeon, although his bedside manner could use improvement."

Feeling a crick in her neck, Marla straightened her posture. "He struck me as being rather cold."

"I think that's because he expects so much of himself. He measures others by his own standards, and that might make him seem standoffish."

"How did he get along with Ben?"

Babs's gaze leveled on hers. "Since his manner can be curt, I can't be sure. But I noticed he avoided speaking directly to the man, so maybe there was something between them."

Marla lifted a curling iron from its holder on the counter, wondering how to phrase her next question. Seeking a reason for someone to be dumping medical waste, she'd thought financial need might be a motivator. But if Dr. Taylor drove a Lexus and wore expensive jewelry, maybe she was barking up the wrong tree.

"Does Dr. Taylor have a family?" Maybe his wife urged him to live above their means.

Babs smiled. "Susan is a lovely woman. They have a teenage daughter, and Russ dotes on her. That girl will want for nothing."

Despite his evident wealth, Marla still thought he was the best bet as a source of medical waste. She wouldn't give up on that angle yet.

"Your cousin had it in for Ben, too," Babs blurted. "You could see it in her eyes whenever she looked at him. They had something going on, but I can't say what it was. I don't suppose she told you?"

No, and you can bet your boots I wouldn't

116

squeal on Cynthia even if I knew what her beef was with Ben Kline.

Tightening her mouth, Marla applied the curling iron a bit too long on one strand until the smell of heat warned her off. Rather briskly, she wound the next section of hair.

"Darren seems very respectable," she said about the banker. "Did he have anything against Ben?"

"He leads a boring life in my opinion," Babs replied. "Such a bland exterior."

Ah, but still waters ran deep. Beneath the calm pool of his dark eyes could lie a seething cauldron. "What do you know about his background?"

"He grew up in Brooklyn, so I guess he can't be the heir."

"I wouldn't discount anyone." *Including you, pal,* she added silently. "Last but not least, what can you tell me about Stefano Barletti, the funeral director?"

Babs's eyes cooled. "We went to his place for a Pre-Need plan, and then someone recommended a different funeral home. Stefano's estimate was way higher than the other one. I don't know what he might have had against Ben, though."

Finished with the curling iron, Marla picked up a comb. Babs didn't like her hair too poofed up, but she still needed height.

Teasing gently, she considered what else to ask.

"Did you ever contact the chef from the Riverboat, Alex Sheffield?" Babs demanded.

"Not yet. Dr. Taylor said Alex had participated in Taste of the World before, but he'd dropped out."

"I can tell you why." Her voice rose. "Sheffield got angry because our president exposed his practice of charging high prices for expensive fish and serving cheaper substitutions. Alex lost a lot of customers over the fiasco. You can ask Jerry Caldwell for more details."

Having met Ocean Guard's president only once before, Marla didn't remember much about him. "Can you give me his number? It's worth checking into, although you'd think the chef would be mad at Jerry rather than Ocean Guard."

"Oh yeah? One of Ocean Guard's goals is to promote stricter regulations regarding the commercial fishing industry, and Alex has invested in that sector."

"So you're saying he might be trying to derail Ocean Guard?"

"It's always possible. But then he wouldn't have anything to do with Ben's murder, would he?"

Marla shook her head. The issues were getting more confusing, and she still had a feeling they were missing something significant. She'd better clear things up fast in order for the fund-raiser to go smoothly. Cynthia couldn't manage on her own; she needed Marla's input. But the way things were going, they were only seeing the tip of the iceberg.

"Marla, how are ya, hon?" cackled an elderly lady with a cane hobbling to the shampoo chair.

"Okay, Rose. You hanging in there?"

"Sure thing. Got my grandkids visiting this week."

"Super. Go on and get washed. I'll be ready for you soon." Sounds permeated her consciousness: spraying water, whirring hair dryers, soft music playing in the background. The pungent smell of perm solution hung in the air. *Comforts of home,* she thought happily, banishing Ocean Guard's troubles from her mind.

"Are you going anywhere special this week?" she asked Babs.

"Just Tampa again on business. Remember, I don't like too much hair spray," Babs cautioned.

Pressed for time, Marla finished her off quickly. At the front desk, she scribbled

Babs's bill and was handing it over the counter when her elbow collided with Babs's purse. Before she could grab it, the handbag tumbled to the floor.

"Oh, I'm so sorry." Kneeling down, Marla stuffed the contents back inside the purse, hesitating as she caught sight of a hotel reservation form. The location given was in Orlando. "I thought you were going to Tampa," she said, puzzled.

Babs snatched it from her fingers. "I am," she snapped. "See?" She withdrew another folder, shoving it in front of Marla's face. Sure enough, that one was for a hotel in Tampa. "Bye, Marla. Thanks for fitting me into your schedule. I'll see you again next week." Handing her a five-dollar bill for a tip, she gave a conspiratorial wink.

Marla straightened, a flush stealing over her features. Obviously she'd seen something Babs hadn't intended to show her. "Well, have a good trip," she ended lamely.

Time flew by until four o'clock. Taking a break, she dashed into the storeroom to call the chefs. She had no trouble getting a substitute for Robbie, the Cajun cook, having had the brilliant idea to contact Carmel Corvinne from The Creole Palace. A rival from New Orleans, Carmel was eager to take Robbie's place and showcase her cuisine. Alex Sheffield was less than enthusiastic, however. If anything, the restaurateur was downright hostile.

"You think I'd support that organization after what it did to me?" he shouted on the phone.

Marla lowered her voice. "I understand you had a problem with Ocean Guard's president, but that shouldn't influence your decision to join us for the fund-raiser. Participating in Taste of the World presents an opportunity to display your skills to an appreciative public. Doubtless your clientele would increase as a result. I can't see why you'd let a personal matter get in the way of such an exclusive invitation."

Bless my bones, if he doesn't buy that bullshit, I've lost my touch. Marla had been a good student of expository writing during her two years of college before she'd quit to attend cosmetology school. If it hadn't been for Tammy's drowning, she might never have made that career choice. In retrospect, being a teacher had been Ma's idea, not hers. After the accident, it had been an easy decision. Marla couldn't bear to work with children who would remind her every day of the guilt she carried in her soul. She chose instead to make people happy by improving their looks and by listening to their problems. Going to your hairdresser substituted for seeing a therapist, or at least that's how she viewed her profession.

Raucous laughter sounded on the line. "You're funny, lady. I'll never forget what Jerry Caldwell did to me. If I can screw him in return, believe me, I will. As for your so-called conservation group, they're just trying to strangle the commercial fishing industry with unnecessary rules. You're seasoning the wrong pot if you think I'd help you."

He slammed the phone with a loud crash, then the line went dead.

7

"Marla, it's me, David Newberg. How are you?"

His familiar voice on the phone brought her a measure of comfort. "Oh, I don't know. I just had an aggravating conversation with Alex Sheffield." David's call had come through just as she hung up from the chef, and her blood was still boiling from their conversation. "Alex has a grudge against Jerry Caldwell, Ocean Guard's president. He isn't too supportive of our organization. I think I'll contact that Moroccan chef if I can find the piece of paper Ben scribbled his name on."

"I have an idea about that. If you're not busy Friday night, let's go to his restaurant. I looked up the Medina. They have a single seating at seven-thirty. So what do you say?"

A ripple of pleasure shimmied through her at his thoughtfulness in relieving her of another chore. If they were going to meet the chef in person, she wouldn't waste time on a phone call. It was a good idea to sample the guy's cuisine anyway before she invited him to join Taste of the World.

"Okay. What should I wear?"

"Choose something comfortable because I understand we sit on the floor. I'll pick you up at seven. And Marla" — his voice lowered — "I'll be looking forward to seeing you again."

He'd hung up before she even realized he hadn't asked her address. For that matter, how had he gotten the salon number? She didn't recall mentioning the name of her establishment at their little tea party. Probably Cynthia had told him, she figured.

Her plans for the rest of the week got way-laid by a heavy workload. Whereas she used to open the salon at ten every morning, she'd changed hours and now accepted clients from nine to six, sometimes staying later. Thursday evening was the first breather in her schedule, so she headed home to get some rest.

Her ears registered the absence of barking before her mind noticed. Usually, Spooks bounced against the window, crazed upon her arrival. But as she pulled the car into the driveway, she missed the poodle's excited greeting. Fear gripping her heart, she braked to a stop in the garage, shut off the ignition, and charged from her vehicle.

"Oh, my God," she murmured upon entering her kitchen. Pots and pans were strewn about the floor, jumbled with the contents of her junk drawer and assorted utensils. Her collection of cookbooks, tossed from the shelves, littered the counters. Stunned, she surveyed the disaster with a sinking heart. *Why?* echoed through her brain. Crouching to her knees, she gathered the broken pieces from a souvenir apple bank she'd bought in New York. Somehow, that hurt the most. She couldn't conceive of how this had happened.

Silence deafened her, bringing her numb mind into focus. Alarmed, she raised her voice. "Spooks! Where are you?" Her heart lurched when he didn't respond. Straightening her spine, she glanced anxiously toward the living room. Was he sick, or worse, lying injured in one of the other rooms? Her pulse rate accelerated as she caught sight of an open patio door through the kitchen window. Ah, he must have gotten out. An instant later, her scalp prickled when she realized what it meant. Someone had been in her house, might even still be there.

Her body shaking, she whirled around

and dashed out through the open garage door to Moss's house. His wife, Emma, answered her frantic knocking.

"I've got to use your phone. Someone broke into my house."

"What do you mean, dear?" The elderly lady peered at her, concerned. "Come on in. You look awfully pale."

"Spooks is missing. I need to call the cops."

"Oh my," Emma warbled. "Use the phone in the kitchen."

"Is Moss home?" She proceeded inside, knowing her way.

"Moss had a golf game today, and then he was going over to Sol Weinstein's house to design a shelving unit. I'm not sure when he'll be back."

"That's all right." While her fingers punched in the code for Vail's direct line at the police department, she took two deep breaths so her voice wouldn't quiver on the phone.

"It's Marla," she said in a rushed voice when he answered.

"I was going to call you," Vail countered, the deep rich timbre of his voice bringing reassurance.

"Yeah, well I have news. Someone's broken into my house, and I'm afraid to go inside. They might still be there. Spooks is missing. He must have run out through the open patio door. And yes, I locked up when I left this morning," she said, anticipating his next question.

"Where are you now?" he demanded.

"Next door at Moss's place. I'll meet you outside. Y-You are coming, aren't you?"

"I'm on my way."

He arrived in less than fifteen minutes, accompanied by a patrol car and two officers. While she waited outdoors, wringing her hands together, they searched inside her house. Her knees wobbling, she ventured several feet down the street, looking for Spooks. A hidden part of her prayed that he wasn't lying lifeless in one of the rooms.

Emerging from the front door, Vail signaled to her. "No one is here. It's safe for you to come inside."

Marla covered her mouth with a hand. "Spooks . . . Did you find him?" Fearful of the answer, she took a few hesitant steps in his direction.

Vail's long stride carried him to her side. His smoky eyes studied her as he took the hand from her face and held it in his own. "Spooks isn't around. Has he ever gotten loose before?"

"Only once. He chased squirrels until he

got winded, then returned home." Tears threatened to spill from her eyes. Violation of the sanctity of her home she could deal with, but not the loss of her pet. She clutched Vail's hand as though it were a lifeline.

"What's that weird noise?" he asked, hunching his shoulders. His feet automatically parted in a fighting stance.

An undulating sound invaded her ears. "Oh, that's just Goat. He's got an animal fetish." Her eyes widened as she realized the import of what she'd said. "God, do you think —"

Without finishing her sentence, she flew toward her neighbor's residence and pounded on his door. Vail's heavy breathing sounded behind her as he caught up. The whale cries swelled as Goat flung open the door, only now they were mingled with wild barking. Spooks charged to greet her, leaping at her ankles and yipping furiously.

Bending down, Marla scooped him into her arms and hugged his small, soft body. "It's all right, sweetheart. You're safe now." His wet tongue licked her face as she grinned happily at Goat. "You found him."

"I figured he must have gotten loose from your yard. I was going to bring him over later." Goat scratched his scruffy beard. Assorted mewling and birds squawks emitted from inside. "Why you got cops hanging out?" he asked, his hooded gaze raking Dalton Vail.

"Someone broke into her house," Vail replied. "You seen anybody around her place?"

"No way, man." Goat shrugged in his sheepskin jacket. "Hope they didn't take nothing good."

"We'll see." Vail steered her down the steps and away. After Goat closed his door, the detective snorted. "He's a character, isn't he?"

"Thank goodness he took Spooks in. My baby could've gotten hit by a car." Cuddling the trembling pet to her breast, she entered her house. The other two officers approached Vail.

"I'll finish filling out the report," he told them. After the policemen left, he turned to Marla. "Look around and see if anything's been taken."

It didn't take her long to do a quick search. None of her jewelry was missing, nor were any important papers that she could see. Mostly her study had been disrupted, some of the kitchen drawers, and her bedside table. Electronic equipment was intact.

Vail's face was somber as he regarded her

in the room she'd made into an office. Papers were tossed everywhere, drawers pulled out. It would take her the entire evening to return things to order.

"Since nothing is missing, I'm going to assume this is another attempt to scare you," he said. "Let's review security precautions." And he spent the next ten minutes instructing her on measures she could take to secure her premises. "Get your alarm system connected, will you?" he grated finally.

In no hurry to be left alone, she invited him to remain for a cup of coffee. "I can fix us a quick plate of spaghetti and meatballs," she offered, hoping he'd keep her company.

"I'm not off duty yet, but I can stay a few minutes to finish this report. Want me to put the coffee on while you straighten up?"

"Sure." Watching him move around her kitchen had a strange effect on her. Stan had never lifted a finger to assist her with what he regarded as women's chores. Dalton, on the other hand, hummed to himself while he added water to the coffeemaker and spooned in the grounds. Once the rangy detective glanced up and caught her staring at him. His wide grin made her heart thud erratically fast. Her cheeks flaming, she resumed her task.

"Any luck on Ben's case?" she asked, sagging into a chair at the table after the place looked halfway tidy. The coffee smelled wonderfully aromatic, and she took a sip from a ceramic mug. *Just right,* she thought approvingly.

Grunting, Vail sat opposite her. "That's what I was going to call you about when you got me on the phone. We've identified the weapon that killed Ben Kline. It's from a knife collection belonging to Darren Shapiro."

Marla gasped. "A knife? I thought you said Ben had been bludgeoned to death."

"Just so."

She considered that a moment. "Whose prints were on the weapon?"

His eyes chilled. "I can't provide any further details."

"You mean you won't. I'm involved in this case, too. If you would share information with me, I might be able to help. For example, I might tell you about the medical waste polluting the mangrove preserve next to Cynthia's house. It may be connected to Ben's murder."

His jaw clenched. "I told you about the weapon and warned you about the board members."

"So you did. I imagine you must have

found something at the crime scene relating to Ocean Guard. Otherwise, why would you advise me to be cautious?" She tucked a strand of hair behind her ear, aware of his eyes following her movements.

"Papers relating to the group were strewn across the floor, some of them smeared with blood. It's my opinion someone was searching through them. Not that it proves anything, but that narrows the field." He took a noisy gulp of coffee, then intensified his gaze. "What's this about medical waste? Don't you have enough sense not to go snooping?"

"I wasn't snooping," she retorted, bristling with anger. "My cousin, Cynthia, invited me to her house and showed me the pollution. We're both committed to making Taste of the World a successful event, and someone is trying to stop us. I won't quit at the first sign of trouble."

Scraping back his chair, Vail stood. "Trouble? There's already been one murder, and you've found a dead duck on your doorstep. If you had an ounce of sense in your head, you'd accept this break-in as another warning. Maybe the killer is someone familiar who doesn't want to hurt you, unless you fail to back off."

Her eyes blazing, Marla leapt to her feet.

"I'll never give up my job with the chefs. Cynthia is counting on me. Whoever is hindering us just better watch out."

"I may not be around the next time you need me."

She couldn't believe her ears. Now he sounded just like Stan. "Excuse me? I can take care of myself, thank you. It so happened I needed a police report in case I have to make an insurance claim. That's the only reason why I called you."

He smirked. "You can let yourself believe that if you want, but I know differently." His expression softening, he stepped closer. "Seriously, Marla, I'm worried about you."

His concern melted her anger. "I'm a big girl. I'll be all right. But you might consider trusting me a bit more. Your case could progress faster if you accepted my input."

"Not when you place yourself in danger. Be on the alert until I see you Saturday. Brianna is looking forward to meeting you."

Marla breathed a sigh of relief when he left. His visit had brought escalating tension instead of the calm she sought.

Ignoring Vail's advice, she went to see Darren on Friday after work. Although she was in a rush to get ready for her date with David, she could spare time for a detour. These activities related to the fund-raiser were consuming all her free hours, she realized with a flush of guilt. When was the last time she'd called Tally, or any of her other friends?

Stop kvetching! Marla told herself as she approached Darren's house, a ranch-style structure located in an upscale neighborhood. *You're doing this for Cynthia. She needs you.*

Yeah, right. And how much of it was to prove her own worth?

An attractive brunette holding an oven mitt swung open the door after Marla rang the bell. "Yes?"

"Hi, I'm Marla Shore," she said, smiling. "I work on the committee for Taste of the World with Darren, and I'd like to ask him a few questions if he's available."

"All right," the woman said grudgingly, "but please be brief. Darren is late for an appointment."

Marla followed her into a comfortable living room. Her gaze swept the furnishings and fixed on the cocktail table, on which lay a couple of long-handled blades ending in curved hooks. Studying them, she didn't hear Darren come in.

"Miss Shore. What can I do for you?"

His curt tone brought her head up sharply. He stood a few feet away, freshly showered if his damp black hair and shaven jaw were any indication. Her gaze widened as she took in the man's physique. Wearing a navy knit shirt and jeans instead of a suit, he couldn't hide his bulging biceps or his muscular torso. Her mouth went dry as she imagined one of those lengthy objects in his meaty hand.

Moistening her lips, she sought a cautious reply.

"I want to talk to you about Ben."

His expression visibly relaxed, which made her wonder what he was afraid she might say. "Horrible, wasn't it? The poor louse must have screwed one of his clients."

"Detector Vail thinks Ocean Guard's board members might be involved." Biting her lower lip, Marla restrained herself from blurting out about the murder weapon.

"I know. We've already had a discussion on the subject." With a weary sigh, he gestured her to a seat on the couch. "I tried to explain to the lieutenant how we're working toward a common goal, or at least I thought so until we began having these problems. Now it seems someone is intent on stopping us."

He studied her from under his thick-set brows. "How is your job going? Were you able to get substitutes for the chefs?"

"I got Carmel Corvinne from The Creole Palace, and tonight I'll meet the guy from Medina." Resisting an urge to glance at her watch, she plowed on. "Our fund-raiser should be a successful event," she predicted.

"I hope you're right." Sitting in an armchair, he twisted his hands. "I realize Ocean Guard has its difficulties, but it is a worthy cause, and I'd hate to think we have a traitor in our midst, not to mention a murderer."

What about your knife that was found near the body, pal?

Marla couldn't mention that without offending him, so she tried a different approach instead. "What do you know about the relationship between Digby Raines and Ben? Babs mentioned something about a sex scandal."

Darren grimaced. "I only remember what I read in the paper, and this is going back eight years or so. Ben had a client who was accused of prostitution. She was a housewife who brought people into her home. Apparently, the woman videotaped her escapades. Ben got hold of one of the tapes and tried to sell it. The whole thing got washed over in a deal with prosecutors."

Clasping her fingers together, Marla leaned forward. "What does that have to do with Digby?"

"The videotape showed the woman having sex with Digby Raines. There may have been nude photos as well."

Marla swallowed a lump in her throat as an incident in her own life surfaced in her consciousness. She'd been in a similar situation when Bertha Kravitz threatened to expose certain photos from her shameful past. But instead of murdering the old woman, she'd succumbed to blackmail. It made her the perfect suspect when Bertha was killed and Dalton discovered their connection.

"Just because Digby might have held this incident against Ben, he didn't necessarily murder him over it," she said, her tone harsher than intended.

"Digby is in trouble at the polls. He might have been afraid Ben would bring the old skeleton out of the closet and cause further damage to his campaign."

"So you believe Digby is capable of homicide."

"I didn't say that." Darren jumped to his feet.

Changing tactics, Marla pointed to the objects on the cocktail table. "What are those? How interesting."

"They're part of my collection."

She lifted one by its wood handle, wrapped in cloth like a mummy. Her arm sagged from the weight. Was this considered a knife? It had a blade, albeit a curved one with a dull edge. Maybe you couldn't stab anyone with it, but you sure as hell could clunk somebody on the head. "What are they used for?" she queried, careful to keep her tone casual.

"Darren!" His wife interrupted, waving an accusing finger as she strode into the room. "Do you know how late it is? You'd better get moving, or you'll lose this job."

Did he have a meeting related to his bank business? If so, that would account for his wife's nervousness.

"Thanks for dropping in, Marla," Darren said, escorting her to the door.

Marla didn't see what he was thankful for. She'd brought up painful topics and hadn't come to any conclusions about his possible involvement in Ocean Guard's problems.

"Do me a favor," he whispered, grabbing her elbow. "Don't mention to anyone that you saw me going out tonight."

"Oh?"

He dropped his hand. "I'm supposed to be — hell, never mind. I'll be seeing you."

Sure, you will, but where are you going now? Outside, she closed the door upon hearing his wife raise her voice.

A neighbor, pulling weeds, gestured her

over. "Are they arguing again?"

Marla strolled by. "What do you mean?"

The gray-haired woman stood from her crouched position, a handful of grass in her gloved hand. "An awful lot of yelling and screaming goes on in that house, and it mostly ain't Helen's voice. I worry about her. Are you her friend?"

"We're acquaintances."

"Did she ever tell you where Darren goes every Friday and Saturday night? It's mighty late when he gets home. Helen never accompanies him."

"Sorry, I'm as much in the dark as you are. Have you known them long?"

Taking a rag from her pocket, the woman wiped her brow. "Long enough to realize Darren appears a quiet type when he's spiffed up in his suit, but behind his mild manner roars the heart of a lion. You don't want to get on his wrong side."

8

Red and blue cushions surrounded tables close to the floor in the Medina restaurant. Marla got the impression she was entering a huge tent as she and David were led to a bench covered in crimson cloth built against the wall. Billowing scarlet drapes and ornate gilded lanterns hung from the ceiling. Illumination was dim, but the lack of lighting appeared less noticeable than the loud volume of exotic music pouring from the speaker system.

Glad she had chosen a comfortable rust-and-black pants outfit, she settled onto the bench, folding her legs under the table. David lowered himself beside her, grunting as his large frame shifted the cushions at their back. His musk cologne drifted into her nostrils, making her glance his way in appreciation. He could have been on the cover of *GQ* magazine with his navy suit and geometric tie. The sky blue of his shirt enhanced the deep cobalt of his eyes.

Leaning against an embroidered fabric covering the wall in an eggshell, azure, and gold thread design, Marla surveyed their surroundings with interest. "Fascinating place," she commented, observing the decorations. Diners filled other tables, but no one had been served.

"I figured you would appreciate it," David said, his warm glance raking over her. "You seem like a person who savors new experiences."

Marla grinned, enjoying his company. "You're right, I don't like to be stagnant. It's fun to explore, especially when Fort Lauderdale has so much to offer. How long have you lived in the area?" Most people in south Florida came from somewhere else. Five years in residence, and you were considered a native. Originally from New York State, Marla retained a faint memory of icy winters, and she had no desire to repeat the experience.

David flicked a lock of fawn hair off his forehead. Her eyes trailed his movement, noticing the Rolex on his wrist. "I've been in the region for over twenty years, but I grew up in Connecticut."

"Did you go to school here?"

"I went to Boston. Couldn't stand winters, so I came back. I joined a firm for a few years and then struck out on my own. My practice has done really well, and now I finally have time to pay attention to the rest of my life." Winking, he lowered his voice. "I'm hoping you can be a part of it. I really like you, Marla. You've got style, intelligence, and looks all wrapped up in one sleek package. In other words, you turn me on."

Marla felt heat suffuse her cheeks. "Let's not get too schmaltzy, okay? We don't know each other very well yet."

"I hope to remedy that soon," David replied, snuggling closer so that his leg pressed against her thigh.

Before she could form a retort, the waitress arrived to pour rosewater from a gleaming silver urn over their uplifted palms for a ritual cleansing. "We'd like to talk to Chef Mustafa," she said to the girl. "We want to invite him to participate in a fundraiser for our organization."

"I'll tell him, miss." The young woman wore a colorful Moroccan vest with a long floral skirt, her thick black hair pulled into a ponytail. "Usually, Mustafa comes out after I serve the entrées to make certain everything is to your liking. You can speak to him then, if you wish."

"That's probably more convenient for

him," Marla agreed. Wiping her hands on a clean towel that served as a napkin, she redirected her conversation to David after the waitress left them alone.

"How long have you been involved with Ocean Guard?" she asked, aware of the warmth emanating from his body.

"I've been their accountant for seven years and got elected to the board two years ago. How about you?"

"I've been going to Taste of the World every year since Cynthia has been hosting it. This is the first time I've been on a committee."

"You're doing a fine job."

The waitress returned with several dishes. Marla put their conversation on hold while she broke off a chunk of sweet honey wheat bread and ate it with cumin-scented lentil soup called *harira*. There weren't any utensils provided so she was grateful for the towel that covered her lap. More courses rapidly followed: a cold salad with chopped tomatoes, bell peppers, cucumbers, and onions in a light vinaigrette sauce; an eggplant dish; pickled beets; and cooked carrots. *B'stella* was a pastry appetizer of baked phyllo dough layered inside with chicken, spiced eggs, crushed almonds, and cinnamon. Marla had her hands full struggling to eat with her fingers as food crumbled from her grasp.

Laughing, David stuffed a mouthful between his lips. "Delicious, isn't it?" he mumbled between bites, as intent on eating as Marla.

"Mmm," she managed to get out, her mouth full. It was too difficult to manage the tricky task of bringing meal to mouth, so she gave up on appetizers. Observing a fork in another diner's hand, she resolved to ask the waitress for utensils when their entrées came. *Being forced to use your fingers is a good way to lose weight,* she thought wryly.

"How are you progressing with the other chefs?" David queried, his face expressing genuine interest.

"Okay, and if Mustafa agrees to join us, I'll need to notify Digby about the changes so he can send a news release. Have you spoken to him lately?" She reached for a glass of water, her tongue flaming from the spicy food.

"Not really."

"I heard he was in the news in an unfavorable light a few years back, and Ben tried to cash in on it. Do you think Digby still harbored a grudge when Ben was killed? Or maybe Digby was afraid Ben would hang his old laundry out to air before the election?"

David frowned. "What do you mean?"

She waved her hand in front of her nose to dispel the smell of cigarette smoke. "I'm just trying to figure out who among Ocean Guard's board members might have had a motive to want Ben dead."

"Some detective questioned me about our group. I can't understand why the cops think it's one of us."

"The killer may be the same person who's discouraging our chefs from participating."

David regarded her with disbelief. "Surely you don't believe there's a connection?"

"What do you know about Dr. Taylor, for example? Or Darren? Or even Babs?" As she said the last name, she decided to phone the hotel in Tampa where Babs supposedly had gone for the weekend. Not that the woman's whereabouts had anything to do with Ben's demise, but if she couldn't be trusted to tell the truth, that was something else to consider.

"Probably not as much as you," David griped, "although I do know Russ was angry with Ben over an investment loss. As his accountant, I advised Russ against selling his interest in a side business involving physician collection services. But Ben offered him a slick deal on the initiative of another

145

client. Russ lost his ass in the ensuing take-over."

"Is he in trouble financially?"

David squinted at her. "I don't believe that's any of your concern."

"Yes, it is, because someone is dumping medical waste on Ocean Guard's mangrove preserve. I don't suppose Cynthia told you about this."

"Medical waste? What are you talking about?"

"You remember the provision in Popeye Boodles's trust that Ocean Guard must maintain the mangrove property in its pristine state? Well, it's my guess that who-ever stands to inherit is trying to make sure we fail to reach our goals. Not only is someone sabotaging our efforts with the chefs, but this same person might be the one responsible for polluting the pre-serve."

David's brows drew together as a troubled look sprang into his eyes. "I see. Then this same fellow could be the one who —"

"Killed Ben Kline. Possibly. Or Dr. Taylor could be saving money by not paying the biomedical disposal company. He has ac-cess to medical waste products. Maybe he's dumping the stuff there because it's conve-niently isolated. That would make sense if he's in financial need. Otherwise, I believe it's imperative to examine each board member's possible motive and alibi. By the way, where were you that night?"

He recoiled, an expression of horror on his face. "Surely you don't suspect me? I'm disappointed in you, Marla."

Playing with her water glass, she glanced at him from under her mascaraed lashes. "I trust you, David, really I do. But in case Detective Vail ever asks me about you . . ." She cut herself off, alarmed by the fury in his eyes.

"He's already interviewed me along with the other board members. What gives you the right to snoop into people's lives, anyway? Is that why you agreed to go out with me tonight, so you could check me out?"

Marla rested her hand on his arm, disturbed to find herself acquiring a suspicious nature like Dalton Vail. See how it ruins relationships? "Of course not," she said hastily, giving him her most demure smile, while part of her wondered if there was a grain of truth in his remark. "I think you're a charmingly attractive man, and I'd want to go out with you even if we were not both involved with Ocean Guard."

"That's better. I'd hate to think you were

using me to get information. Honesty is of crucial importance, Marla. I should make that clear straight off."

Realizing she'd ruffled his feathers, she attempted to appeal to his ego. "Oh, I agree. I understand how you must possess a high degree of integrity to work with people's money. As an accountant, you've got to be accountable to your clients. Ha-ha." She laughed at her own pun, relieved when his shoulders relaxed. But even as she switched topics, she realized he hadn't answered the question about where he had been the night Ben died.

The tension between them dissipated when their entrées arrived and a belly dancer shimmied into the center of the dining room. After requesting utensils, Marla dug into her lamb roasted with apricots and onions served with couscous, while a crescendo of music accompanied the dancer's graceful gyrations. During an interval when the sequined performer went to change props, David inquired about her work and other activities. She was glad to focus on mundane conversation until their desserts arrived. Chef Mustafa came out to circulate among the guests, and she extended an invitation for him to join Taste of the World.

"I'd be delighted, beautiful lady," he said, grinning.

Marla breathed an inward sigh of relief. At least they still had enough well-known chefs for the fund-raiser to be a success. A few loose ends warranted checking out, however. She intended to visit Pierre to see if he'd determined the cause of the explosion during his cooking class, and she needed to talk to the president of Ocean Guard about Alex Sheffield. If she could get a handle on who was baiting the chefs, it might help identify the person plaguing their organization, not to mention who had sent her that disgusting package the other day. A shudder racked her frame, but she quickly put aside any further disquieting thoughts so the remainder of their evening could be pleasant. David was an attentive escort, and she shouldn't risk losing her chances with him over her obstinacy to ferret out the truth.

"Excuse me, sir," the waitress cried, as they were on their way out the door. "I think you didn't fill this out correctly."

A look of puzzlement on his face, David retreated a few steps and grabbed the credit card form from her hand. "What's the matter?"

"You left off the gratuities. I'm sure that

was just an oversight, sir."

"Isn't the tip included?" he retorted, pointing to the paper.

"That's the tax we add in, which is part of the subtotal. If you'll give me your credit card back, I'll run it through again and tear up the old receipt."

His expression darkened ominously. "You must be mistaken. I'm sure the menu said a service charge is included with the price of the meal."

"But sir —"

He grasped her by the arm, squeezing her elbow. "Nobody accuses me of cheating them."

Fear entered the girl's eyes, and she struggled to pull away. "Let go, you're hurting me!"

"Bring me a menu and I'll prove you're wrong." Releasing her, he muttered to Marla: "She must be new here. I could've sworn the service charge was part of the thirty dollars for each of our dinners."

Aware of the stares from other patrons, Marla felt embarrassed and hoped for his sake that David was right. Sure enough, he pointed to the fine print under the food choices which said a fifteen percent service charge would be added to each bill.

"You see?" he chortled triumphantly. "I

always pay my expenses properly. You should fire her," he directed at the chef, who'd come bustling from the kitchen upon hearing the commotion. "Come on, Marla, we won't let this pitiful incident ruin our evening."

On the way home, he apologized, giving her a boyish grin. "Sorry if I blew my stack back there. I'm old-fashioned in that I don't like it when anyone disparages my honor. Guess I would've made a great swashbuckler, eh?"

Marla nodded. "Integrity means a lot to you, and it's a value that's important to me, too. At least you stood up for your rights."

His expression softened. "I knew you'd understand."

They drove in companionable silence back to her house. David walked around to the passenger side and opened the door for her. "I can be as chivalrous as you want, milady," he said, bowing. On her doorstep, he took her hand and raised it to his lips. "Alas, sweet lady of the night, if you would invite me inside your humble abode, I can prove my gentlemanly intent." His mouth brushed the back of her hand, sending a warm tingle through her body.

Temptation warred with common sense. "Not tonight, it's too late. I didn't think we'd get back after midnight, and tomorrow is a workday." He was so close she could smell his cologne. The musky scent warmed her blood, driving away any remnant of reason. Leaning forward, she kissed him boldly on the lips. "But let's get together again soon, okay?"

She went to bed with his taste on her mouth and awoke refreshed to a clear morning. Saturdays were always busy, and this one was no exception. Marla found herself tied up with a number of phone calls at work and had to shift some of her clients to Miloki and Nicole.

"That fund-raiser is taking more of your time than the salon," Nicole complained, organizing her curling irons.

"We're getting down to the wire with Taste of the World," Marla said, brushing cut hairs from a recent client off her chair. "I've got to make sure everything runs smoothly."

"Oh yeah? I thought that was your cousin's responsibility."

Tally said the same thing when Marla phoned her. "I don't see you anymore, and you hardly ever call. You're so wrapped up in working for Cynthia that you don't care about anyone else."

"That's not true." Standing behind the

front desk, Marla glanced at the receptionist. Anything she said would be fodder for gossip. "Can we talk about this later?"

"Sure, Marla. You know where to find me."

Marla gritted her teeth in frustration. Didn't they understand? Working for Taste of the World was an important responsibility. Cynthia had requested her help, and she couldn't refuse. Relations with her extended family had been delicate since that incident in her past. She was especially proud that Cynthia regarded her as someone to rely on. The chance had come to prove her mettle by ensuring the fundraiser was a success, but in order to do so, Marla had to stop whoever was opposing Ocean Guard. She wouldn't risk losing Cynthia's respect just because Nicole and Tally were acting childish. When Taste of the World was over, she'd shower her friends with attention. But right now, she hoped for their understanding.

As though conjured from her mind, Cynthia strode through the door, glanced around the busy salon in bewilderment, then fixed her gaze on Marla. "Here you are! We need to talk."

Marla glanced at her cousin's hairdo, which reminded her of a mile-high sundae. *You need a new hairstyle, cuz, and damned if*

I'm going to let you leave here without one. "Oh? How about I give you a trim while we chat? You'd look great in a layered cut. Consider it a complimentary session. If you like what I do, you can tell your friends."

Cynthia lifted her chin. "I like my hair the way it is."

"You can always grow it out. Seriously, you'd look a lot younger if you let me give it a try."

Cynthia's expression clouded with doubt. "Well, I don't know." She studied the other stylists, noting their work. "My beautician comes to the house."

Marla took her cousin by the elbow and guided her to a workstation. "I can accommodate you in that way," she crooned, indicating Cynthia should take a seat. "Occasionally, I'll get a client who needs me to come to her home, either to get her ready for a special occasion or because she's been ill. And we do weddings a lot, going to the hotel to do the entire wedding party. I believe in being flexible to meet your client's needs."

"Quite the businesswoman, aren't you?"

Marla resented Cynthia's surprised tone. "This is a business. What did you think? That it doesn't take any brains to do people's hair?" Not that some of the stylists didn't give that impression. Marla encouraged a certain dress code among her staff, so she didn't feel that was a problem at her salon. But she could see how potential customers might be put off by the mini-skirted, overly made-up gals in some of the places.

Cynthia's gaze met hers in the mirror. "You never finished college."

"No, but I went through twelve hundred hours of cosmetology school, and I'm licensed by the state board. To renew my license, I take an AIDS course every two years. I attend hair shows to learn new techniques. Maybe I haven't earned a bachelor's degree, but I assure you I've got more business savvy than many graduates."

Cynthia look chagrined. "I-I didn't mean that you weren't intelligent," she sputtered.

Sure you did, cuz. "That's all right. Now let me show you what I can do. Your coloring is a bit too brassy. Is it all right if we give you a rinse to tone down these highlights? You'll like the effect, believe me."

"Okay."

"Wait here, I'll be right back."

Marla hastened into the storeroom to select the products she needed. While she was there, the phone rang.

"Cut 'N Dye Beauty Salon," she warbled into the receiver.

155

"Hey, luv, it's Lance. Gotta minute?"

Her scalp prickled. "I always have a minute for my favorite computer guru. What's up? Did you get anything on Dr. Taylor?"

He chuckled. "Seems like you have a nose for rotten scents. The good doctor owns a major interest in a surgical outpatient center. With all the managed-care problems, its financial health is faltering. Why did you say you wanted this information?"

Marla took a moment to reply. "Someone is dumping medical waste on a mangrove preserve adjacent to my cousin's estate. It relates to Ocean Guard, and Dr. Taylor is on the board. I wonder how much money he'd save in bypassing payments to the waste disposal company. It bears checking into, wouldn't you say?"

9

Promising to treat Lance to dinner, Marla hung up, her mind in a turmoil. So Dr. Taylor's clinic was suffering from financial woes. Possibly, the HMOs had taken a bite out of his private practice as well. Would these give him a reason to pollute the mangrove preserve? Her theory would only be valid if the fees he paid to the waste disposal company were high enough. Of course it would shatter her idea that the heir to Popeye's estate was contaminating the land to void Ocean Guard's mandate, but different options were worth considering if she hoped to find the culprit. Next week, she'd take advantage of the opportunity to question Dr. Taylor in his office. Meanwhile, Cynthia waited for her attention.

Her cousin was tapping a foot impatiently when Marla returned holding a bottle of coloring solution. "I thought you must have taken a break," Cynthia snapped.

"I got a call from a friend who's handy with computers. I'd asked him to check into Dr. Taylor's business practices." Wrapping a plastic cape around Cynthia's shoulders, she related what Lance had said. "I'm hoping to learn more when I see Russ next week."

Her cousin's gaze darkened. "There's been more medical waste washing inland. Bruce said he'd hire someone to clean it up. I asked him about the heir to Popeye's estate. He said the trustee, Morton Riley, would have the most information. When I called his office, Mr. Riley's secretary said he's currently abroad on business. We're trying to track him down."

"How about the attorney who drew up the trust?"

"Bruce confirmed that it was Ben's firm. I left a message for his legal assistant, but the woman hasn't called back. Apparently, she's the one who found his body. I imagine she's still upset."

"That's another avenue to explore, then. Is this news what you came to tell me?" Once her cousin was adequately draped, Marla pulled on a latex glove and began applying the solution. *You're going to love the results, cuz.*

"Partly." Her gaze skewed away from the

158

mirror. "Annie is a problem."

Okay, Marla thought, *now we'll really get down to what's bothering you.* "You mean she's still going out with Shark?"

"Worse. I think she's stealing money from me."

Marla couldn't help her inadvertent gasp. "How so?"

"Bruce and I have a special place where we keep extra cash. The bills don't add up to what I counted at the beginning of the week. I think Shark is encouraging her to pilfer our funds."

"Have you confronted Annie?" Working the solution into Cynthia's roots, she felt the knots of tension plaguing her cousin. She'd have to tell the shampoo assistant to give Cynthia a good scalp massage. It was amazing how relaxing that could feel, and the extra care always made her clients feel better.

Cynthia shook her head, damp hair plastered to her scalp. "No, I have no proof. It breaks my heart that I can't trust her anymore. That boy is a terrible influence, but she won't listen to me. She says I dislike all her friends."

Marla set the timer for twenty minutes. "Teenagers don't listen to their parents. Young people think they know everything, until they make a mistake. Unfortunately, that's how many of them learn." She glanced away, unwilling to meet her cousin's sympathetic gaze. They both knew she spoke from her own tragic past experience. "I wish I could help you."

"You're a good listener, Marla." Cynthia twisted in the chair. "To be honest, I didn't take you seriously before we started working together on this fund-raiser, and I'm sorry for my snobbish attitude. When you get to my station in life, sometimes you forget to look beyond appearances. In your case, I was totally wrong. I hope you'll consider yourself my friend."

Marla's eyes misted. "Of course," she croaked.

"It's not easy when Annie screams that she hates me."

Patting her shoulder, Marla smiled. "Maybe your daughter takes out her anger on you, but I doubt it's how she truly feels. This is a difficult time during which she's testing her limits. I'm sure you and Bruce will manage."

Suddenly Cynthia stiffened, her eyebrows arching. "Well, look who's here. If it isn't Digby Raines, our mayoral candidate. I wonder what he wants."

As soon as he spotted Marla, he broke

into wide grin and crossed the distance between them. "Marla, darling. I see your cousin is getting her hair done. I was hoping you'd be free to give me a trim."

Marla accepted his handshake, figuring she was never going to finish work at this rate. At least she was having a profitable afternoon in terms of information gained. Glancing at her watch, she frowned. She still needed time to get ready for her date with Dalton and his daughter.

"I can squeeze you in until Cynthia is ready for me again. Come on, let's take a look." She led him to Giorgio's station. The male stylist was out of town for the weekend, so she could use his chair. She didn't want to inconvenience Cynthia by asking her to move. "What can I do for you?"

He winked at her through the mirror. "Now that's a leading question. Which answer do you want, the politically correct one, or the one that's really on my mind?"

His leering face turned her stomach. Instead of showing him to the door as impulse drove her, she spun his chair so he was forced to meet her narrowed gaze. "I'll do your hair, but that's the only body part in which I'm interested. Get my drift?"

He gave a low chuckle. "Sure, doll face."

161

"Do you want a similar style?" As her fingers riffled through his frosty white hair, she grimaced. His strands were as stiff as petrified straw. What did he use on them, shellac? Swirling off his forehead was a strong cowlick, slicked back so his darkened eyebrows highlighted his firm-jawed face. No doubt he was careful of the image he presented on television and in the newspapers. With his kindly expression, the man could easily pass for a benevolent philanthropist. His Wedgwood blue eyes crinkled when he smiled, but if you looked beyond, you could see the false gleam accompanying his wide-toothed smile.

Her glance dropped to his manicured nails. Now she liked him even less. In her opinion, men should keep their nails clean and blunt-cut but leave polishing to females.

"I know just what we'll do," she crooned. "You'll look absolutely fabulous when we're finished. Go on and get shampooed, then return to my station." Accompanying him to the shampoo bowl, she ordered the assistant to give him a good conditioning. His hair needed it after such a heavy application of holding spray.

Cynthia's timer went off just when Digby approached, his wet hair smelling of fresh herbs. She sent Cynthia to the shampoo area while she worked on the politician.

"I'm still upset about Ben Kline," Marla mentioned. Selecting a comb and pair of shears, she began snipping an inch off his ends.

His mouth sagged, and he cast his eyes downward. "Terrible, wasn't it? Makes you wonder."

"About what?" Marla leaned forward to hear over the noise of Nicole's blow-dryer at the next station.

"Who killed him. Ben rubbed people the wrong way, but you don't just clobber someone you dislike."

"Tell me about it. The murderer must have been harboring a lot of rage."

"Who knows what goes through people's minds? I attended the funeral. It surprised me to see Stefano there."

"Where was the burial?" Most likely Ben's remains went to a Jewish funeral home. Stefano's place wouldn't qualify.

"Levinson Memorial Gardens. There was quite a crowd. I can't imagine why Stefano showed up. Maybe he committed the evil deed and came to watch the finale."

"That's a nasty accusation."

"There was bad blood between them. I

don't suppose you knew Ben was suing Stefano?"

"No, I didn't." She paused expectantly, scissors in hand.

"Ben had initiated a class-action lawsuit on behalf of Stefano's customers. You'll have to ask Stefano about it if you want to know more." He grinned broadly, showing a row of perfectly even teeth. "Maybe Stefano decided to get the shyster off his back."

"Not by murdering him, I hope," Marla said dryly. Her glance caught Nicole's in the mirror. The stylist's mouth curved upward in a knowing grin. Doubtless Nicole had picked up on every word. Dear Lord, if any customers overheard, gossip would be flying around like static-laden hair. She finished the cut, then picked up a blow-dryer. "What do you know about Dr. Taylor's relationship to Ben?" she asked, lowering her voice.

"They had a falling out a while ago over some financial deal," Digby commented. "Russ isn't a happy guy, but I don't think it's because of that loss."

Switching on the blow-dryer, Marla lifted his damp strands. "What do you mean?"

Digby unfolded his arm from under the cape. "He's got another problem that he'll never be able to solve."

"The doctor seems so self-assured. What could bother him that much?"

"You'd have to ask him."

Moving her body, she aimed the blow-dryer at another section of his hair. "It seems as though you know an awful lot about these people." And he didn't want to fill her in, either.

He shrugged. "I make it my business to know what the voters' interests are. By the way, I've tried to get in touch with Babs to run the new press release by her before I send it out. Have you heard from her lately?"

"She's out of town."

"Again? Don't tell me, she went to Tampa."

Marla's jaw tightened. Why did she get the feeling he knew something he wasn't sharing? "I believe so."

Snorting, Digby's eyes roamed her length. "If you believe that, I can sell you a piece of real estate in the Everglades."

"Why don't you just level with me, Mr. Raines?" At least his hair was short, so it dried fast. She turned off the dryer and began styling his hair with a comb and brush.

His gaze fixed on her breasts. "This level

is just fine, thanks. But if you want to get deeper, honey, that can be arranged." As she changed position, he reached around and pinched her behind.

"Watch it, pal," she gritted, twisting a strand of hair until he winced.

He wasn't put off by her warning gesture. "Come on, we all know hairdressers like to accommodate their customers. How about if I buy you a drink after work?"

Seething rage blurred her vision. "I don't think so. Detective Vail and I have an engagement this evening for which I'm going to be late if I don't get you out of here and finish my cousin. Not that I'd ever consider going out with the likes of you. Aren't you married?"

"My wife is very understanding."

"Poor woman." Picking up a can of holding spray, she aimed the nozzle at his eyes. Her fingers twitched. Tempting though it might be to damage the bastard, she couldn't actually hurt anyone. After spraying his cowlick and the crown of his head, she untied his cape. "I'll write your ticket," she said, scribbling figures on a bill of sale. She handed it to him to take to the receptionist, not even caring if he gave her a tip.

He returned while she was cleaning off his

chair to clear the space for Cynthia. "Here, doll face, maybe you'll reconsider and give me a call."

Marla stared at the twenty-dollar bill in his hand. "Thanks, but I don't accept bribes. Give it to your wife instead. She deserves it more than I do for putting up with you."

His expression darkened. "Be careful, my dear. My tolerance goes only so far."

She faced him squarely. "And then?" *What do you do, pal, murder people?*

"You don't want to find out." Whipping around, he stalked out of the salon.

"What was that all about?" said Cynthia's voice from behind.

Taking a deep breath to calm her nerves, Marla turned to her cousin. "I believe Digby just propositioned me."

"Oh, so what else is new?" Her tone indicating that was a common occurrence, Cynthia dropped into the chair.

Marla worked quickly, creating a layered, more natural look for Cynthia's hair. By the time she was done, the lighter coloring and softer style lifted years from her cousin's appearance. "How do you like it?" she asked anxiously.

Cynthia studied her new look in the mirror. "It's different. I guess it's okay."

Marla mashed her teeth together. "That's all?"

Cynthia's eyes glowed. "I like it, really I do. I had the other hairdo for so long that I just need time to get used to this. I'd love for you to do Annie's hair, but I doubt she'd be willing to come in here."

"I could always do her at your house. I can be flexible." An inner glow of satisfaction warmed her. If Cynthia wanted her to do Annie, that meant she was pleased. "In fact, I'll stick a pair of shears into my purse right now so that I don't forget. If she's home tomorrow, give me a call, and I'll come over." Before it slipped her mind, Marla added the scissors to her handbag stashed in a drawer.

"Thanks, Marla." Standing, Cynthia hesitated. "I hope you'll forgive me for looking down on your profession. You're very talented."

When Cynthia started fumbling inside her purse, Marla waved a hand. "You don't need to give me a tip. I'm glad you stopped by. If Bruce learns anything, you'll let me know?"

Smiling, Cynthia touched her arm. "Of course. I'll be in touch soon, if not tomorrow."

As soon as she left, Marla rushed to clean her space. It was getting late, meaning she'd have to hurry to be ready by the time Dalton picked her up. She made one quick stop in the storeroom to sweep stray supplies off the counter and shelve them, and rinse out the sink.

As an afterthought, she opened the drawer where she'd put Ben's envelope. Now that she'd been to the Medina, she didn't need his note anymore. Halfway to tossing it into the trash, Marla changed her mind. It might be necessary to confirm arrangements with Mustafa at a later date, and she'd forgotten to ask for his business card. Better keep this just in case. After tucking it back in the drawer, she rushed out.

"Sorry to leave you in the lurch," she said to Nicole. "Will you lock up after everyone is finished?"

The dark-haired beauty grinned. "Only if you promise to let me know how your date went."

Marla rolled her eyes. "I doubt it'll be that exciting since Dalton's daughter will be along, but I'll get back to you."

She'd have to scramble to get ready in time. Fifteen minutes in the shower, fifteen more to get dressed and put on her makeup. "Sorry, Spooks. You've got to be quick." She let him out into the fenced backyard, then glanced around her kitchen with a wary eye. Ever since the break-in, she felt nervous coming home. It annoyed her that she couldn't regard her home as a safe haven like before. The end of a workday always meant relaxing in her own domain, and now that peace had been shattered. She should do what Dalton suggested and connect the alarm system, but it was another phone call on her long list and would have to wait its turn. Better to identify the person responsible for harassing her.

After Spooks completed his business, she opened the door for him to scoot inside. Then she was off and running to get ready.

She'd just finished applying her lipstick when the doorbell rang. *Lord save me, the guy is early! All right,* she thought while fastening her pearl earrings, so it's six-twenty. She'd have appreciated an extra ten minutes of preening. Shutting Spooks in her study so he wouldn't dash outside when she opened the front door, she went to greet her date.

Her smile faded when she viewed the tall man who stood on the doorstep. "You!" she cried. "What do you want?"

"Hello, Marla," said her ex-spouse Stan. His face wore its usual supercilious grin as he peered at her, hazel eyes raking her attire. She wore a burgundy-rayon dress with a

170

scoop neckline that showed off a single strand of pearls. "I see you still have that necklace I bought for you in St. Thomas. Going somewhere special?"

"It's none of your business." Shit, she didn't need this now. Anxiously, she scanned the street, hoping Stan would leave before her date arrived. She noticed Stan hadn't come alone. Wife number three, alias Kimberly, was sitting in his Mercedes studying her fingernails. The blond bimbo had a vacuous expression on her oval face.

Stan's shoulders hunched, a sign which told her he was prepared for battle. "I remembered the lease on your Toyota is up next month. Are you going to trade it in for another vehicle or pay the balance? Because if you want to own the car for a change, I have a proposition for you."

She rolled her eyes heavenward. "I can't wait to hear it."

"You agree to sell your portion of our jointly held property, and I'll pay for the rest of the car. It's in your best interest, you know. One less payment to make each month, and you can use the break."

"Don't tell me what I can use. And I'm managing just fine, thank you. No matter what you say, you won't convince me to give up my share of the rental income."

She turned to slam the door in his face, but he wedged his foot in the way and pushed his bulk inside. She heard Spooks bark furiously, and was sorry she hadn't let the dog loose. Spooks liked to tear at Stan's leg, a sport she'd love to encourage right now.

"I know how you struggle to make ends meet," he sneered. "You're just too ashamed to admit it. You had a good thing when we were married. A good thing."

"Maybe you thought so, but I got tired of being bullied. Does Kimberly let you push her around, too?"

His condescending glance set her blood to boiling. "Unlike your unworthy soul, Kim accepts my guidance."

"You mean your authoritative, domineering, superior attitude. Bastard. Don't ever call me unworthy."

Stepping closer, he leaned his face near enough to hers so she could smell his cheese breath. "We both know why you married me. You were a poor, lost child involved in a terrible tragedy. You needed someone with my knowledge and experience to help you."

She gripped the door to steady herself. "You were a lawyer in the firm I hired to defend myself against the lawsuit filed by

Tammy's parents. You took advantage of my vulnerability!"

"You were on the verge of a nervous breakdown. I helped put the pieces back together. Why don't you admit how much you owe me?"

She snorted, so furious her voice shook. "I suppose you want me to pay you back by signing over my half of the property. Well, forget it. I'll admit I was very malleable at that stage in my life. I needed someone to give me emotional support, and you fitted the bill. You made me feel wanted and attractive, and my mother was overjoyed I was seeing a wealthy Jewish lawyer. Was it any wonder I folded under pressure? Yet you never told me I was a worthy individual. You kept putting me down, until I felt I couldn't exist without you. Thank God Tally pulled me out of that slump by suggesting I go to cosmetology school. That, not marrying you, was the best thing I ever did."

"You're being stubborn just to annoy me, aren't you? Or are you jealous of Kimberly? It'll make her happy if we move into a bigger house, but we need the money from the sale of that property. Maybe you're just being obstinate to spite her."

Marla bit her words out from between clenched teeth. "You're the one who's being a stubborn ass. You won't give up, will you? I've said no before, and I'll say it again. Now get out of my house before I call the cops."

"Did I hear my profession mentioned?" Dalton's voice boomed.

Craning her neck, Marla spotted him marching along the walkway to her house, a thunderous expression on his craggy face. Relief washed through her, but she cast an anxious glance at the young girl by his side. Her wide-eyed look of apprehension tugged at Marla's heartstrings. This wasn't the kind of introduction she'd hoped for in meeting the girl.

"Dalton, allow me to introduce you to Stan Kaufman. Stan's my ex, and he was just leaving."

"What's the matter, honey?" Kimberly screeched, slamming the car door and stumbling in their direction. Her spiked heels made walking in a straight line difficult. "Is that bitch giving you trouble?"

10

Marla bit back a scathing reply. If she uttered the invective trembling on her tongue, she'd confirm Kimberly's low opinion of her in front of Vail's daughter. Aware of Brianna's watchful gaze, she forced a smile to her face. "I'm afraid Stan has outstayed his welcome. He was just leaving."

A stray thought entered her mind, and she turned to him. "In your eagerness to get me to sign over my share of our property, did you by any chance leave a package on my doorstep the other day?"

He lifted his nose. "Do you think I would leave you anything? You made your bed. Now lie in it." Whirling around, he cast Vail a hostile glance before stomping off toward his car. Kimberly stumbled after him, her tight skirt clinging to a set of firm thighs.

Flushing with embarrassment, she addressed Vail's daughter. "I'm so sorry. You must be Brianna. It's so nice to meet you."

Brianna didn't look anything like her father. Instead of the harsh angles delineating his face, hers was oval with less pronounced cheekbones and a narrower forehead. She shared his naturally thick eyebrows, but not the even divide of his chiseled lips. Chocolate brown eyes instead of Vail's steel gray regarded Marla above a nose with a slight upward tilt. Her gaze held a certain innocence that was reassuring, especially because Brianna's full lower lip gave her a sexy pout which would bring the boys in droves when she was older. Unaware of her potential allure, Brianna wore her toffee hair in a high ponytail. Marla glanced approvingly at the girl's black skirt and two-piece dusty rose sweater ensemble. Brianna had good taste, wearing stylish clothes suited to her slim figure.

She didn't respond to Marla's overture, but after the spectacle she'd just witnessed, Marla wasn't surprised. Before she had a chance to offer an explanation, Moss swaggered over holding an enormous bouquet of mixed flowers.

"Ahoy, mate. What's all the ruckus? These came for you earlier but you weren't home so I took them in." His keen glance surveyed her guests. "Whooie. This looks like a hot night. He send these to you?"

Vail's guarded expression gave her the answer. "I don't think so. Thanks, Moss. I'd better put these inside."

"Hey, wait a minute. Here's the card." He read the lines: "Last night was wonderful. Let's do it again next weekend. I'll call you soon. Love, David."

Lord save me, the night is going from bad to worse. Snatching the bouquet from her neighbor's hands, she whirled on her heels. "Please excuse me, Dalton, while I put these away. I'll just be a minute."

Inside, she freed Spooks from the study before staggering into the kitchen. The poodle, who'd been getting his jollies barking at the window, bounded after her. Arranging the flowers in a vase of tepid water, she took a deep breath to steady her nerves. This wasn't how she'd planned the evening to go.

"What a disaster," she told Spooks who'd settled for licking her ankle. "My one chance to make a good impression on Vail's daughter, and I blew it. He'll never ask me out again. I don't know why it should matter so much, but it does." Facing the counter, she pressed cool fingers to her throbbing temples.

Spooks dashed away, and a moment later she understood why. The dog pranced into the kitchen, giving his special greeting bark. Before she could turn, a large hand patted her back.

"It's all right, Marla," Vail's voice rumbled soothingly. Grasping her arms, he spun her around to face him. Brianna was nowhere in sight, presumably waiting outdoors. Humiliation sank into her stomach like a heavy matzoh ball.

"I'm sorry," she murmured, wishing she were witty enough to make a flippant remark. But the hurt went too deep, surprising her in its intensity.

"I'm the one who regrets that I didn't arrange this date with you earlier. Who the hell is David? And what the devil did you do with him last night?"

Marla glanced at him, startled. No, the man couldn't be jealous! "David Newberg is a friend of mine. We went out to dinner last night, that's all. Since when do you keep tabs on my activities, anyway?"

"When it involves your safety," he growled. "Didn't I warn you about Ocean Guard's board of directors? Newberg is a member. Is your interest in him personal, or are you snooping again?"

"We're just getting to know each other." She lifted her face, and his grip tightened. His masculine warmth seeped into her veins until her limbs turned rubbery. Never mind his furious expression. He was worried about her, and that realization made desire ripple through her.

"You're a damned distraction, you know that?" he said, thrusting her away. "You make my job that much more difficult. I get too worried about you to think clearly. My daughter warned me about women who cast a spell on unsuspecting men, and she was right."

Marla laughed, the sound bubbling from her chest. "I think I'm going to like that girl." Feeling lighthearted, she picked up her purse from the counter. Her glance fell to the card with the name of Babs's hotel scrawled across it.

"I know Brianna is waiting, but I need to make a quick phone call," she said. Without offering an explanation, Marla picked up the receiver and dialed one of the numbers she'd looked up earlier. When the Tampa operator answered, she gave Babs's name.

"Ms. Winrow isn't answering her room, ma'am. Would you like to leave a message?"

"Not at this time, thanks." Hitting the flash button, she listened for a dial tone then punched in the number for Orlando.

"Hello? Jen, is that you?" Babs's voice rasped on the other end of the line, when the hotel operator rang her room.

Marla replaced the receiver, her face grim. Babs had lied to her, and perhaps to her husband as well. She turned to Vail. "Remember Babs Winrow? She's the senior vice president of Tylex Industries who's chairperson of Ocean Guard's board. Babs told me she was going to Tampa on business, but she's in Orlando. She just thought I was someone named Jen."

Taking her by the elbow, Vail guided her toward the front door. "Snooping again, are you? Let's discuss it later. I'm sure you're eager to share what you know about my case. My daughter is waiting, and Brianna is not the most patient person."

Dalton had made a reservation at the Parisian Bistro off Las Olas Blvd. Its casual ambiance suited her mood. Munching on a crunchy piece of French bread and butter, Marla swallowed before focusing her attention on the girl.

"You have a beautiful name. What does it mean?"

Brianna, slurping a spoonful of savory onion soup, glanced at her. "Mom said it means strong. That's what I have to be to take care of Dad since she went to heaven." Bending her head, Brianna twisted a ribbon of melted cheese onto her spoon.

"Oh, I see. I'm so sorry about your mother."

"We're managing just fine. Carmen helps with the cleaning and cooks our dinners. I look after Lucky when I get home from school," she added proudly.

Marla raised a questioning eyebrow at Dalton who appeared tense by the stiff set of his shoulders and the tight angle of his jaw. *It must be difficult getting his daughter to accept the idea of a new woman in their life,* she thought, feeling a rush of sympathy. *How awful to deal with the loss of your mother at such a young age.*

"Carmen is the housekeeper," he explained quietly, fingering his wine glass. A lock of peppery hair tumbled onto his forehead as he tilted his head. "Lucky is our dog. Brianna is responsible for her care."

"What breed is it?" Maybe she could connect with the preteen over pets. Marla had always been a dog lover.

The girl shrugged. "Golden retriever. She needs a lot of attention." Her brows furrowed as though that meant something special.

"I have a poodle. Next time you come over, I'll introduce you properly. His name is Spooks. Tell me, what grade are you in?"

"Sixth. I go to Cypress Middle School."

"Do you have a favorite subject?"

"No. Everything sucks."

Marla leaned back while the waiter served their entrées. She'd ordered poulet parisienne, chicken in wine sauce. It came with garlic mashed potatoes and fresh asparagus.

"How about after school activities?" she tried, feeling it was getting more difficult instead of easier to get the girl to talk.

At least her appetite didn't suffer. Brianna dug into her steak with gusto. "I take ballet and jazz. Look, can we just eat in peace? I know you're trying to impress me and my dad. That's what they all do, but he stops seeing them after awhile."

Marla nearly choked on a piece of chicken. Speechless, she gave up on her attempt to win the girl's approval.

"This is delicious," Dalton said quickly, glancing between the two of them. "Want a taste?"

"I don't eat pork, thanks," Marla stated.

"Daddy said you're Jewish. Jewish people don't believe in cremation," Brianna said matter-of-factly.

Marla's mouth gaped. "Where did that come from?"

"My wife requested that she be cremated when she died," Dalton rasped. "Brianna has a hard time with it." His eyes glistened, and he put down his fork. "So do I."

My, aren't we having fun. I'd better lighten this up or we'll be sucking lemons for dessert.

"I meant to tell you what happened this week," she told him. "We got chefs to replace the ones who dropped out from Taste of the World. A new press release will go out soon."

"Uh-huh." Sparing a glance at his daughter, Vail resumed eating his dinner.

Brianna rolled her eyes. "Daddy, you tell me everything about your cases. I'm not an idiot. I know you want to discuss it with her since she's involved."

The corner of his mouth quirked. "I can't hide anything from you, can I?"

Marla could clearly see the understanding look passing between them, and somehow it warmed her heart to realize Dalton confided in his daughter. She supposed he needed a sounding board but wished he'd trust her as well. Maybe if she made the first move, he'd offer more information. A social setting might be just the impetus she needed to loosen his tongue.

"Regarding the chefs, I approached Alex Sheffield since someone told me he'd participated in Taste of the World before. He seemed very vindictive when he refused my offer, admitting he has a grudge against

Ocean Guard's president, Jerry Caldwell. It's possible, although unlikely, that he's behind the attempt to sabotage our fund-raiser."

"Sabotage?" Dalton's slate-colored eyes nailed her.

She took a gulp of water. "There's more going on behind the scenes at Ocean Guard than you would believe. Chefs have been receiving warnings against participating in Taste of the World. A couple of them have experienced disasters resulting in temporary closure of their establishment or significant fines. Someone at Pierre's cooking class was responsible for doctoring the bottle of rum that caused an explosion."

Now she'd caught his interest. His food forgotten, he leaned forward, eyes intent on her face. "Did you find out who it was?"

"Stupid me, I'm such a *shnook* I forgot to follow through on that one. But it's a viable lead if we can finger the culprit."

"Maybe Alex sent a spy to work in Pierre's kitchen," contributed Brianna who'd apparently been listening with keen ears. "If he hates Jerry Caldwell so much, he could be trying to sabotage Ocean Guard by ruining your party."

"It's a fund-raiser, not a party," Marla explained. "People buy expensive tickets to attend, and the money goes to the organization. This year is especially critical for the group."

"How is that?" Vail compressed his mouth when a busboy came to refill their water glasses.

"I'll tell you in a minute, after I finish about the chefs. I got Carmel Corvinne from The Creole Palace to replace Robbie from the Cajun Cookpot. He was nasty when I went to see him, and I didn't care for the unsanitary conditions in his kitchen. That place is a sewer."

She rattled on, the need to sort things out in her head taking precedence over other topics. "Dmitri Sarvik is sticking with us, but Max quit from the seafood place. When I saw him last, I got the impression he had something else to say. I've been meaning to get back to him on that. Mustafa is substituting for Pierre so we're okay in that respect."

"You were saying about this being a critical year for Ocean Guard?" Vail persisted.

Marla glanced at Brianna. "Maybe we should continue this discussion another time. I really wanted to get to know your daughter."

Brianna snorted. "Go ahead and talk

business. It's better than the two of you getting mushy."

Her face reddened. "You needn't worry. We don't have that kind of relationship."

The girl smirked. "Oh yeah? You're just showing interest in me to please him, aren't you?"

"Brianna," Vail growled, a thunderous look on his face.

Marla smiled sweetly at him. "I know. I'm just like all his other girlfriends, right?"

"Exactly," Brianna concluded with a smug expression.

"Well, you're wrong. I'm not looking for a serious relationship. Dalton and I are merely friends."

"Is that why he mentions you all the time?"

Marla gave him a thoughtful glance. "I wouldn't know about that, but we help each other. Right now, I could use his input. I'd like to learn more about you, honey, but you don't seem to want to talk about yourself. So you can just listen to us."

Ignoring the sullen expression on the girl's face, Marla returned to their earlier topic. "I was saying about Ocean Guard that this year is especially important. I'll tell you why."

Stuffing a piece of chicken into her

mouth, she chewed quickly. "The founder of Ocean Guard was Popeye Boodles, a rich benefactor who established a trust. He owned the mangrove preserve adjacent to Cynthia's estate. Under the terms of the trust, Ocean Guard inherits the property five years after his death if certain conditions are met." She explained the terms. "Someone is voiding the antipollution provision by dumping medical waste in the preserve."

"Dr. Taylor?" queried Vail, familiar with Ocean Guard's board members.

She ate a forkful of potatoes. "I thought of him immediately. His clinic isn't doing well financially, but I don't know if he'd save enough money by avoiding fees to the waste disposal company. Or he could be Popeye's heir. If Ocean Guard fails to meet the terms of the trust, his beneficiary wins the property. Cynthia and I suspect this person is a member of Ocean Guard's board of directors."

Vail paused midway to taking a bite of his pork tenderloin. "Do you think Ben Kline's death relates to this trust? If so, I've been following the wrong path. I figured the board was involved, but I'd assumed personal motives prompted the murder. Nearly every one of those people hated Ben and would have liked to see him dead."

Brianna piped in, having finished her meal. "I need a Coke, Daddy," she ordered in the tone of a child used to getting her way.

"Sure, honey," he agreed, signaling the waiter. "Marla, you want coffee?"

"I don't think so, thanks. It's getting late. We need to go to the theater."

"How about alibis?" Brianna interrupted.

Marla and Vail both stared at her as though she were some precocious genius.

"Gee, you're turning her into a regular Sherlock Holmes." Marla failed to keep a hint of disapproval from her tone. *You'd think he'd want to protect his child from the adversity of life.* Instead, Brianna was the one protecting him from an onslaught of predatory women. Not that Marla believed Dalton played the field that much. He hadn't given her that impression. Brianna was probably making up stories to scare Marla off.

Her thoughtful gaze fell upon him. The man exuded appeal with his thick ebony hair streaked with silver, intelligent gray eyes, and commanding jaw structure. His wide shoulders stretched the fabric of his charcoal sport jacket in a manner that suggested musculature beneath the fine wool cloth, and his confident air proclaimed self-assurance. All in all, the guy presented a damned sexy package, Marla concluded wistfully.

He must have sensed her change of attitude because his gaze smoldered back at her as if throwing a challenge. *Let's see what happens if we get closer*, she interpreted his message. *No thanks, pal*, she thought, needing more space. *I'm not ready for that just yet. And neither is your daughter.*

They didn't get a chance to resume their discussion until later at the Broward Center for Performing Arts where *Rent* was playing. Their center seats were adequate even in the rear orchestra section. Marla glanced at a control console situated in the middle of the high-ceiling room. It boasted enough lights and switches to qualify as an airplane cockpit. People filtered in, chattering loudly. Senior citizens wearing formal white and black served as ushers. While waiting for the music to begin, Marla scanned the hair styles of the people in front of them. *Look at that guy, the one who is bald on top.* He'd combed his mat of hair from the nape to his forehead. It looked ridiculous with a tuft sticking straight up. What some guys would do to preserve their masculine image. Didn't they know bald men could be sexy, especially if they look like Patrick Stewart? She could always tell if a man had implants, too. You could see the plugs. They weren't fooling anyone but themselves.

Vail sat between her and his daughter. His arm leaned against Marla's, making her acutely conscious of his nearness and the rock-solid hardness of his biceps. Her nerves were so attuned to his touch that she quivered inwardly from the contact.

"Brianna mentioned alibis," she said, hoping to coax him into revealing more information. "Did you have a chance to investigate each of the board members?"

He shifted away from her, leaving in his wake the fragrance of spice cologne. "I've checked out anyone who might be involved."

"Of course, you're very thorough. It makes me wonder how you determined the murder weapon belonged to Darren Shapiro." Crossing her legs, she swung her foot back and forth.

Snorting in exasperation, Vail glared at her. "You're not going to give me any peace, are you? Stop moving your leg like that. It's giving me ideas."

"Really? What kind?"

"You know."

"I know a few things, but I'd like to learn

more. For example, what time was Ben killed? I seemed to have forgotten what you told me before."

His eyes narrowed. "For your information, Ben's murder occurred around eight o'clock Monday evening after your board meeting. Ben died from a blow to his head by a blunt instrument, a special type of curved knife used in Samoan ceremonies. His legal assistant said Darren Shapiro had given the knife to Ben as a gift in return for a favor. Ben displayed it on his wall."

"So you're saying the murderer grabbed this weapon off the wall and bonked Ben on the head? Whoever did it must have been angry and wanted to strike out. He snatched whatever was handy and hit Ben, maybe not even intending to kill."

"It would appear this was a crime of opportunity," Vail agreed, scratching his jaw. "The weapon was put back on the wall, the area partly cleaned up, but not enough to conceal all the trace evidence. We've got some good samples, and a set of prints for which we have no match. They don't belong to Shapiro, although he admitted the knife came from his collection."

"So you've eliminated him as a suspect."

"Not necessarily, but I am inclined to believe it was someone else. Motive is what I can't figure out. So many people had grudges against Ben."

"Any alibis not hold up?"

"Babs Winrow was home with her husband, Walter. Digby Raines was the guest of honor at a campaign dinner. David Newberg was at the movies; he showed me his ticket stub. Stefano Barletti went bowling with friends. Darren claimed he was visiting an acquaintance, but he wouldn't reveal his name. Dr. Taylor attended Digby's dinner. And then there is your cousin."

Marla stiffened. "Cynthia? Surely you don't count her as one of the murder suspects?"

His mouth twisted wryly. "I don't discount any possibilities, including the fact that you were at that meeting. Regarding your cousin, she was home alone that night. Or so she said."

A knot twisted her stomach. "But Cynthia has no motive. She had nothing against Ben."

Vail's expression clouded. "Oh yes, she certainly did."

11

As the orchestra began its overture, Marla sizzled with curiosity. She bit her lip to keep from firing questions about her cousin during the blaring musical introduction to *Rent*. The decibel level made conversation difficult anyway, so she suppressed her concerns and watched the curtain rise.

Her attention was diverted to the show which she found difficult to comprehend. Her ears couldn't distinguish the lyrics, although she understood most songs bemoaned the sad lives of the unfortunate characters. Either the acoustics were faulty, or the generation gap left her in the dark. Between the loud music and youth-oriented theme, she was ready for a drink by the time intermission rolled around.

"Isn't it awesome?" Brianna gushed, grinning happily on their way to the lobby.

"Oh yeah, it's wonderful," she muttered. "I think my ears are still ringing."

"Me, too," Vail said, a bemused expression on his face. "What happened to musicals with melody and romance? This one is a bummer. I'd just evict those people and be done with it."

They got in line at the refreshment stand. "You don't get it, Daddy," Brianna chided, her ponytail swinging as she bounced on her heels. Scorn crossed her features. "Just face it, you're a dork."

"Perhaps his taste in music is different from yours," Marla said soothingly.

"My taste in everything is different from hers," Vail grated, the creases around his eyes deepening.

It couldn't be easy for him to understand a girl on the verge of puberty, Marla thought with a swell of compassion. Or had his daughter already reached that milestone? Not being a maven on adolescence, she didn't presume to offer advice, although sometimes her insights were useful. Many of her clients described their troubles with teenaged children, and she'd learned a lot from acting as listening post. But Brianna had problems that stemmed from deeper roots, Marla decided, and she didn't feel experienced enough to deal with them.

Hoping to steer the conversation away from personal issues, she returned to an earlier topic, blurting out the question that plagued her. "What about Cynthia? You didn't finish telling me about her. What did she have against Ben?"

Vail quirked an eyebrow. "I think that's something you'll have to ask Cynthia for yourself."

"Is her motive strong enough so you believe she could have committed murder over it?"

"You and I don't think the same way as a murderer, Marla. What we regard as insignificant, a killer embellishes in his mind. Or else he's just after something in particular, like money. Explain to me how Popeye's trust works again. If Ocean Guard fails to meet its obligations, who inherits the property?"

"No one knows. Cynthia's husband was supposed to ask the trustee, Morton Riley, but he's out of town. Ben's firm originally drew up the trust. Maybe Ben was murdered to hide the identity of Popeye's heir. This might be the person responsible for sabotaging our fund raiser and dumping medical waste on the mangrove preserve."

"That doesn't work for me," Brianna proclaimed merrily. "Because if the heir gets the goods, everyone will know who it is. The heir can't be the murderer."

Marla was surprised by the girl's astuteness. "That's a good point, but this person might still be desperate enough to commit a crime, especially if rational thought doesn't enter the equation like you suggested," she added to Dalton.

"I'll see what I can find out," he promised. "What would you like to order?" They'd reached the front of the line.

She scanned the menu items. "I'll have a glass of Chardonnay, thanks. I'm still full from dinner."

"And I'll have a Coke. Man, I wish some of my friends were here," Brianna whined, looking bored.

Marla realized she was neglecting her duty in getting to know the girl, so the rest of intermission she spent querying Brianna about her interests while carefully keeping away from painful topics like parents. She figured they were both glad when the show started again.

When he brought her home, Vail left his daughter in the car to walk Marla to her door. "Listen, if I need your help with this investigation, I'll let you know. Otherwise, please steer clear of trouble, so I don't have to worry about you."

"I'll be careful," she hedged. "Thanks for a delightful evening. I'm glad I had the chance to meet Brianna. She's a lovely girl."

"Yeah, when she isn't mouthing off. Look, I'm not sure about my schedule right now, but I'll call you." He hesitated, wavering as though he wanted to say something else.

Marla felt the heat from his powerful frame even from where she stood. And she felt something more, vibes emanating from him that struck a chord within herself. In the lamplight, ribbons of silver gleamed in his hair. His intense gaze snagged hers, stealing the breath from her lungs.

"Brianna is watching," he said huskily.

"Yes."

"You know what I want to do."

"Yes."

"Next time."

"Is that a promise?" Her lips curved in a wistful smile.

"You bet." His jawline tightened. "Do as I say, Marla, and don't interfere with my case. I'm looking after your welfare."

"I know." Although she appreciated his concern, those words rankled. After living with Stan, she'd vowed to make her own decisions. No man would direct her path ever again.

Thus when Cynthia called to make her an offer she couldn't refuse, Marla felt no guilt in accepting. It was her life, and she'd do whatever she damn well pleased.

"Bruce has tracked Morton Riley to the Bahamas," Cynthia told her on the phone Sunday afternoon. "Ocean Guard has authorized the expense of sending you and David after him. David is stopping by to pick up the tickets, and he'll meet you at the airport tomorrow morning at eight for the flight to Nassau."

Marla's mouth gaped. A free trip to the Bahamas? "W-Why me?" she stuttered.

"I have to get the house ready for Thanksgiving," Cynthia explained in a coaxing tone. "You're the most logical person to go. Besides, this will be a great opportunity for you and David to get closer."

"Just how close do you mean? And whose idea was this, yours or my mother's?" Marla regretted the words as soon as they left her mouth.

"Actually, it was his idea. David is quite enamored with you, darling. I'm so thrilled for you. He's a brilliant catch."

Marla had mixed feelings. She wasn't that much of a fool to let a good man get away if he had potential. Not that matrimony was on her mind. Companionship was the key word here, that's all.

"When are the flights? I have to go back to work Tuesday."

"Get someone to cover for you. Your plane leaves Fort Lauderdale airport tomorrow at nine a.m. It's a half hour nonstop flight on Bahamasair, so you'll get in quite early. You may be able to finish your business in one day, but I've made a hotel reservation at the Marriott on Cable Beach just in case you have trouble locating Morton Riley. Your return flight is Wednesday evening."

"That's three days from now!" She'd have to call Nicole to cover for her. The stylist wouldn't be pleased, but this was important. "Don't you want me to come over and do Annie's hair today?" she asked, remembering Cynthia's request.

"Annie isn't home," Cynthia snapped. "She went off with Shark again. I swear that boy is a bad influence, but the stupid girl won't listen to me. Her eyes are blinded where he's concerned." Her cousin's voice lowered. "Now I'm noticing things missing from the house, Marla. Small objects, but expensive ones like an Lladro figurine and some Hummels. I've put my staff on alert, but no one's seen anything."

"Are you getting a background check on him?"

"I hired someone, but the report isn't ready, yet. Oh, before I forget, I'm giving

David spending money, so let him pay for all the meals."

Lord save me, this should be an interesting vacation. Doubtless Cynthia would expect to hear the intimate details of their relationship when she returned.

She didn't dare consider what Vail would think about her going on a jaunt with one of his suspects. But if David were the heir, he wouldn't be chasing after the trustee who could finger him on sight. David's integrity impressed her as being of paramount importance to him. Marla felt certain he was every bit as eager to locate Popeye's beneficiary as were she and her cousin. Ocean Guard's future viability was at stake, and so was Marla's continued regard in her relative's eyes. If she and David had the power to blow this case wide open, it was worth a try.

Opening her calendar, she confirmed that her appointment with Dr. Taylor wasn't until Thursday. Maybe she wouldn't need to keep it if Morton Riley pinpointed the heir.

Her hopes soaring, Marla waited for David at the check-in counter inside terminal three at Fort Lauderdale international airport. It was just past eight on

Monday morning, and already the concourse was crowded. She'd left her car in the economy parking lot for five dollars a day, bringing a wheeled piece of carry-on luggage as her only piece of baggage.

A hand on her shoulder made her whip around. "David!" she exclaimed, a flush of pleasure lighting her features as she regarded him. His twinkling cobalt eyes were accentuated by a blue dress shirt tucked into a pair of navy pants. A sport coat was flung over his arm. He'd combed his fawn hair into a side part so a lock of it hung appealingly across his forehead. His freshly shaven jaw smelled like lime as he gave her a quick embrace.

"You look lovely this morning," he said in a low, sensual tone. His gaze roamed from her clean, blow-dried hair to her scoop neck ivory shell with the cinnamon blazer and dark tobacco slacks. A pair of sturdy flats supported her feet.

"It's a little early for flattery, isn't it?" she joked. "Let's get in line." It didn't appear as though many people would be on their flight until they went to the gate. Mostly older passengers were present, presumably gamblers eager to try their luck at the casinos before the weekend crowd arrived.

"Can I get you a cup of coffee?" David

asked as they took seats facing a wall of windows.

"No, thanks, I'll wait until we get to our hotel. It's such a short flight." She smiled. "Besides, I'm already wired. I had two cups earlier."

"Have you been to Nassau before?"

"No, I haven't. I'd like to travel more often, but it's hard for me to get away from work, and I have to worry about Spooks. I put him in the kennel while we're gone, but I hate to do that to him."

He nodded. "I take my vacation in the summer, after tax season is over. Usually, I'll combine business and pleasure in Europe, where I've got some multinational accounts." He grinned broadly, showing two small dimples in his cheeks that she hadn't noticed before. "It's a minimal amount of work time that I put in, I assure you. Maybe if we're . . . You might like to go with me next year."

She raised her eyebrows. "In what capacity?"

"That depends. We'll have the chance to get to know each other better on this trip. I can't wait until we're alone."

Uh-oh. She'd neglected to ask Cynthia about the hotel arrangements. They'd better not be booked together in the same room!

Swallowing, she regarded him warily.

"Our purpose is to interview Morton Riley, remember? It's possible we might finish our business there today."

"Our return flight isn't until Wednesday," he pointed out. "There wasn't anything available before then."

"Oh, I see." Her hopes of leaving earlier flew out the door. Nicole wasn't too happy about covering for her again, and she had to take time out on Thursday to see Dr. Taylor. Ocean Guard's affairs were monopolizing her life.

Her excitement swelled as the time neared for boarding. At eight-thirty, a mint green and yellow twin-engine jet taxied to the gate. She grasped her bag as flight personnel pronounced the plane available for boarding a short time later. It wasn't a big jet, with rows of three seats each on either side of a center aisle. After settling in, she leafed through a copy of *Island Scene* magazine. Too wound up to concentrate, she put the issue away and twisted her hands in her lap until their plane taxied onto the runway. Her ears clogged as the cabin pressurized, and the engine noise once they took off made hearing difficult. They climbed above a cloud bank and veered away from the coastline within minutes.

"Beautiful view, isn't it?" David asked, cocking his head in her direction.

"Sure," Marla replied, staring out the window. He'd kindly offered her the window seat, so she watched, fascinated by the sea below.

His warm hand clasped one of hers. "You're not nervous, are you?"

Her laughter sounded shallow. "About what?"

"About us being together."

She glanced at his serious expression. "Of course not," she lied. "I'm just anxious to find Morton Riley. Aren't you?"

For a moment, a look of hostility marred his features, but then he smiled, a bit too brightly. "Certainly, but I'm not going to let business distract from our pleasure. This is a rare opportunity for us to be together, away from everyone we know."

A shiver wormed up her spine. What if he was the killer? She shouldn't discount the possibility that he was Popeye's heir just because he was rich and didn't need money.

Nah, that was nonsense. David was just coming on to her, that's all. She could handle him, or she could relax and see where things went between them. Time would tell.

The landing went smoothly. After they

passed through customs and immigration, a driver with a minibus took them into town. It was a bumpy ride, worse than the flight. What made it tolerable was the ocean view around every corner. Marla clutched her armrest, glad they hadn't rented a car. She didn't want to bother learning how to drive on the left side of the road.

They halted in front of the towering rose pink facade of the Marriott Cable Beach Resort.

"Your rooms aren't ready yet," a pleasant receptionist told them in a singsong voice. "If you come back at three o'clock, I should have the keys for you then."

Marla perked up at the plural words. Thank goodness Cynthia had the sense to reserve separate rooms. Pushing them together could only go so far without boomeranging.

"Let's find a phone and call Morton Riley," she suggested, after they'd checked their luggage with a bellhop. "Where is he staying?"

"He's renting a place in town. Riley works on international trade agreements," David explained, pulling a notebook from his jacket pocket. Ruffling through the pages, he showed her Riley's local address. "Once a year, he makes the rounds in the Caribbean basin. His house is probably near the government center."

"The phones must be downstairs where the shops are located. There's an escalator to the lower level. Let's go." She'd just as soon accomplish their mission right away. They could worry about what to do until Wednesday later, after they'd met the trustee.

Nobody answered when David dialed Riley's number. "Now what?" he said. "It's early yet. Riley may not get home until after working hours."

"We'll have to wait." Disappointed, Marla began strolling toward the shops. The lure of a sale could always distract her attention. Unfortunately, the price tags made her lip curl. *Who's gonna buy these baubles, pal? Casino high rollers?* she thought, peering in the window of a jewelry store.

They passed more reasonable shops beyond the casino at an interior corridor leading to the Radisson, an adjacent resort. Other women cast envious glances in her direction as they sized up her companion. Was this so bad? Here she was in the sunny Bahamas on a free ticket. Why couldn't she relax for a few hours?

"I wish this business with Ocean Guard was finished so we could get on with our lives," she remarked with a grimace of impatience.

David pursed his lips, examining her face. "I want you to have a good time while we're here, Marla. Why don't you let me worry about Ocean Guard? I can see Riley on my own."

"Are you kidding? I didn't come all this way to get shuffled aside. I'm just as concerned as you."

"I know that. I'm trying to save you needless aggravation. You work too hard. As you said, you don't get away very often. Why don't you regard this trip as a mini-vacation?"

"I can't, at least not until we see Riley."

They headed outdoors to a spectacular pool area with a cascading rock waterfall and waterslide. The beach area was crowded with sunbathers eager to catch the early-morning rays.

Squinting in the sunlight, David gave an engaging smile. "Even after we see Riley, we have to wait for our flight. We might as well make the best of the situation. You're too uptight, Marla."

A sigh of resignation escaped her lips. "I can't help it. Time is marching on while we try to get answers to so many questions. Before we know it, Taste of the World will be upon us. We have to move quickly to expose the saboteur before he does any more damage . . . or any other chefs quit the fund-raiser."

He took her by the elbow and guided her back inside where they could talk out of the heat. "We'll get the guy, don't worry. Now chill out, sweetheart. We've got a few hours to kill. Let's enjoy this place."

"Thanks for being so understanding." He was right, of course. Why beat herself over the head with their problems when there was nothing they could do at the moment? David might decide she wasn't worth the effort if she didn't lighten up.

Lunch provided a pleasant diversion. They ate in the Goombay Mama restaurant off the main lobby. David talked her into ordering a Bahama Mama, a fruity orange rum drink with a whopping punch.

"Wow," she said, feeling its effects in terms of reeling senses. "They're not stingy with their liquor here."

A silly grin split his face. "These conch fritters are the best, better than I've had in Key West. Want a taste?"

She hadn't ordered an appetizer, deciding an entrée of grouper fingers would be enough. "No, thanks. Where should we go for dinner tonight?" Forcing herself to play tourist, she was gratified at David's delighted response.

"I've heard of a place called the Café Johnny Canoe," he said enthusiastically. "It's next to the Nassau Beach Hotel which is on the other side of this resort. I'll bet they have some other rum concoctions you can try. You sure enjoyed this one." Nodding toward her empty glass, he signaled the waiter for a refill.

"Hey, wait. I don't want to sleep all afternoon." A relaxed mood put her mind at ease. David had been correct in surmising she'd been too uptight.

"You're on vacation. Take advantage of it." He grinned disarmingly. "And if you want to take advantage of me, I'm available."

She flushed beet red, having just been thinking how charming he was and how sensuously curved his lips appeared. Their food arrived, and she hid her embarrassment by digging in with alacrity. The fish was crisp on the outside, flaky and warm as it slid down her throat. Having something solid in her stomach might dilute the effects of the rum.

After paying the bill, they checked in with the receptionist again, but their rooms still hadn't been cleaned.

"Let's go next door and take a look at that restaurant for tonight," David suggested.

Feeling as though her limbs were made of styling gel, she allowed him to guide her downstairs, where they headed outside toward the Nassau Beach Hotel. Tropical greenery shaded a walkway that wound a path to the adjacent resort.

Marla, feeling woozy, was carefully watching where she stepped and hoping the effects of the rum would wear off quickly.

"Look out!" David suddenly shouted.

Glancing up, Marla gasped. A coconut plummeted straight at her head.

12

As Marla stood frozen in place, a shadowy figure bolted from a balcony several stories above them. The coconut, an airborne missile, plunged earthward. Even as her mind registered the danger, strong hands shoved between her shoulder blades from behind. She pitched forward, taking the brunt of the fall on her hands and knees. Sprawling on the ground, she shook her spinning head. Thankfully, she'd landed on soft soil rather than concrete, but she hadn't escaped unscathed.

"Are you all right?"

David's solicitous inquiry penetrated her stunned consciousness. "Yes, I think so." Rising unsteadily to her feet with his assistance, she gingerly stretched her arms and legs. "No broken bones, just some scrapes." The fleshy part of her palms burned, but she managed to brush the dirt off her clothes.

"You're hurt." His gaze darkened, lifted to

the balcony. "Sonovabitch. Someone hurled that coconut at you. I can go after the bastard, unless you need me." His voice wavered indecisively.

"Whoever it was probably got away," she said in disgust. "I'd like to get cleaned up. By any chance, did you bring Band-Aids? I might have scraped my knees."

"There's some in my shaving kit."

"I'll look for the ladies' room while you access your luggage. Maybe you can urge the receptionist to get our rooms ready if you tell her about my accident." Holding his arm, she retreated toward their hotel.

"It wasn't an accident."

She heard the ominous note in his voice. "Do you really believe someone tried to bash my brains? Who else knew we were here besides Cynthia?" A feeling of dread assailed her. Surely her cousin couldn't be involved. More likely, they'd been followed onto the airplane. If so, who had given orders that she was to be put out of action?

"Popeye's heir must have gotten wind about our trip," David said in a grim tone. "That's the only thing that makes sense."

It became more imperative to contact Morton Riley, but when she phoned his number again, no one answered. "We could hop into a taxi and wait for him on his doorstep," she suggested, although her body craved rest. She'd cleansed her wounds in the rest room, but that only made her hands and knees ache more.

"Our rooms are almost ready. Why don't you lie down for a while? You look tired, and events have taken their toll. I'd rather you be well rested to enjoy our dinner tonight." His eyes crinkled as he smiled kindly.

Her heart warmed at his obvious concern. "What about Riley? Do you think the person who threw that coconut will go after him next? If Riley can identify the heir, he's in danger."

"I don't know. Maybe the guilty party just wants to put you out of commission, believing that will screw up the fund-raiser enough for your cousin to cancel the affair. That would achieve his objective if Ocean Guard fails to meet its commitments. You might be his sole target."

"Oh, joy. That's reassuring."

Loud music blared, and she noticed people were crowding the lobby. A band marched into sight. Dressed in colorful Junkanoo costumes, the players paraded for the tourists, pausing for photo opportunities.

She caught sight of the receptionist signaling. Their rooms were ready, and they finally received their keys.

"You go ahead and get some rest," David commanded. "I'll keep trying to reach Riley. If we connect, I'll let you know right away. Otherwise, why don't you and I meet back in the lobby at six? If Riley is meeting with government officials, he should be finished by then."

"Okay." Nothing appealed to her more than crawling into bed just then and seeking oblivion. Although her fears weren't abated, it felt good to put them aside for a brief interval. Deciding to let David carry the burden of worry, she succumbed to sleep within the hour.

When six o'clock drew near, Marla felt refreshed and prepared to tackle any difficulty. She'd showered and changed into a dressy pantsuit for the evening and descended the elevator, looking forward to greeting David.

His familiar countenance did not grace the lobby until fifteen minutes past their meeting time. When he appeared, a harried expression carved lines on his face. His skin showed an unhealthy pallor, and his hands, when he grasped hers, trembled.

"What's wrong?" she asked, her gaze scanning the lobby for hidden dangers.

He gave a weak smile that didn't reach his

eyes. "I couldn't rest. Too wound up, I suppose. How about you? You look ravishing tonight." His posture eased as he regarded her with a mock leer. "Maybe we should just go to dinner and forget about Riley until tomorrow. It's not often we get the chance to be alone together."

How could he ignore their reason for being there? "If you're not going to Riley's place now, I am. Will you come or not?" A hint of annoyance spiced her tone. She couldn't help it; here he was romancing her when they had business to conduct. *I'm not some sappy female, pal. Normally, I can face the tough issues. When someone isn't trying to bash my brains in with a coconut, that is.*

His mouth curved downward at her decision. "Of course I'm coming. I was just trying to save you some grief."

"Why? Do you know something I don't?"

He glanced at her before averting his eyes. "You're being unusually hostile."

"You're being evasive. You looked upset when I met you."

"I'm concerned about your safety."

"Your face was white, like you'd seen a ghost."

"All right, I'm worried because Morton Riley still isn't answering his phone. I don't want us to get involved if the Bahamian police show up. They might detain us."

She raised her eyebrows quizzically. "What for? Detain us over his absence?"

His lips tightened into a thin line. "We'll find out soon enough. Let's go and get this visit over with."

Outside, the weather had become cloudy and windy with the heavy ambience of impending rain. A crowd milled about the valet stand, while a line of taxis waited for customers.

"Let's take a jitney," David suggested, peering about with a guarded expression. "If anyone is keeping tabs on our movements, it'll be harder to track us with people getting on and off along the route. We'll take a taxi back to the hotel."

Rubbing her sore hands, she followed him down the curving driveway to street level, where they found a bus stop. It wasn't long before a lumbering vehicle rattled to a stop in front of them. Climbing inside, Marla took a seat at David's indication.

"The fare is seventy-five cents each, due when we get off. I'll take care of it," he whispered, pulling out his wallet.

"Some people are paying a dollar," she observed, realizing US currency was readily accepted on the island. "They must be leaving a tip for the driver."

"I noticed."

Staring out the window, she watched as they passed by a verdant golf course, brightly painted residences, and an empty schoolyard. Pink, coral, lime green, and turquoise were popular colors for most of the buildings. On the left, the ocean reflected slate gray from clouds scudding overhead in a darkening sky. Soon night would descend, and the air would be filled with perfumed fragrances of tropical flowers.

They got off near the British Colonial Hotel. "Which way?" she asked since David seemed more familiar with the place. He must have been to Nassau before, she assumed.

"Up this street." Trudging past the Conch Fritters Bar & Grill, he turned right and headed up a series of winding streets.

Marla became increasingly uneasy as they entered a residential district where few tourists were visible. Electric power lines crossed a street broken by uneven paving, which made walking difficult. A stray dog, black except for white forelegs, blocked their path, baring its teeth as they skirted around. Older-model cars littered a sandy lot like cast-aside toys. No lights shone from within an adjacent house, almost as though

217

the residents had abandoned their home like the drivers who'd discarded their dilapidated vehicles.

Beyond the hillside, Marla was relieved to find a more affluent community with single-story homes and lush landscaping. "This is it," David said, gesturing at a house with a white-tile roof and brick-paved driveway. Streetlights cast a dim glow on the sand-colored structure. David paused to kick a few pebbles out of his path.

Marla's stomach growled, reminding her it was mealtime. If Riley had been home, she'd have expected to sniff the spicy aroma of conch chowder emanating from his house. But the only scent was an earthy odor of rotting vegetation. No sounds came from within the house, which was dark as a ship's cargo hold. Maybe Riley had a dinner engagement in town. That would account for this unusual stillness.

Approaching the entrance, she hesitated when David didn't follow. "What's the matter?" she asked him with a puzzled frown.

"Things seem awfully quiet. Do you think it's right to show up unannounced like this?"

"Of course it is. Riley should be home by now, unless he was detained in town. In that case, we can leave a note on his door. I've got a pad of paper in my purse."

Raising her hand to ring the doorbell, she froze upon noticing the entry was slightly ajar. "Hello," she called, pushing the door open a crack.

"Marla, don't go inside," David warned, looming up beside her. "You'll be . . . It wouldn't be wise if no one's home."

It sounded as though he'd meant to say something else, but Marla ignored him, curiosity compelling her onward. A gust of wind swept by her legs, widening the crevice. Boldly, she shoved the door open and stepped inside.

"Mr. Riley?" Her voice came out as a hoarse cry. Hearing no response, she searched for a light switch. A hall light provided illumination for comfortable living-room furnishings. An open briefcase lay on an armchair, papers strewn on the floor. Marla glanced down an empty corridor, her heart thumping.

"Let me look for Riley. You stay here," David commanded, tapping her arm.

"Not on your life."

Pushing past him, Marla crept down a darkened hallway toward what she figured must be the kitchen. "Mr. Riley!" she called again. No response. The open archway into the kitchen beckoned.

Marla took one step inside, then stumbled backward. "Dear Lord. David!" Even in the faint light coming from the single window, she'd seen the blood. Everywhere. On the walls, countertops, covering the floor like a slippery, congealed mass. She hadn't missed the body either, or the butcher knife impaled in the man's chest.

Slapping a hand to her mouth, she whirled around to flee and collided with David's solid form.

He caught her by the shoulders. "My God," he mumbled. Without loosening his grip, he leaned sideways to peer into the kitchen. "That's Riley. His face . . . I've met him before." His tone deepened. "We've got to get out of here."

"Shouldn't we call the police?"

"Not now. Let's move."

Too stunned to comprehend, Marla followed him outside, where she wrapped stiff arms around her trembling body. A cool breeze ruffled her hair, tossing strands into her eyes. Her hand shook as she pushed them away.

David led her along the road, presumably heading toward the main thoroughfare where they could catch a taxi. "We can't afford to get involved with Bahamian officials," he explained. "We might miss our flight home. They might even think we had something to do with his death."

David's earlier words came back to her as she trailed him down a hill. *I don't want us to get involved if the Bahamian police show up. They might detain us.* Why would he have said that earlier unless he knew something was wrong? Other than Riley's not answering the phone, that is.

She halted in her tracks. "Hold on. Where were you while I was resting in my hotel room?"

David stopped and turned, his expression inscrutable. "I was getting changed."

"That wouldn't have taken two hours or more."

"What are you implying, Marla?"

"You came here, hoping to scoop me on Riley's interview. He was dead already when you found him, wasn't he?"

Gliding forward, David took her hands in his large palms. "I was hoping to spare you the trouble," he said earnestly. "If I could get the information from him, you wouldn't have had to bother. So I set up an appointment once Riley answered the phone. I got here within thirty minutes, but it was too late."

"If you knew he was dead, why didn't you tell me?"

"Would you have believed me? You'd have insisted on coming yourself, and you'd have been angry with me like you are now." He hung his head like a remorseful child. "I'm sorry. I made a mistake, but I was only trying to protect you."

"Dammit, David, I don't want to be protected." Stomping ahead, she fumed at the machinations of controlling men. Now their best lead was gone, and his killer might still be on the island. The residential district seemed deathly quiet for a Monday evening, and even the birds who were normally vocal had silenced their songs. Cedar pines scented the air, a light wind rustling through their branches. It sounded as though the night whispered against her, stealing her security and firing her blood with wild imaginings.

"I'm going to notify the authorities," she hissed to David once they'd reached their hotel safely. "I'll call from a pay phone and give an anonymous tip. That way, we won't get involved." She didn't want to miss their flight home any more than he did, but it wasn't right to leave Riley's body lying there. The Bahamian police would carry out an investigation. Besides, it was only conjecture on her part that someone from the mainland was involved. Riley might have had other enemies unrelated to their concerns.

Dinner at Café Johnny Canoe was a somber affair. Marla could barely eat her meal of grilled mahimahi, pigeon peas and rice, and macaroni and cheese Bahamian style. Something was very spicy, either the seasoning on the flaky fish, or those green things in the square of macaroni and cheese with its crusted top. Tears sprang into her eyes, but maybe it wasn't from the food. A lump clogged her throat, and she realized it was her reaction to Riley's death. Hoping to allay her horror of the night's events, she gulped down a rum-laden Goombay Smash.

Feeling numb, she was grateful when David gave her a chaste good night kiss on her forehead outside her room.

"Lock your door and go to sleep," he urged, his eyes dark with concern. "We've still got another two days before we can leave. Tomorrow we'll go shopping downtown. There should be safety in numbers, and I need to get gifts for a few people. It'll be better if we pretend things are normal."

She saw what he meant by safety in numbers after they took the jitney downtown in the morning. East Bay Street was mobbed with cruise-ship passengers bustling from

223

one shop to the next. Glad she had worn her sweater as a cold front had moved in, Marla suggested they work their way down one side of the street first.

Souvenir shops, perfumeries, china and crystal emporiums, and jewelry stores tempted her with their wares. Stopping in one of the latter, she bought a few trinkets for her staff. David showed her the heavy sterling silver bracelets he'd bought for his mother and sister as they strolled farther along the street.

"Damn, the link just broke!" he cried, showing her the damaged item. "I'll have to return it." In the store, he handed the receipt to a clerk. "I'll take this other bracelet," he proclaimed, "but see how you gave me fifteen percent off on both these items as they were priced the same? I think I'll owe you money back if I get this other one."

Marla regarded him with admiration. "Not everyone would be so honest," she said. "If the store clerk didn't notice the discount, it would be her fault."

His jaw dropped in horror. "That's being untruthful, Marla. I always tell the salesgirl when she's made a mistake, even if it's in the store's favor."

"Of course." But even as she agreed,

Marla wondered why he'd been untruthful to her. David should have told her he'd been to Riley's house and found him dead. Instead, he'd led her to the murder scene, where she had to discover the unpleasantness for herself. Nonetheless, she'd insisted on going despite his attempts to discourage her. She supposed he'd tried to protect her, although his approach rankled.

Lunchtime brought them to the Conch Fritters Bar & Grill. She ordered grilled grouper, baked sweet potato, and steamed zucchini. Painted wood parrots dangled from a thatched-roof ceiling where fans revolved to the lazy accompaniment of island music. It was a respite from their worries, although she couldn't dismiss the sensation that they were being watched.

Aware of her disquiet, David suggested they take a taxi that evening to Traveler's Rest, a popular native restaurant facing the ocean. Arriving after seven o'clock, they asked for a seat outdoors under an awning.

"No one followed us," she whispered so the other diners wouldn't hear. "We rode in the only vehicle coming this way."

David, looking handsome in a striped shirt and navy trousers, visibly relaxed. "I hope you're right."

As the sun descended, a calm settled over the sea that reflected her mood. She soaked in the peacefulness of the scene as though it were balm for her soul. No one had hassled them all day, and she felt relaxed enough to think clearly.

"So what are your theories about the heir?" she asked David, purposefully avoiding the subject of Morton Riley. She couldn't bear to think of the scene in his house.

"I haven't a clue." He sipped a banana daiquiri, gazing thoughtfully at the darkening sky. "There's Babs Winrow. It's always possible the heir is a woman, you know. She strikes me as a determined personality who's willing to do whatever it takes to achieve her goals."

"I think she's been lying to her husband. She told him she was going to a meeting in Tampa, but I happen to know she was in Orlando instead. I wonder what her purpose in going there was." Marla chewed on a piece of soft warmed bread that melted in her mouth. "Then there's Digby Raines whose political aspirations include flirting with every woman in sight."

David nodded vigorously, a lock of hair falling across his forehead.

"Raines was involved in some dirty dealings with Ben several years ago. I don't know if you heard about that."

"His porno flick? Yeah, I did, but I thought that was over with." She took a tentative taste of her grouper smothered in tomatoes, onions, and green peppers. It came with the ever-popular pigeon peas and rice along with cole slaw.

"It wasn't over with if Raines held a grudge or was afraid Ben would remind the public about that fiasco in an election year." He pointed a finger at her. "Don't forget Stefano Barletti. I've heard things about him, too."

"The funeral director?" She sniffed the balmy ocean air, wishing they were talking about lighter matters. Until the fund-raiser took place, she supposed none of them could rest easy.

"I heard Ben was suing Stefano on behalf of some clients."

"I need to talk to that guy," Marla mumbled half to herself. "I'm seeing Dr. Taylor on Thursday," she announced. They spent a few minutes discussing the medical waste problem Cynthia and her husband were handling. "I'd like to determine if Dr. Taylor is involved. He seems the logical choice."

David stuffed a barbecued shrimp into his mouth. "How about Darren Shapiro? He's always so quiet. Maybe he is secretly Pop-eye's heir, and he's the one who's been plot-ting against us."

Marla remembered what Vail had told her, that a weapon from Darren's collec-tion had killed Ben. "Who knows?" she said, suddenly edgy. "Anyway, what's on the agenda for tomorrow? We have the en-tire morning before we go to the airport. Where can we go that'll be safe?" Riley's murderer might still be waiting for an-other opportunity to take a potshot at her, and she didn't want to give him the chance.

David's expression brightened. "We'll go to Crystal Cay. It's an island park with an undersea exhibition where you can view the coral reef. Should be a good way to kill time."

Apparently someone else thought *kill* was the appropriate word. After she and David viewed the underwater observatory at Crystal Cay the next morning, they split up. The island, accessible via bridge from Nassau, had a beach, nature trails, and a seafood restaurant. Marla wanted to check out the Marine Gardens, while David headed for the Shark Tank. Tropical shrubbery made a thick jungle lining the walkways. Not many people were around, but that didn't bother Marla until she heard a loud *crack*. Startled, she quickened her pace. The thick foliage made seeing beyond the winding path impossible. Another loud noise sounded, and she felt a whoosh of air fly by her cheek. Her heart raced as realization dawned.

Someone was shooting at her.

Screaming David's name, she charged along the path searching for his familiar form. Trees obstructed her view as she rounded one corner after the next. Finally, Marla spied him trotting in her direction from the Turtle Pool. "We've got to get away from here!" she cried. "The killer is nearby. He has a gun!"

As though to emphasize her point, a crack sounded from behind, followed by a thudding sound on a nearby tree.

David's face blanched. "This way," he rasped, gesturing.

They wound up at the entrance without further incidents. Too many people were milling about the ticket window just after a new bus arrived for the murderer to fire at them.

"We'll take a taxi," David determined, eyeing the empty bus. He flagged a cab nearest to the curb, and they tumbled inside. "Marriott Resort," he ordered, before turning to Marla. "Let's get our bags and head to the airport, even if it's early."

Her voice shook as she replied. "I agree. I've had it with this place. Let's go home."

13

The waiting room in Dr. Taylor's office made Marla feel like a piece of meat in an inspection plant. Furnishings were nondescript, magazine selections were unappealing, and the receptionist displayed all the charm of an ice cooler. Marla was a patient number waiting to be called, examined, and signed off on a list. Glancing at the table where magazines were tossed haphazardly, she perused the titles: *Boating, Sports Illustrated, Skiing* (that was a good one in Florida), *Popular Mechanics,* and a three-month-old issue of *Newsweek.* Didn't Dr. Taylor realize women had different reading tastes than men?

After relieving her boredom by studying the hairstyles and clothes of the other patients cramming the small space, she turned her thoughts inward. Spooks had been ecstatic to greet her that morning when she'd picked him up from the kennel. She'd barely had time to take him home, let him out in the yard, and drink two cups of coffee before going to work at nine. Nicole hadn't been too happy to learn Marla had an afternoon appointment which would again mean foisting customers off on her colleagues. Marla felt guilty already, having ignored the messages on her answering machine in her rush to get to work that morning. Anita was eager for a report on her progress with David. Marla couldn't help wondering what part her mother had played in Cynthia's invitation to them. Cynthia wanted to know how she and David had gotten along as well as what they'd learned. Tally was concerned about her absence, making Marla regret she hadn't notified her friend that she was going away, and Dalton Vail demanded an immediate return phone call. From the fury in his voice, she'd prefer to avoid responding to him at all.

Bless my bones, I'm making a mess of everything. Not only had she failed to learn the name of Popeye's heir, but she'd left David with the impression that his courtship was on track. She had been so rattled by the disastrous events on their trip that she'd clung to him through the plane ride home and weakly promised to get together with him again soon. She'd even let him kiss her good-bye. Obviously, he had mistaken her numb state of mind for something more, while part of her brain noted his embrace didn't fire her senses the same as Dalton's. Anyway, she'd sort out matters between them another time. David had a lot going for him: looks, an easygoing manner, and a secure position in life, but maybe that wasn't enough.

Or maybe she was a *schnook* who didn't know a good thing when she saw it.

A nurse called her name, scattering her thoughts. Grasping her purse, she followed the woman into a treatment room. Another long wait followed, during which Marla had plenty of time to study the red plastic biomedical waste container, disposable latex gloves, gauze pads, metal instruments, and sterile solutions laid out on the counter.

"Marla, what seems to be the problem?" Russ Taylor asked after an overly enthusiastic greeting. The surgeon wore a white lab coat over a shirt and tie and pair of navy slacks. Fatigue lines etched his face, but they were offset by a tilt to his mouth that indicated he possessed a sense of humor.

Before her trip to the Bahamas, she'd debated what to tell him, but now she had some legitimate concerns.

"I was a *klutz* and tripped over a curb last week." She turned her hands up to show him her skinned palms, hoping he wouldn't notice the scrapes were recent. "My wrists have been sore, so I wanted to make sure nothing else was damaged." That much was true; she'd found herself rubbing her wrists on the flight home yesterday, and today they ached. With the volume of work awaiting her, she didn't need any more delays.

His examination was brief but thorough. "Those bruises will go away with time," he said, combing his fingers through a thick head of hair. She liked his style, a reasonable length brushed off his forehead and groomed on his nape. "Your wrists are tender, but I don't see any further problems developing there. Just give your hands a rest and they'll heal."

No, thanks. Been there, done that, she thought, remembering the hand injuries inflicted on her by Bertha Kravitz's killer.

"I was in the Bahamas the last few days to learn about Popeye's heir," she blurted, as he headed for the door. That stopped him cold. "David Newberg and I got word that the trustee for Popeye's estate was there on business, so we went to see him. Since Ben died, I've been wondering who's trying to

234

sabotage Ocean Guard's fund-raiser. The heir has the most to gain."

Russ Taylor regarded her impassively. "And?"

"Morton Riley was dead when we arrived. Murdered." She'd hoped by offering information, Taylor would react, but his heavy silence prompted her to continue. "I was there. I saw . . . the body." She visualized Riley stretched out on the floor, a knife protruding from his chest. The coppery scent of blood fouling the air. David's reassuring presence as they stumbled through the night to reach their hotel and safety.

"Aren't you wondering who killed Ben?" she demanded. "Don't you want to know who's been obstructing our efforts for Ocean Guard? Someone dangerous is out there, killing people to get his way. Any one of us might be next."

He lifted his nose. "You're not a member of the board, so I don't see why you're so concerned."

"Cynthia asked for my help. Did she tell you someone is dumping medical waste in the mangrove preserve next to her estate? That contamination diminishes Ocean Guard's chances of fulfilling the terms of the trust."

Casting a glance at the red sharps container on the counter, she lowered her voice meaningfully. "Whoever is guilty must have access to the stuff."

"I have no idea what you're talking about. My other patients are waiting." With a brusque movement, he thrust open the door and marched out.

Well, he'd sure given her the shaft. She still needed to know something about his personal background to determine if he might be the heir. Then there was the matter of his financial health. Maybe his staff could provide information.

Outside in the hallway, she asked a nurse the way to Dr. Taylor's office. "He wants to discuss my condition," she confided with a bewildered expression designed to gain sympathy.

Directed to the end of the corridor, she hooked around a corner and entered a spacious room overlooking tropical greenery beyond a wide picture window. Mahogany and leather dominated the furnishings, while her shopaholic-trained vision noted expensive accessories. Even if Dr. Taylor's investment in the outpatient clinic was doing poorly, his practice must be doing well, she thought. Other doctors had been forced to give up their solo practice to join groups because managed care had reduced their income so drastically. Or maybe Dr. Taylor cut his expenses by dumping medical waste illegally. That would only make sense if he paid high fees to the waste disposal company, she repeated to herself, anxious to confirm or eliminate the prospect.

Drawn to the photographs on his desk, she studied a picture of Russ Taylor flanked by an attractive brunette she assumed was his wife, and a girl about fifteen. Other photos showed happy family scenes with the three of them. In orderly fashion, the frames marched across his desk like troopers lined up for inspection. Two pens, black and gold, were aligned parallel to the desk blotter in neat precision with a mechanical pencil. Like soldiers on patrol, she observed.

A cough from behind alerted her to someone else's presence. Whirling around, she saw one of the nurses eyeing her curiously.

"May I help you?" the nurse asked. She was a pleasant-faced young woman with gold-highlighted hair that needed a good trim.

"I was just waiting for Dr. Taylor, thanks. These are lovely photographs, aren't they?"

The nurse, smoothing her uniform, smiled. "Dr. Taylor is very devoted to his children. I-I mean his family," she stuttered, looking faintly alarmed.

"Really? He's fortunate that the HMOs haven't affected his business. It's expensive having a teenage daughter these days."

"No kidding. I've got two preteens myself." She seemed amenable to chatting, for which Marla was grateful.

Marla kept a careful eye on the doorway while she kept the conversational ball rolling. "The doctor is involved in that outpatient surgical clinic that's near here, isn't he?"

"Sure, a lot of the doctors in the building were invited to participate. From what I hear, things aren't doing so well over there because managed-care plans don't want to pay. But Dr. Taylor has been doing all right, thank goodness. After all, he has to cover our salaries and benefits. He's got a family to support, and then there's his . . . well, he has quite an extra expense every month."

"How's that?" Marla's pulse accelerated. Now she was getting somewhere!

"The poor man, he never talks about it. You know how he is, such a perfectionist about everything. That's why he's such an excellent surgeon. But it must break his heart to have —"

"Ladies, what are you doing in here?" Dr. Taylor's icy tone interrupted them.

The nurse's hand flew to her mouth. "Oh, I'm sorry, sir. This lady said she was waiting to speak to you."

"That will be all, Sheila." He waited until she left before letting an ugly scowl betray his emotions. "I thought I was finished with you," he said to Marla.

Feeling like a rat caught in a trap, she floundered for a response. "I, uh, had another question."

"Yes?" His suspicious gaze traveled from her to his desk, as though he were afraid she might have moved one of his precious possessions.

She decided to be bold. "How much do you pay per month to the waste disposal company? I'm just trying to get a handle on who might be polluting the preserve. Any information would be helpful."

His eyes hardened. "I have no idea. Why don't you let your cousin deal with that problem?"

"She's got enough to do. We're having Thanksgiving at her house this year. Normally, my cousin Julia has the family over in November, and Cynthia does Passover in the spring. But Julia and her husband will be away on a cruise during Thanksgiving week. Cynthia volunteered to switch even though Taste of the World is next month." A nervous chuckle bubbled from her throat. "If she's smart, Cynthia will keep the tables set up for the few weeks in between."

His lips tightened in response to her prattle. "I see. Well, if you want information on who picks up our red containers, ask the girls at the front desk."

"Thank you." Scurrying away, she was surprised by his apparent cooperation. Maybe she was looking in the wrong direction to think him guilty of dumping the waste in the preserve. But then again, according to his nurse, he had some major expense every month that he didn't like to talk about. And Lance had said the clinic's financial balance was faltering.

Unfortunately, none of his staff could provide the information she needed. She had to find out if the disposal fees were significant enough for her to pursue this tract. That left one alternative; she needed to speak to someone in the waste disposal company itself.

In her car was the information given to her by the dentist. Sifting through the papers, she found a local address in Davie, about fifteen minutes from her current location. Checking her watch, she cursed at the time that had elapsed. Her clients must be stewing by now. She'd just have to make it up to them later. Offering a discount on the next appointment might be useful.

Driving by a warehouse district, she searched for the street address for UFO Medical Waste Systems. She found it in a two-story white concrete building with green trim. Pulling into a parking lot, she watched a large truck with the company's insignia rumble by from a yard in the back.

A receptionist sat at a desk in the front office. On one side, a closed door led to an inner sanctum. On the other side, a stairway climbed to the second level. A couple of roughly dressed men were chugging Cokes and chatting in a corner. Furnishings were sparse, mainly a threadbare couch, a Formica table, and a soda machine of an early vintage.

Ignoring the men, who had broken off their conversation to stare at her in blatant interest, Marla got to the heart of the matter. "I work for Ocean Guard, a beach preservation society," she told the girl at the desk. "We're having a problem with medical waste washing up on the shore, and I'd like information that may help us pinpoint the culprit. Would you be able to tell me how much the monthly disposal fee is for a doctor's office and for a surgical clinic?"

The girl tapped a painted fingernail to her chin. "I don't have a clue, honey. If you've got a few minutes, I'll ask Woody upstairs."

"Okay." Marla paced idly while the girl made the call. Color warmed her cheeks when one of the men winked at her.

"If anyone can help you, doll, Woody is the fellow. He knows everything that goes on this place."

"Great." She hoped they were right. Time was rushing by, and she needed to get back to work.

The receptionist signaled. "Woody can talk to you. Go on up those stairs, hang a right, and go to the room at the end."

After passing a row of cubicles where workers toiled diligently, Marla entered the room indicated. Instead of an office, it was a conference center, complete with a long polished wood table and stately chairs with space enough for about twenty people. At the far end sat a man in shirtsleeves and tie. Concentrating on a stack of papers spread out on the table, he didn't look up until she cleared her throat.

"I appreciate your taking the time to see me," she began.

"Please, take a seat. What can I do for you? My name is Woody Erikson, and I'm a major account executive."

They shook hands, then Marla lowered herself into a chair at a ninety-degree angle from his. "I'm Marla Shore, and I represent Ocean Guard. We're concerned about someone illegally dumping medical waste on a private beach owned by our organization. We think we have a lead on the individual who might be responsible, but I need more information. How much does a doctor's office pay per month to your disposal company?"

Woody leaned back in his chair, exposing a paunch. "Well now, that depends. A private office may pay seven dollars per reusable sharps container or twenty dollars per thirty-gallon box for general medical waste. Say they use eight boxes per month. That's one hundred sixty dollars."

"Or nineteen hundred twenty dollars a year," said Marla, doing a quick mental calculation. Hardly an amount of money worth committing an illegal act to save. "And a surgical clinic?"

"There you're talking from five hundred to three thousand a month. Hold on, let me give you a copy of the regulations."

While he left the room, Marla pondered the implications. Would Dr. Taylor risk exposure for up to thirty-six thousand dollars a year? It sounded substantial to her, but that might be peanuts to his purse. She wasn't sure if saving money was a valid enough motive in this case. And that brought her right back to Popeye's heir who had more to gain.

"Here's a copy of the Florida Administrative Code for biomedical waste," Woody said, handing her some stapled papers. "That one lists rules and gives definitions. The waste acceptance protocol are the instructions we give out to our generators. It explains the types of waste we accept, how it should be packaged and labeled, and describes transportation and treatment facilities. Generators must use only registered transporters to remove biomedical waste. Our company provides a receipt for each service."

"Can this receipt be a way to track the user?"

Woody scratched his jaw. "Maybe. A tracking document accompanies all waste transported from the generator. This gives the type and quantity of waste products; the generator's name, address, and phone number; information about the transporter and the medical waste treatment facility. The customer retains a signed copy. We file them for at least three years."

"So if I can find a labeled biohazard bag

or sharps container, you might be able to trace its origins?"

He nodded. "It's more likely that your culprit is using unauthorized containers to haul the stuff wherever it's being dumped. In that scenario, you wouldn't have means to trace its source. May I offer a suggestion?"

"Of course."

"I wouldn't ask you to touch the stuff, but maybe you can take photographs and bring them to me. That might give us some hints of where the material is originating."

"How so?" She regarded him in puzzlement. Wasn't all biomedical waste the same syringes, bandages, and such?

He rolled his shoulders as though stretching his muscles. "Some items are peculiar to the type of generator. For example, nursing homes dispose of a lot of diapers. If you've got those in your waste, I'd look in that direction."

Marla grimaced. "Next time, I'll inspect the debris more carefully." Definitely not a prospect she anticipated with any glee. Rising, she smiled and extended her hand. "I really appreciate your help, Mr. Erikson. If I get those photographs, I'll be sure to bring them to you for your expert opinion."

She'd pass on the advice to Cynthia as

soon as she could spare the time to make return phone calls. After finishing off her last two customers for the day and wrapping things up in the salon, she picked up a few groceries and went home. Having let Spooks out the back door, she headed into her office where the blinking red light on her answering machine made her groan. Too much to do, not enough time!

Fielding questions from her mother about David and filling Tally in on recent events took over an hour. Her conversation with Cynthia was brief but more upsetting.

"David told me about Morton Riley," Cynthia snapped. "I can't believe you didn't give me the news right away. Where have you been all day? I'd half a mind to drop in at your salon, but I wasn't near that end of town this morning."

"Sorry, I had a lot to do." Feeling remorseful, Marla stooped down from her desk chair to scratch Spooks behind his ear. His yapping had compelled her to let him back inside the house after her first phone call. His affectionate presence brought her comfort as she sought to appease her cousin.

"Riley was the only one who could tell us the identity of Popeye's heir," Cynthia replied. "Now what are we going to do? That disgusting waste is still washing through the preserve, and we've lost our only chance to learn who's responsible."

"Not necessarily," Marla replied soothingly. "Your husband may still connect with Ben's legal assistant and get the answers we need. Or there's another alternative. If you can get me photos of the debris, I'll show them to a man at the waste disposal facility. He may be able to help us pinpoint the source."

"I'll try." An exasperated sigh came across the line.

"How's it going with Annie?"

"Don't ask."

"Things will turn out okay. Have faith, cuz."

Hanging up, Marla considered whom to call next. The hell with it. She'd rather take a bath than talk to anyone else.

Soaking in the tub surrounded by sudsy bubbles, she sifted through the mental list of chores for the next day. Babs had an after-noon appointment, meaning Marla would be able to question the woman about her decep-tive trip to Orlando. That encounter should prove interesting, but she wasn't as eager for the other item on her list. Interviewing Stefano Barletti about Pre-Need funeral ar-rangements would be a somber affair.

14

Marla stood outside the funeral home gazing at the colonial white two-story building with its circular driveway in front and its discreet side entrance, where a hearse was parked. Located in a busy commercial district of town, this was the main facility for Stefano Barletti's family, who owned a series of parlors.

I can think of better things to do on a Friday morning, Marla thought, glad there wasn't a funeral in progress when she entered the foyer. A couple of chapels branched off on either side, rows of empty chairs facing forward. She gave her name to a man who bustled out of a small office to greet her.

"Oh yes, Mr. Barletti is expecting you. Please come with me." He led her down a hallway and halted at an elevator. After a brief pause, they boarded the lift to the second floor.

Upstairs, a hive of people busied themselves in a series of offices. Stefano, attired in a dark suit, greeted her warmly.

"I was so glad to get your call. You're doing the right thing, Marla. A Pre-Need plan will save you money and relieve your family of the burden during a difficult time."

His office was a cluttered space personalized by family photos and potted plants. Marla sank into a chair opposite the desk. Her glance surveyed the standard furnishings. *How unlike Dr. Taylor's ostentatious place,* she thought.

After rummaging on his desktop for a printed form, Stefano dropped into a seat and folded his hands. "Can I offer you a cup of coffee before we get started?"

"No, thanks." She crossed her legs. "Tell me, how's your part going for Taste of the World?"

"The flower arrangements will be magnificent. And you? Any further problems with the chefs?" Something glinted behind his eyes for a brief moment, then was gone.

Marla gave him a shrewd glance. For all she knew, he might be the one sabotaging her efforts. "Everything is on target," she said airily.

"No more dropouts?"

"Not at this time."

Frowning, he examined his hands. "I heard you went to the Bahamas with David Newberg."

"Really? Who told you?"

"I don't remember. I keep in close contact with all the board members, you understand."

"Were you informed about the results of our trip?"

His eyes glazed. "Word got around. Riley bit the dust."

You don't seem particularly upset, pal. "He was the trustee for Popeye's estate. I was hoping he could tell us the identity of Popeye Boodles's heir. Someone has been dumping medical waste on the preserve next to my cousin's property, not to mention discouraging the chefs from participating in our fund-raiser. Whoever stands to inherit has the most to gain."

She leaned forward. "Ben's firm was involved in drawing up that trust. Do you think he was murdered by the heir?"

Stefano looked at her incredulously, his thick-set eyebrows rising like wings on a plane. The expression elongated his face, giving him a gaunt look accentuated by his perpetually startled brown eyes. "Why are you asking me that question?"

"Your family has been around town for a

250

while. You might have heard things."

"The only thing I hear is you're snooping where you don't belong." Gripping a pen, he clicked it on and off. "Did you come here to discuss Pre-Need arrangements or to interrogate me?"

Brushing a strand of hair off her face, she smiled sweetly. "Forgive me, I'm just trying to help my cousin. Cynthia is getting nervous now that we're a few weeks away from the fund-raiser. Anyway, let's talk about funeral plans."

From the way he glowered at her, Marla figured he was wishing she could make use of one right now.

"Is this going to be a package for two people?" he snarled, pen poised in his fingers. His glance dropped to her ringless left hand.

"No, this is just for me."

"You should think ahead. At some point in your future, there may be a significant other. I assume we're talking about a traditional ground burial rather than a mausoleum?"

"I guess so." She had no wish to be preserved for eternity in a tomb like Romeo and Juliet. Besides, she believed her religion required a ground burial.

"Purchasing two plots now will save you

money because land prices keep rising. In the event you don't need the second plot, we'll buy it back from you. Consider it a hedge against inflation." Pushing a chart in front of her, he pointed to various sites marked out in squares. "Which cemetery section appeals to you?"

Marla moistened her lips. "It doesn't matter, whichever costs less."

"That would be the newest section." He circled two spaces. "Do you prefer a chapel or graveside service?"

She gave it serious consideration, mortality being on her mind after viewing Riley's body and being shot at herself. "A graveside service would be easier on my family, so let's go with that one. Is there a price difference?" Squinting, she tried to read what was on the upside-down form.

"It's $420 for use of the chapel as opposed to $275 for a graveside service." At her nod, he continued. "Next there's a basic charge for the professional services of the funeral director and staff. That's $1870. This includes arranging conferences between family and clergy, filing necessary permits, planning the funeral, placement of obituary notices, and coordination with other responsible parties. It also includes administrative expenses for the use of our facilities."

"I see."

"You have a choice about embalming. May I ask your religious preference?"

"I'm Jewish."

He nodded sagely. "Jewish people usually don't embalm unless you're going into a mausoleum. It's my understanding, and correct me if I'm wrong, that the religious directive is to return to the earth as quickly as possible."

"Okay, no embalming." She felt uncomfortable discussing these choices, but it made sense before you needed them. What a relief to your relatives to make one phone call in the event your prearrangements became necessary. Ma had paid for a plan, and Marla was grateful. She dreaded the day when she'd have to use it, but that was better than making hasty decisions later.

"You're going to have other expenses." Stefano reversed the general price list so she could see for herself. "Transfer of remains to the funeral home is $290. Use of a hearse will be $275. Dressing and casketing is $145. Since you're not embalming, refrigeration is required, which costs $395."

I'd always wanted to die broke, she told herself sardonically. "What's this opening and closing that you've circled?"

"That's for opening the gravesite and closing it after the service. Also, I recommend a concrete vault. It gives more protection than a concrete liner, which is more porous. Now let's discuss choice of caskets." He stood, gesturing for her to follow. "We have a casket room so you can see the selections."

Oh, joy. She couldn't wait. Trailing behind, she entered a room where up to twenty coffins were on display. Detaching herself emotionally wasn't hard. She didn't want to think about herself lying in one of those boxes.

"The Jewish religion calls for your casket to be made of all wood, meaning pegged and glued with no metal parts so the body can get back to the earth quickly." He showed her a few samples. "See, no nails or metal hinges. Or, if you go into a mausoleum, embalming is required along with a sealed metal casket. Choices include steel, copper, and bronze, like this one here."

Her eyes bulged. The price tag of $37,995 made her choke. Hopefully the ones made from wood were more reasonably priced. She surveyed the different styles ranging from solid mahogany with a polished finish and a champagne velvet interior at a cost of $19,995 to a plain pine box for $795.

"How about this one?" she asked, pointing to a solid poplar design with a polished maple finish and beige crepe interior. It ran midprice range at $2,695.

Stefano ran his fingers lovingly over the smooth service, his dark eyes gleaming in appreciation. "Beautiful, isn't it? Of course, if you prefer a velvet interior, we have a similar one for an extra $800."

"No, I like this. What's next?" Uncomfortable in the confined space with Stefano looming beside her, she headed through the door and back toward his office.

"Clergy fees, death certificates, prayer books, yarmelkes, acknowledgment cards, a guest sign-in book. Then there's an archiving fee and sales tax on the merchandise."

He'd been writing everything down on a proposal form, and now he pulled out a calculator to get the total. "Here's the best package I can give you," he said circling a number that made Marla cringe. "We have a payment plan available if you'd like to stretch this out over four years with no interest. It includes our personal protection program. If, God forbid, something happens to you after a year, the rest of the premiums are waived."

"Terrific. Can I take this home to study?"

She'd contact another funeral home to compare prices. Babs had told her Stefano charged exorbitant fees. Upon his approval, she folded the papers and stuffed them into her purse.

"Who handled the arrangements for Ben's funeral?" she asked, knowing the answer but wondering how he'd react.

He grimaced. "One of the Levinson places took care of him."

"They weren't the ones involved in that voodoo case, were they?" She'd read a news article about a mortician convicted of performing voodoo rituals by stuffing dolls stuck with pins into a dead man's chest cavity and chopping off his hand.

"No, that was somewhere in north Florida." Thrusting stiff fingers through his gray hair, Stefano regarded her from beneath heavy brows. "Levinson's is a nationwide chain. Conglomerates now own more than fifty percent of the mortuaries in this county. Most people don't realize it when they choose a place. Ownership may have changed hands, but the old names remain on the signs."

"Doesn't that hurt your business? Yours is one of the few family-owned firms left."

"We still provide more personal services than the chains, and their prices tend to be higher. Did you know they charge up to sixty-two percent more than independents for the same items?"

Yeah, right, pal. Like your prices are cheap? "You've managed to stay viable."

"So far."

"I heard a rumor that Ben was suing you on behalf of some former customers," she said, switching topics glibly to provoke a response. "Did that have anything to do with Pre-Need plans? What guarantee is there that I'll get what I pay for?"

He shifted uneasily. "You have to trust me, Marla."

No problem. I'd trust you like I would a snake. Digby had mentioned that story, she recalled. Had it been an attempt to discredit Stefano and throw blame off himself? Deciding to pursue that angle later, she directed her attention to a photograph on his desk. A handsome couple, attired in earlier-era swimsuits, stood in front of a palm tree on the beach.

"Nice picture," she commented. "Your relatives?"

"My parents. That was taken not long after they met."

"Any sisters or brothers?"

"No, I was an only child. But I made up for it with my own family." He pointed proudly to another framed photo. "That's my wife and our four sons."

"How lovely." Wishing she could get a closer glimpse, she squinted. One of those faces looked vaguely familiar.

"Is there anything else you want to know?" Stefano said, his lip curling in a sneer.

Smart man. "I've got enough information for now, thanks." Gathering her purse, she rose. "I guess I'll see you at Taste of the World." Heading for the door, she paused and turned. Stefano's expression made her catch her breath.

A look of utter hatred on his face was quickly replaced by an oily smile once he noticed her looking at him. "Yes?"

"One more thing. Detective Vail is investigating Ben's death. In case he asks me, where were you that night?"

"You think you're so clever, don't you? Well, the lieutenant has already questioned me. I told him I was out bowling that night, and he's confirmed my story."

Moving around his desk, he stalked closer, spearing her with his bulging dark eyes. In his narrow face, they reminded her of movies featuring the walking dead. Unlike a zombie, however, his menacing tone was laced with emotion. "Nosy *yentas* get in trouble, Marla. You'd better make a quick decision about your funeral plans. You may be needing them sooner than you think."

His warning echoing through her mind, Marla returned to the salon in time for Babs's appointment. She spared a moment to call Anita and ask her about final arrangements.

"I'd like to get a quote from the person who helped you," she told her mother.

"That won't be necessary. I've got all the information here. If you're free tonight, why don't you come over after work? I'll show you my Pre-Need policy."

"I have a date with Ralph. Remember him? He's the guy from the auto body shop. We haven't seen each other in a while."

"What happened to David?" her mother's indignant voice responded. "You haven't broken off with him already, have you?"

Marla grimaced with annoyance. "Of course not. I just felt like being with Ralph for a change. He's a good friend."

"So what is David to you, something more? Just how far did things progress while you were in Nassau?"

Marla laughed at her mother's hopeful tone. "Not that far. David acted like a perfect gentleman." She was grateful David hadn't taken advantage of their situation but wasn't ready to confront her deeper feelings about him just yet.

"David will be upset if he finds out you're seeing someone else," her mother warned. "Cynthia told me he's smitten with you."

"We don't have any commitment to each other."

"How about that cop fellow? You're finished with him, aren't you?"

"You wish. Seriously, I don't think he'll be happy when he hears I went off alone with one of the murder suspects." A guilty flush stole over her. She'd never returned Dalton's phone call.

"Baloney. David wouldn't hurt a fly."

"You never met him! How do you know?"

"I'll meet him at Thanksgiving. Cynthia invited him."

"Oh, great." Sooner or later, she'd have to decide what she wanted from their relationship. David's smiling face and pleasant demeanor made him an enjoyable companion, but that alone didn't seem like enough for a long-term commitment.

"Marla, Babs is here," shouted Nicole's voice from the salon.

"I've got to go. Maybe we can review those funeral plans on Sunday? I have some free time then."

"Come for lunch. We'll have gefilte fish and challah."

Babs was in a cheerful mood when Marla greeted her. Looking the competent businesswoman in a crisp linen suit, she was on a late lunch break for her appointment. They made small talk through her wash and blow-dry.

When Marla was using the curling iron, she broached what was on her mind. "I'm thinking of going to Orlando to visit the theme parks. Can you recommend a place to stay?"

Babs studied her reflection in the mirror. "Orlando is teeming with hotels. It's best to stay near your destination."

"I like the Courtyard by Marriott chain. Which one were you at last weekend?"

"I was in Tampa."

"Oh, that's strange." Finished with the curling iron, Marla picked up a comb. "I wanted to confirm your appointment this week, so I called the one in Tampa. You were registered as a guest but didn't answer your phone. I recalled seeing a brochure sticking out of your purse with an Orlando address. When I tried that number, you picked up."

Babs's eyes narrowed. "I don't recall speaking to you over the weekend, nor do I recall showing you that number. I told you, I was in Tampa."

"Maybe Walter believes you, but I don't." Marla leaned over, lowering her voice. "Why are you lying, Babs? You can tell me. My lips are sealed, and it may help you to share this burden you carry."

Shoulders slumping, Babs covered her face with her hands. "No, it — it's my secret. You mustn't let Walter know. He'd be devastated."

Was she having an affair? Feeling shameful for prying, Marla refrained from posing that question. Instead, she put a comforting hand on Babs's arm. "I won't say anything, but if you need help, please feel that you can come to me."

Instinct made her raise her head just as someone entered through the front door. *Oh, no.* Dalton Vail stomped toward her, brows furrowed on his craggy face. His charcoal sport coat hung open, showing a tie with crimson slashes that reminded her of blood. Her blood, which in his boiling rage, he might want to spill if she didn't appease him.

Babs's eyes widened. "If you're finished, I'll be running along now. Looks like Lieutenant Vail is about to lose his cool."

Marla, heart thumping wildly, applied a

mist of hair spray. Even though reason told her to flee, she couldn't go without finishing her client's coiffeur. Besides, cowering in the storeroom wouldn't accomplish anything. Better to face your foes and disarm them.

Babs shrugged out of her cape and stood. After digging into her purse, she handed Marla a five-dollar bill. "I'm glad it's you he's after and not me," she whispered, winking. "Good luck."

Marla plastered a fake smile on her face and rounded on Vail who'd been impatiently tapping his foot while she finished with Babs. "Hello, Dalton," she said pleasantly. "What brings you into the salon?"

His steely eyes assessed her coolly. "We need to talk. Privately. You'll come with me now." Grasping her elbow, he propelled her toward the door.

"Wait a minute! I can't leave. My next customer —"

"Can be handled by your staff. Right?" Raising a bushy eyebrow, he directed his query at Nicole.

Nicole's alarmed glance moved between them. At Marla's barely perceptible nod, Nicole agreed. "Yes, sir," the stylist intoned, seemingly as awestruck by his commanding air as the rest of her suddenly silent staff.

Her face flaming, Marla allowed him to lead her outside. "Let's go to Bagel Busters," she suggested, figuring Arnie would serve as an ally at the deli.

"I don't think so. Get in my car."

"Stop manhandling me, Dalton," she snapped, as he dragged her along the pavement.

"You've been wanting to play with fire. Feel the heat." He thrust her inside his vehicle, its interior hot as an oven in the afternoon sun.

She had a feeling that wasn't the kind of heat he meant, and her skin prickled in a deliciously wicked sort of way. Gads, had she brought this upon herself on purpose? Why else would shivers of anticipation be skimming along her nerve endings like this? Glancing at him as he levered his large frame into the driver's seat, she felt her mouth go dry. No doubt he was angry because she'd gone away with David, but was that because David was a murder suspect or a rival suitor?

Dalton didn't speak as he put the car into gear and headed onto the main road. He stared straight ahead, his jaw firm, hands clenched on the wheel.

Marla swallowed hard, afraid to break the silence. She'd wait to see what he had in mind before defending herself. Going to the Bahamas was the easy one. Cynthia had requested she contact Morton Riley in Nassau, and Ocean Guard had provided the tickets. Through no fault of her own, Cynthia had assigned David to accompany her.

Keeping it from Dalton was another matter. She should've answered his phone call as soon as she'd returned. Maybe he hadn't known about Riley. Maybe he'd assumed she was going on a tryst with David. In that case, they needed to clarify their relationship. Marla felt no obligation to Dalton, but she didn't want to lose him, either. Introducing her to his daughter had been a serious step. If she wasn't careful, she might chase him away, and that possibility filled her with dread.

"Where are we going?" she ventured, noticing they were entering an older residential neighborhood where overhanging branches from banyan trees shaded the road. At least he wasn't taking her to the police station. For an intimate conversation, that was not the place she'd choose.

"My house," he stated, his tone flat.

"Isn't Brianna home from school?"

"She's at the mall with a friend. We'll be alone for as long as it takes."

15

Marla entered Dalton Vail's house through a foyer, where she got a quick glimpse of an umbrella stand made out of a tree trunk and silk ferns in a white-rattan basket, before Vail hustled her into his living room. The brick exterior of the ranch-style home gave no indication of its contents, she thought, as her eyes feasted on a display of scented candles. From the rear came a dog's loud barking, presumably their pet Lucky in the backyard.

"I had no idea you liked antiques," she remarked, running her hands over the smooth surface of an old-fashioned wooden school desk. Her glance skimmed the sofa with its curved arms and Cabriole legs, the wing chairs and lamp tables.

Dalton regarded her with an unreadable expression. "Not me. My wife was into this stuff."

"Oh, I'm so sorry." His wife had passed

away two years ago, and apparently he hadn't redecorated.

"Sit down, Marla." A fatigued look entered his eyes, as though being at home had defused his anger. Raking his fingers through his peppery hair, he remained standing while she sank onto the silk-upholstered couch. "Tell me why you went to Nassau with that Newberg fellow."

She grasped a velvet throw pillow and cradled it in her lap. "Ocean Guard sent me. Cynthia traced Morton Riley to the Bahamas, where he was involved in negotiating some sort of trade agreement with the government. Riley is the trustee for Popeye Boodles's estate. We figured he could give us the name of Popeye's heir. It was Cynthia's idea to send David along as my escort."

"And?"

Averting her eyes, she refused to meet his accusatory gaze. "We found Riley. He was dead . . . murdered."

Vail grabbed the desk chair, whipped it around, and sat facing her straddling the seat. "Give me the details."

Waving a hand in the air, Marla swallowed. "What's there to tell? We'd been given his address. We went to the house Riley was renting and found him lying on the kitchen floor. He'd been stabbed."

"Did you call the authorities?"

"I used a pay phone and left an anonymous tip." Her heart raced as the scene replayed itself in her mind. "We were afraid of being detained. I needed to return to work on Thursday and couldn't afford any delays. We went back to the hotel and pretended as though nothing had happened."

"What day was this? What time did you go see him?"

Relating the details, she left out the coconut incident and the killer at Crystal Cay.

His mouth tightened. "Let me see if I got this straight. You went to your room to rest for a couple of hours. Later, you and Newberg took the trolley into town, then walked the rest of the way to Riley's address. Newberg knew exactly where to go."

"Yes, that's right." She didn't see where this was leading.

"According to his story, Newberg had already been there and found Riley dead."

"So? He knew I'd insist on going anyway to see for myself."

"Maybe not. Riley never answered his phone. Maybe Newberg hoped you'd give up your quest, believing Riley was unavailable."

David had tried to dissuade her from

seeing Riley, Marla remembered. She'd thought he was being protective, but what if his efforts had been more self-serving? How did she know David didn't commit the deed?

No, that was ridiculous. Someone tried to clunk her on the head with a coconut while David was with her. And the killer at Crystal Cay had shot at them both, right? Or had the gunshots only come when she'd been separated from David?

Rubbing her temples, she gave Dalton a resentful glare. "What are you trying to do, make me suspicious of David? Do you think he killed Ben, too?"

His eyes were hard as flint. "In my book, everyone is suspect. You're interfering where you don't belong."

Rising, she tossed the pillow onto the sofa. "Oh yeah? Taste of the World is a few weeks away. A new trustee will be assigned now that Morton Riley is dead. In January, this person will decide whether or not Ocean Guard receives the mangrove preserve. We're running out of time."

He stood slowly, pushing the chair out of his path. Towering over her, he exuded menace with his hunched posture and clenched fists. "You're only doing this for your cousin. It's getting too dangerous, and

I want you to sign off the project now before you become the next victim."

"Do you really care that much about me, or are you just concerned I'll screw up your investigation?" she retorted. "I would've thought you'd have taken Ben's killer into custody by now." She lifted her chin, defying him to respond.

His eyes smoldered dangerously. "I'm worried about you, damn stubborn woman."

Before she could protest, he hauled her into his arms, and his mouth descended upon hers. His kiss was brutal, crushing, but it made her knees weaken and a lazy warmth steal through her limbs. Clinging to him, she molded her body against his rock-solid length. A groan ripped from his throat before he thrust her away.

"I didn't mean for that to happen," he rasped, his dark gaze raking her with blatant hunger before his expression closed, and a blank mask fell into place.

"Didn't you?" She barely recognized her breathless tone.

"No . . . yes. You're driving me crazy. I can't think straight on a case when you get involved."

"Please understand," she said gently, pressing his arm. "I have to see this job through to the end. Cynthia is counting on me."

He snorted, and she withdrew her hand as though she'd touched fire. "I realize her regard means a lot," he tempered, "but I'm sure Cynthia wouldn't condone risking your life. It was a dumb move to go off on your own with one of the suspects."

"You know what I think? You're jealous because I didn't bring you along."

"I am not. I'm only concerned for your safety."

"That's part of it. Don't try to hide your feelings, Dalton. I can see right through you."

His lips compressed. "Good, then you can see this discussion is finished. You *will* listen this time."

Damned stubborn man, she told herself during the silent drive back to her salon. Why did he have such power to aggravate her? His hidden depths tantalized her, constituted a challenge she couldn't refuse. The man's complex personality invited further exploration like the layers of a client's hair. Yet how deep did she want to go?

As she adjusted her seat belt, she cast him a quick glance. His stern profile made her heart rate soar. Beneath his implacable exterior lay a passionate, vulnerable man, but it would take a gentle touch and a kind heart to draw him out. Many women would accept such a task with alacrity. Was this the path she cared to choose?

Marla didn't seek a commitment, didn't want one. Her freedom was too precious and hard-won to yield so readily. On the other hand, Dalton's mystique fired her guns, and she didn't recall anyone else who could keep her primed like he did.

Not even David affected her so strongly, and he had the background, position, and wealth that could provide security and status for whoever snagged him. But although she was attracted to David, he didn't sizzle her blood like the ruggedly handsome detective.

Marla considered what to say to David when she saw him at Cynthia's on Thanksgiving. *I like you, but our relationship isn't going anywhere?* Or, *it's too early yet. I'm not sure how I feel.* Maybe she wasn't giving him enough of a chance.

David seemed to think they were already a duet, judging by his effusive greeting on Thursday.

"Marla, darling, I've missed you," he crooned, sweeping her into his outstretched arms. Brushing his lips lightly across hers, he released her after a brief squeezing embrace. He appeared casually dressed in a navy knit shirt and trousers, his fawn-colored hair neatly styled into a side part. His eyes twinkled as he regarded her. "So what have you been up to?"

"I could ask you the same thing." She smoothed down her silk cranberry blouse that went with dressy black slacks. An earring pinched, so she rotated the diamond stud until it loosened. "I expected you to call."

"Work kept me busy." He glanced at her cluster of relatives chatting outside by the pool. Marla had just entered Cynthia's house when he'd accosted her in the courtyard. "Your cousin wasn't too happy with our report."

"We failed to accomplish our mission in Nassau. We're still no closer to learning the identity of Popeye's heir. Can you blame her for being disappointed?"

He shook his head. "I'm just as concerned about Ocean Guard's future. You haven't experienced any further setbacks for the fund-raiser, have you? The chefs are working out okay?"

"Oh yes, everything is fine. I even spoke to Stefano, and he said the flowers will be magnificent."

"Good. Nothing must get in the way of

Ocean Guard's getting that property, Marla. Nothing. We've all worked too hard at this to fail now."

"I need to talk to Cynthia." New information had come to light that she wanted to impart to her cousin. David would have to manage on his own.

Striding ahead of him, she pushed open the French doors to the patio. Her name rang out as various relatives sauntered over to greet her. Michael and Charlene each gave her a hug, after which Marla kissed her mother. Reclusive Aunt Polly shyly patted her arm. Shark was there, following Annie around like a puppy. Didn't he have his own family?

Her gaze meandered to the children playing beside a rocker. "Rebecca and Jacob, don't get too near the pool," she warned her niece and nephew, a flutter of panic in her breast. The water sparkled invitingly, its aqua depths holding hidden danger.

"The kids have heard your warnings enough times now to remember, Marla," Charlene admonished.

"It's never enough. Drowning is the —"

"Number one cause of death for children ages four and under in South Florida. I know, you've told us a hundred times already. Jacob has had swimming lessons, and he'll be five in a few months. He helps us watch his baby sister."

Charlene's warm, tawny eyes assessed her. She wore her golden oak hair straight down her back which gave her an earth mother look, but her delicate features added refinement and sensitivity. Her gentle but firm nature provided the perfect personality for an elementary school teacher.

Marla smiled as she watched Charlene scoop Rebecca into her arms and snuggle the toddler.

"Aren't they growing fast?" Anita's voice said from behind. Marla turned to engage her mother in conversation, but she quickly lost Anita's attention. "Tell me, Charlene, what's the baby eating these days?" Anita asked, beaming at the toddler.

Marla's gut clenched as she observed their interaction. Charlene was everything Anita might have desired in a daughter. First her mother had been devastated when Marla dropped out of college as an education major; then she'd been crushed by Marla's divorce. It was only recently that Anita had accepted Marla's career choice. Thank goodness her brother had provided grandchildren, because Marla didn't need that guilt trip on top of all her other emotional baggage.

Seeking her cousin, Marla found Cynthia in the kitchen instructing her staff. "Cynthia, I have to talk to you," she said, her tone urgent.

"Hey, Marla. What's up?" hollered Bruce, a carving knife in his hand. Her cousin's husband stood so tall he had to stoop to trim a large roasted turkey.

She grinned at him. He looked silly wearing an apron, but his tailor-made clothes needed protection from his labors. His hair, black and spiky, shone with spray as polished as his shoes.

The sugary fragrance of baked sweet potatoes wafted into her nostrils. "Watching you slice that bird is making me hungry," she commented. "Cynthia, I have some news."

Her cousin lifted the lid on a simmering pot, sniffed the contents, then closed it again. "This just needs a few more minutes," she told a girl in a maid's uniform. "Marla, let's go outside."

The afternoon sun warmed Marla's back as she faced Cynthia who stood under the veranda's overhang. Sometimes November brought cooler air but not this year. After a brief cold spell, the weather had heated up again. The lower humidity and clear skies were a delight to beachgoers, but natives hoped for a winter chill. Not so Marla. Her early years had been spent in New York State, where she'd experienced enough snow and ice to last a lifetime.

"Pierre called me. He learned that one of his kitchen assistants used to work for Alex Sheffield," she said.

"So what does that mean?" Cynthia's face crinkled in puzzlement.

Marla's gaze shifted from her cousin's flawless makeup to her newly layered hairstyle. It looked a lot better than Cynthia's previous upsweep, more natural and flattering to her bone structure. Gads, she still had those shears in her handbag. When did Cynthia want her to do Annie's hair?

"Sheffield may be responsible for the chefs withdrawing from Taste of the World," she explained. "He has a grudge against Ocean Guard's president, Jerry Caldwell. It's logical that Alex might be the one sabotaging our organization's fund-raiser."

Waving a hand, Cynthia snorted. "I know Alex, and I doubt he'd go so far. Jerry is pushing for stricter regulations regarding commercial fishing practices, but so are other marine conservation groups. On a more personal level, Jerry accused Alex of serving a cheaper substitute for what listed on his restaurant menu as mahimahi. Alex got in trouble, but I can't believe he'd blame Ocean Guard for Jerry's actions."

Marla brushed a strand of hair from her eyes. "Well, someone put an explosive substance into Pierre's rum bottle. Other chefs are being persuaded to quit Taste of the World, like Max. If it isn't Alex Sheffield, who else is responsible?"

Her cousin's gaze intensified. "I like your first theory, that it's the same person who's dumping medical waste. You should take another look, Marla. Bruce has hired some people to clean up the mess, but we've got to stop the source."

"You've got to stop what?" Annie repeated, her arm linked into Shark's as the youngsters ranged into sight.

Marla wondered how long they'd been listening. "We've got to stop your hair from frizzing like that, honey," she said in a teasing tone. "Try one of the anti-humectants on the market. Any silicon-based product will do. Put it on when your hair is dry, otherwise it'll get too greasy. When would you like me to do your cut?"

"Huh?"

Cynthia caught on. "Marla did a great job on my hair, so I told her she could do yours next." Smiling, she fluffed the wispy bangs

Marla had given her. "Now I need to update my wardrobe to go with this new look."

"Mom, you're so retarded." Hooking her thumbs into the waistline of her skin-tight black pants, Annie thrust out her bosom, shown off to advantage in a low-cut mustard sweater. "Come on, Shark. Let's go for that walk you wanted."

Shark wore an ivory guayabara shirt that contrasted sharply with his swarthy complexion. Marla's perusal halted at his scornful eyes. Something in his expression struck a familiar chord, but she couldn't place it. He bared his teeth, exhibiting a row of incisors that must have worn braces. Costly item, Marla thought, contemplating his origins.

"Isn't your family celebrating the holiday?" she asked him.

His grin widened, but she saw no mirth in his eyes. Malice gleamed brightly in their depths as he met her gaze. "I'd rather spend time with Annie. She invited me to come today, so I'm hanging here."

"Is that your blue Chevy out front? It must be a very popular car. I've seen a similar one cruising around my neighborhood. Just this morning, in fact, I spotted the same model when I took my dog for a walk."

"Coincidence, man. Let's move out, Annie. I wanna see that swamp you mentioned."

Marla watched in dismay as they headed toward the bridge leading across the lagoon. She wouldn't go near the mangrove preserve while they were in the vicinity. Turning to her cousin, she shrugged. "I'll take a look there later. Did you get the photos I'd requested? I meant to bring my camera but left it on the kitchen counter."

"Sorry." Cynthia frowned. "I haven't had the chance; too many preparations for the holidays. I'll call you when I've got them, I promise."

Marla slipped away to chat with her relatives while dusk fell and the sky darkened. A game of croquet got started, which didn't interest her. She sat beside Aunt Polly, wanting to visit with the elderly woman whom she didn't see that often. Aunt Polly was describing her latest foray into the neighbor's trash.

"They threw away perfectly recyclable tuna cans," whined Aunt Polly. "I washed the things out and put them in my bin. You'd think people would have more sense. They're *schmucks*, all of them."

"*Tanteh*, stop *kvetching*. I know how much

you enjoy sifting through garbage. Where else would you have found that pretty rose-colored jar you use to store your kosher salt?"

A frown creased Aunt Polly's wrinkled face. "This world is going down the tubes, you mark my words. It's a *shanda*."

"That's not true. Folks like you make a difference."

Marla smiled fondly at her relative attired in a homemade shirtwaist dress. Aunt Polly didn't believe in technology. Environmental concerns and frugality ruled her life, which she lived alone in a tiny, hot apartment. She rarely turned on the air-conditioning, made her own soap, and refused to buy insurance to save money. It galled Marla that although she'd offered to cut Aunt Polly's hair for free, the woman insisted on trimming it herself. *Looks like it, too,* Marla thought, noting the gray split ends that hung loose down her back.

"That's odd." Aunt Polly's filmy eyes squinted behind her spectacles, a piece of white adhesive tape wrapped around one of its arms. "Did you see it?"

"See what?" Seated on the patio, Marla faced the house while her aunt had a view of the grounds. Twisting her neck, she peered into the darkness but saw nothing.

281

David, who sat beside her stuffing down chopped liver on crackers, leapt from his chair. "Look at that."

This time, Marla observed a dot of light moving faintly among the trees. "What can it be?" Tossing her napkin onto the table, she rose. Her gaze scanned the company, but all her relatives were present. Annie and Shark giggled together in a private corner, the children played by a swing set, and her brother chatted with their cousins.

Michael glanced up, sensing her eyes on him, and winked. "Nice chap," he'd told her earlier, referring to David. "You could do worse."

"Gee, thanks, pal." Giving him a sisterly punch, she'd complimented his children's manners. Rebecca and Jacob went about their horseplay in a quiet fashion, although she knew they could be quite vociferous in their own home. "Just keep your eye on them," she'd pleaded, aware of the close proximity of the swimming pool.

No chance of the pool lights reflecting into the distance, she figured, watching the night swallow any gleam of brightness beyond. Had it been her imagination, or was something there? Aunt Polly had seen it, and so had David.

"I'm going to check things out," she

hissed. "That's the direction of the mangrove preserve."

David fixed his shirt, tucking it into his expanded waistline. "I'll come with you."

"Got any insect repellent?" she joked, a trek into the woods at night not being very appealing. *This might be your chance to catch the culprit dumping medical waste, silly. Bug bites you can deal with later.*

A camper mentality she didn't possess. David, ever thoughtful, conned a can of *OFF!* from Bruce, and they spritzed themselves before trekking into the wilderness. Grateful she'd worn long pants, Marla traipsed behind David, who took the lead. Footlights spaced at regular intervals illuminated the sandy path that wound through woods alive with sound. Buzzing insects competed with hooting owls for dominance, but they were both overruled by a chorus of crickets. Strange rustling noises coming from the bushes added to Marla's unease.

Her nostrils tickled from a spicy scent, and she squeezed them shut to avoid sneezing. She could barely make out a faint light dancing through the trees ahead and didn't want to alert the intruder to their presence.

At the entrance to the preserve, the footlights ended. A boardwalk continued into the tropical hammock, a pitch-black void that no sane person would enter at night.

"Damn, we forgot to bring flashlights," Marla muttered.

"Ssh," David hissed. "There's enough moonlight. We don't want to give away our position."

"Well, maybe you're better at seeing in the dark than I am." Slippery from fallen leaves, the boardwalk felt treacherous. Marla groped for the railing and clutched her way along. After a few feet, the boardwalk divided.

"Now what?" Her pulse raced, and her hands felt clammy. Despite the sea breeze, a sheen of sweat covered her forehead. If she were smart, she'd have stayed behind and let David investigate. Vail's words came to mind as the utter folly of her situation revealed itself. *Don't be alone with any of them.* How did she know she could trust David?

"You go left, I'll go right. We'll meet somewhere up ahead," he said quietly, his matter-of-fact tone dissolving her fears.

"What if I meet the fellow out there?"

"Wait for me. I'll deal with him."

"How? We don't have anything to use in our defense." When David didn't respond, she glanced at him sharply. A muscle twitched on the side of his jaw.

"I don't need a weapon. That guy has done so much to harm Ocean Guard, I could kill him with my bare hands."

16

The tropical hardwoods of the coastal hammock gave way to lower vegetation of saw palmettos and scrub oak as Marla proceeded farther into the preserve. She crossed into the mangrove wetland, with its tangled web of roots and buttonwood trees extending to the shoreline. The stench of rotting organic debris mingled with briny sea air, and she heard water lapping against a surface somewhere ahead. Was she getting close to the slough that ran out to sea?

Loud honking noises made her wonder if alligators could crawl onto the boardwalk in search of prey. Despite the unseasonably warm autumn air, a shiver wormed its way up her spine. Shadowy shapes enveloped the night, her imagination twisting them into ghouls and ghastly creatures ready to spring at human flesh. Insects buzzed at her exposed skin, but veered off at the scent of insecticide. *That won't keep all the preda-*

tors away, she thought nervously. Her rubber-soled shoes padded softly on the boards underfoot as she slinked forward, holding on to the weathered wooden railing.

David's tall figure had moved out of sight. She'd never felt more alone and aware of peril than standing in a deserted marshland, listening to the sounds of the night. That lapping noise seemed to be growing closer. As her eyes discerned a barely visible outline, she realized she was looking at a boat gliding in her direction. An empty boat.

A crunching noise from behind brought her head up sharply, but it was too late. A hand slapped across her mouth and nose, smothering any sound she might have made. She felt a strong arm wrench under her chin, tilting her head backward. Struggling for breath, she could not resist when forced to the handrail. Release came momentarily as the hand lifted from her face, and she sucked in a strangled gasp. Before she was able to recover her wits, her assailant grabbed her by the shoulders and cracked her skull against the bar. Stunned, her senses reeling, she was barely aware of being tossed over the railing. Dank wetness enveloped her, and she realized belatedly she was sinking into the slough. Deep water, and cold. Drowning.

Like Tammy.

Horror flung her eyes open, flooded her mind with awareness. Holding her breath, she forced her panic-stricken gaze to search for the surface. Eyes stinging from salt water, she blinked desperately. Which way was up? Inky depths extended into a void all around her. So this was the way of it. Retribution at last, her fate being to end life in the same manner as the toddler whose doom she'd sealed.

No, that won't happen. She'd made amends and turned her life into something valuable. It was worth fighting for, and she wouldn't give up and die in this inhospitable place.

While her lungs threatened to burst with pain, she made herself relax to see if she could float. Her blouse ballooned, and her body began to rise. When she felt she'd have to breathe in even if it meant taking in water, her head broke the surface. She took a shuddering gulp of air, then kicked her feet to stay afloat.

"Marla!" David's voice hollered her name.

"Over here." Her hoarse cry went unheeded. Gathering strength, she tried again.

"I'm over here, in the water."

"Oh, my God."

She swam toward his voice, and the railing came into view in the faint moonlight. The boat had long since disappeared, its owner probably hoping she'd drowned or worse. An ominous sound reached her ears, water thrashing from behind. *Oh, no. Reptiles. Hungry reptiles.*

"David, there's an alligator!" No, alligators wouldn't be in salt water. Must be a snake. Oh hell, did it matter? "Help me!"

Muttering an expletive, he leapt over the railing and splashed into the water beside her. Clamping a hand around her waist, he lifted her to the landing.

"Hurry," he urged, as her fingers fumbled for a holding.

She grasped a slimy post and hauled herself over the handrail, tumbling into a bedraggled heap on the boardwalk. David scampered after her, not a moment to spare judging from the angry splash rending the night. Then the danger slithered off into the watery depths.

Breathless with relief, Marla forced herself to her feet. She eyed David's sodden form as he gazed at her with concern. "I . . . I was attacked," she murmured, teeth chattering. "Someone pushed me." Swaying dizzily, she stumbled into his arms.

"It's all right. You're safe now." Holding her, he patted her dripping hair.

"Ouch! I must have a bruise there. He hit my head against the railing, then tossed me into the water. Did you see him?"

"I saw a moving figure but couldn't discern who it was."

"What should we tell my family?" she croaked as they trudged toward the house, their wet shoes making squishing noises.

"We had a craving for alligator meat but the big one got away," David suggested, a twinkle in his eye. "I think we should keep quiet about what happened. If we're lucky, we can sneak inside and get cleaned up before anyone sees us. Your cousins must have some clothes we can borrow."

But as they approached the brightly lit house, screams pierced the night, bloodcurdling cries that turned Marla's veins to ice. A cluster of her relatives gesticulated wildly as she and David rushed toward the patio.

"Rebecca fell into the pool," Aunt Polly told her. "Do something!"

Marla watched, horrified, as Bruce lifted the girl's limp body into the waiting arms of her father. Michael stared down into his daughter's lifeless face and howled in anguish.

"Call 911," Marla yelled. Scooping Rebecca from her brother's arms, she laid the girl on the ground and began CPR. David knelt to assist her. With crushing relief, Marla saw the girl's chest rise in a shuddering breath. Water spewed from her mouth as she vomited. Marla tilted her to the side, glad to see her bluish color receding as breathing was restored. By the time the paramedics arrived, Rebecca had regained consciousness. She couldn't have been under very long, Marla thought, muttering a prayer of thanks to the Almighty.

Charlene and Michael left to accompany Rebecca to the hospital, where the toddler would get a thorough checkup and remain for observation. They left their son, Jacob, in Anita's solicitous care.

Reassured that everything was under control, Marla disappeared into a bathroom to scrub the swamp mud from her skin.

"Marla, are you in there?" called Cynthia, knocking on the door. "David said you had an accident and would need something to wear. Here's a shorts set I can loan you."

Marla swung open the door, a towel wrapped around her hair.

"Don't give me that look," Cynthia cried, cringing. "I know, we'll get a pool fence. I'll order one first thing in the morning. You were right."

"I'm just glad I was here to help." Marla's voice shook with emotion. This event was too reminiscent of the last time.

Cynthia bowed her head. "Thanks," she whispered. "I — I don't know what else to say."

Marla blinked, moisture tipping her eyelashes. Too choked up to speak, she merely nodded.

"What happened to you and David?"

Marla told her about the intruder in the swamp. "It was definitely a man, someone who isn't spending Thanksgiving with his family. You'll remember to take photos of the stuff he dumped tonight and call me, right? That may be our only way to trace the medical waste polluter. Now tell me how Rebecca ended up in the pool."

Cynthia handed over the clean clothes. "I'm not sure. We thought the kids were playing together. Bruce announced that the buffet was ready, and everyone went inside to fill a plate at the dining room table. I was supervising the staff to see that the chafing dishes remained full. Next thing I knew, Charlene was screaming."

Marla didn't learn anything new when she questioned the rest of her family. Although their responses were subdued, they wolfed down their meals. Knowing that Rebecca would survive had brought back voracious appetites. She managed to grab the last spoonful of sweet potatoes before Shark helped himself to seconds. Glancing at him curiously, she noticed water spots on his clothes. He hadn't been around when she'd worked on Rebecca, had he? Come to think of it, she hadn't noticed him or Annie in the vicinity.

Waiting for the distraction of dessert, Marla drew Annie aside. "So when would you like me to cut your hair? I've got my shears in my purse." She gave an encouraging smile.

"Not now." Annie thrust her thumbs into her belt line. Her glance followed Shark, who swaggered to the table holding a plate heaped with brownies and ruglach. "At least *he's* having a good time."

"What does that mean?"

Annie glowered. "He's been stuffing himself all night, and I don't like the way he's been ordering me around. First he wants me to put the hummus spread on crackers for him. Then he tells me to get him a plate of food. When he said I should get him a piece of pie, I told him to get it himself. What a conceited prick."

"You filled his plate for dinner?"

Annie's eyes downcast. "Yeah, like I'm his doormat."

"Where was he?"

"Huh? He was waiting out here."

"On the patio. Alone?"

"Heck, no. The kids were playing over there." Her glance rose to the swing set. "Actually, Jacob came inside. He said he needed to use the bathroom."

Marla's pulse rate quickened. Making Annie promise to call her for a haircutting date, she excused herself and wandered over to the little boy. Busy eating a cookie and smearing chocolate around his face, he grinned through a mouthful of food. His thick head of wheat-colored hair and wide round eyes gave him an impish appearance. Anita hovered next to him, beaming with a grandmother's glory as she watched him chew.

"Hey, Jacob," Marla said, crouching down to his level. She exchanged a few words with him, ruffled his hair, then rose. "Ma, did he say why he went inside and left Rebecca?" she whispered out of the kid's hearing.

Anita's face pinched. "He had to use the bathroom. Someone told him to wash his hands or he wouldn't be allowed to eat."

"Who? Charlene?"

"No. She'd gone to get the kids their plates. I've asked Jacob, but he won't tell me. I think he's scared he'll be blamed."

"Or afraid to tell for other reasons." Marla's glance swung to Shark, who was peering at them intently. Their eyes met, and she stared him down until he looked away. Damned if she'd let him screw her family.

"You're still coming over this Sunday, right?" Anita said.

"Yes, I'll see you then." She hadn't been able to make their date this past weekend due to a last-minute wedding party. Another beautician had canceled, and Marla had been asked to substitute. Being a sap for a hard case made refusal impossible. Besides, the pay had made it worthwhile.

Taking her leave, she retrieved her purse and headed into the house.

David waylaid her in the living room. "Where are you going? You're not leaving, are you? We haven't made any plans to see each other again."

His eyes regarded her fondly, and she felt an answering warmth. After all, the man had saved her life earlier.

"I'm afraid I'm busy for the rest of this weekend," she said, a hint of regret in her tone. "Tomorrow after work, I promised my colleagues to take them out for pizza. I've had to rearrange so many appointments lately that I feel I owe them a good time. Saturday night, I'm treating my friend Tally to dinner. Her husband will be out of town, and we haven't seen each other for a while. And Sunday is the day to visit my mother and get all my chores done."

"Well, aren't you the busy lady. I guess things will be more frantic with only three weeks to the fund-raiser. Say, I want to call Mustafa to request he include a certain item from his menu for Taste of the World. Do you still have that envelope Ben gave you with Mustafa's phone number?"

She gazed at him quizzically. "Yeah, I put it somewhere, but didn't you get the chef's business card? You can call him at his restaurant."

David smiled, reaching out to pull her close. The smell of fresh air and earth clung to him. A lock of hair swept his forehead, crowning arches of bristly eyebrows. "You're right, as always. Let me know if you hear anything new regarding Popeye's heir."

"I will." She gazed into his face, her eyes searching his. How did she really feel about this man?

His gaze darkening, David lowered his

head to graze his lips against hers. "We make a good team," he murmured. "I see something permanent in our future."

You see more than I do, pal.

Marla drew back, detaching herself from his embrace. His kisses were so lukewarm, almost obligatory. Was he merely being polite, saving his passion for later? While she felt drawn to him, the reasons eluded her. Sure, he acted like a gentleman, but was that his appeal? Or did her family's approval have more to do with her attraction? Perhaps she was falling into the same trap as she had with Stan. Craving respect from her relatives after her disastrous past, it had been easy to succumb to Stan's powerful personality. She didn't need to go down that same road twice. *Let's get past the fund-raiser,* she told herself, *and then I'll examine my motives.*

Saturday night, she confided her concerns to Tally. Purposefully avoiding restaurants owned by chefs participating in Taste of the World, she'd suggested a local steak place. With her hearty appetite, Tally had happily agreed.

"How can Vail think I may be endangered in David's company?" Marla said between bites of salad. "He's been looking after my safety."

"So who does that leave as suspects in Ben's death?" Tally asked, flinging a strand of blond hair from her eyes.

Marla held up her fingers as she ran through the list. "Babs Winrow, who visits Orlando when she's supposed to be in Tampa. Dr. Russ Taylor, who needs money to cover a mysterious debt. Darren Shapiro, the banker who slinks away on weekend nights. Stefano Barletti, whose Pre-Need funeral arrangements are probably over-priced. Digby Raines, a politician who likes women as much as the polls."

"And your cousin Cynthia. Means, motives, opportunity?"

"You sound like Vail!" Marla laughed. "Stefano was being sued by Ben on behalf of disgruntled former customers. Digby may have felt threatened by Ben on election eve. They were entangled in a scandal years past which gave Ben a hold over him. Darren inadvertently provided the murder weapon." She paused. "Whoever is Popeye's heir had reason enough to kill the lawyer as well as the trustee in order to hide his identity."

"Temporarily," Tally wisely pointed out. "If Ocean Guard fails to meet its obligations and this person inherits, you'll all know who it is."

"Tell me about it. That makes no sense, does it?"

"What's Vail's opinion?"

"He's not very forthcoming with information. I have no clue which one of the board members he thinks is guilty."

Wishing to eliminate Cynthia from her list, Marla queried her mother the next day. As usual when she visited Anita, Marla found herself seated at the kitchen table and served a meal.

"What did Cynthia have against Ben Kline?" she asked.

Anita smoothed a manicured hand over her sleek white hair. "I didn't want to mention this earlier, *bubula*. You must promise not to tell anyone what I'm about to reveal."

Marla's ears perked up. She'd thought only her past held a dastardly secret.

"You know Corbin, whom we haven't seen for a while? Well, I can tell you where he is: spending time in the clinker. Cynthia hired Ben to defend her brother against felony charges, but Ben screwed up, and Corbin got put away. Cynthia felt she'd paid Ben for nothing and accused him of ripping her off."

Marla swallowed a bite of gefilte fish before she replied. "How angry was my cousin?"

Anita frowned. "Not enough to kill Ben, if that's what you're thinking. Shame on you, daughter, for suspecting a member of your own family."

"I'm just covering all the angles," Marla said in her best imitation of Vail's impassive voice. *Damn,* why did that man keep creeping into her consciousness? "Anyway, you were going to tell me about your Pre-Need funeral arrangements." Reaching into her purse, she retrieved a bunch of papers. "Here's the estimate I got from Stefano Barletti."

Anita took a seat and perused the forms. "These numbers are way out of line. Mine came to less, but don't forget, your father and I bought our plans many years ago. I called my Pre-Need counselor, and this is the quote he gave me for you."

She picked up a scrap of paper. "You can get a decent casket in poplar for $1295. Professional services, removal of the body, refrigeration, and use of a chapel shouldn't cost more than $1400. Cemetery services come to $650. Adding in the plot and extras, your total comes to approximately $5000."

"Wow, that's quite a difference. Babs was right. She said Stefano charged higher prices than elsewhere. I wonder if he'd do a price match."

"You can shop around, even for funeral expenses," Anita advised, "but you only have that luxury if you plan things ahead of time."

"Can I take this paper? I may need it as an excuse to see Stefano again."

"Why don't you leave the murder investigation to your policeman friend?"

"Someone has targeted me, Ma. I didn't want to worry you before by telling you. David and I must have been followed to Nassau, because someone tried to clunk me on the head with a coconut, and Popeye's trustee was murdered. A dead duck was left on my doorstep at home, and my house was invaded. Dalton isn't revealing his findings, so I have to act on my own."

"My God, Marla. Why didn't you tell me any of this before?"

"Why? So you wouldn't look as upset as you do now." She smiled reassuringly. "Look, I don't want to disappoint Cynthia. She's relying on me to keep the fund-raiser on track."

"Yes, but you're putting yourself at risk!"

Marla raised a hand. "Say no more about it. I'll watch my back, but I won't quit."

Anita gave a resigned sigh. "I liked the way you did Cynthia's hair. It's about time she changed her style."

"She wants me to cut Annie's hair," Marla said, beaming with pride.

"That girl is a problem. She's blind-sided by that fellow, Shark. I don't like him."

"Neither do I." Marla had left a message for Vail on Friday, giving Shark's tag number which she'd copied down upon leaving Cynthia's house on Thanksgiving. It brought to mind something else she needed to do.

17

As soon as she got home from visiting her mother, Marla put Spooks on his leash and walked over to Goat's house. "Hey, pal," she said when her neighbor opened the door. A strong scent of pine spray wafted from the interior.

Shirtless, Goat sported a sheepskin cap and wore some kind of jungle-printed fabric wrapped around his hips. A necklace of polished shark's teeth adorned his neck.

"Marla! Bringing your pooch over for a grooming?" Chewing on what looked like a twig, he regarded her closely.

She glanced at his minivan parked in the driveway. The words, The Gay Groomer, were emblazoned on its side in brilliant aquamarine against a background of canary yellow.

"Not today, thanks. I was wondering if you'd seen that blue sedan around here again."

A strange light entered his eyes. First his head bobbed, and then he began undulating his body. *"Ugamaka, ugamaka, chugga, chugga, ush,"* he sang. "One bird in the heather, one in the bush! Grab it, twist it, until it goes *squoosh!"*

"What does that mean?" Marla asked, squinting. "You chanted those same words before, right after the dead duck landed on my doorstep."

"Squoosh," he repeated, twisting his hands as though wringing out a wet cloth.

Marla caught the note of agony in his voice. "Please tell me, Goat. Did you see something that upset you?"

Reason brought him to a standstill. "He shouldn't have done that. Poor helpless creature. Grasping its neck and then —"

Grimacing, Goat shut his eyes.

Excitement coursed through her. "You saw someone kill the duck?"

Goat sniffed. "H-He put the remains in a bag."

"Who did?"

"Stupid punk." Anger contorted his features. "He drove by and tossed the bag at your door. What are kids coming to these days?" Slapping a hand to his mouth, Goat glanced over his shoulder. "Sorry, I wasn't referring to your children, Becky." A loud *baa* sounded from within. A guilty flush rising on his face, Goat snatched the sheepskin cap from his head and clutched it between his hands.

"Don't tell me you've got a real goat in there." At his silly grin, Marla shook her head. "What did this guy look like?"

"Light brown hair with a buzz cut, decently dressed dude. Must have been in his late teens. Drove a blue Chevy. I was too upset to mention it before." He peered at her curiously. "Why do you look so sick? You think you can identify him?"

Slowly, Marla nodded. "I believe so. From your names, you'd think both of you were animal lovers, but I don't think he shares your affinity for furry creatures. His name is Shark. He's more the carnivorous type."

So why would Shark be stalking her while playing up to Annie and hanging around Cynthia's house?

Later, after completing her chores, Marla sat in her small family room curled up on an armchair. Sipping a mug of hot coffee, she reviewed the details from the few times she'd met the youth. *Schmo, isn't it obvious? He's spying on us!*

The more she thought about it, the more convinced Marla became. Shark had seduced Annie in order to get closer to

Cynthia and keep tabs on her cousin's movements. He was also responsible for intimidating her. That both of them should be targets told her the saboteur was involved. Whoever didn't want their fund-raiser to succeed was attempting to destroy them mentally, hoping to upset their plans for the big event. Popeye's heir? Presumably. Could Shark have been the person who followed her and David to the Bahamas? Chilling logic followed on this trail. Was he . . . Could he be the killer?

She brought the steaming brew near her face, seeking comfort in its warmth. If Shark had pushed Rebecca over the edge of the pool, clearly he was capable of dire deeds.

Afraid for Annie's safety, Marla put down her mug, then snatched up the telephone to call Cynthia's house. Their answering machine came on, inducing a swell of disappointment.

"Cynthia, please call me as soon as possible." Thoughts racing through her mind, she wondered what she could say to alert her cousin without Shark overhearing if he was present. "I-I need to pick up my clothes, and maybe you'll have those photos ready for me. If you get home late, it's okay to call."

Her anxiety didn't abate through the

night as she waited futilely for the return phone call. In the morning, she tried again but received the same response. Perhaps they'd gone out of town, she reasoned. Or Cynthia was just too tired after coming home late. She could always accomplish a few of her chores and run over there.

Mondays were hectic because Marla saved her business errands for this one day off during the work week. She'd taken care of Spooks, done the dishes, and changed the linens when the telephone rang, making her jump. *Bless my bones, you'd better calm down, or you won't help anyone.* Her clammy fingers gripped the receiver.

"Yes?" Hopefully, it would be Cynthia saying everything was okay.

"Marla, this is Babs. I-I'd like to see you."

"Oh." Her stomach sank. It wasn't her cousin after all. "You want to make a hair appointment?" Sometimes favored clients called her at home.

"No. I mean, I need to see you privately. This isn't easy for me, but there's something I have to say."

Marla's curiosity peaked. "All right. When?"

"How about if we meet at Barnes & Noble? I'll buy you a cup of coffee. Ten o'clock okay?"

Precise and to the point, that was Babs. "Sure. See you later," she agreed.

What could Babs possibly want to tell her? Marla wondered as she finished paying bills. Maybe the businesswoman's guilty conscience had been nagging her, and she was ready to confess her sins. Was Babs sneaking off to Orlando to meet a lover? That's the only thing that made sense, especially if she was hiding these trips from her devoted husband.

At ten o'clock, Marla waited inside the bookstore by a display of best-sellers. A smile lit her face as Babs rushed through the entrance, but it quickly faded at the woman's obvious distress. Dressed in a navy suit with an ivory shell, Babs might have looked her usual sophisticated self except that her blond hair was in disarray and her cinnamon lipstick was smeared. Presumably, she'd completed her toilette in haste, or else she'd been so distraught she hadn't cared.

"What's wrong?" Marla asked after they were seated in the café. She sipped a cup of hot coffee while Babs stared unblinkingly at her espresso.

Babs glanced up, her hazel eyes clouded with anxiety. She reached for a paper napkin, twisting it while a range of emotions crossed her face. "I want to tell you about Orlando because you probably have the wrong impression about me. But you must promise never to reveal a word about this to anyone, least of all Walter. I love him, Marla, and I don't want to hurt him."

Marla put her cup down, leaning forward to hear the juicy details. She'd heard so much in her venue as a hairdresser that nothing surprised her anymore.

"You know, Walter and I never had any children. We'd so hoped for a family, but it turned out we couldn't . . . he couldn't . . . conceive. We swallowed our disappointment, but mine was a lot less than his."

Folding her hands on the table, Babs focused downcast eyes at an imaginary speck on the floor. "I-I had a daughter when I was very young and gave her up for adoption. She found me, thanks to the lawyer representing her."

"Ben Kline." Marla knew it instinctively.

Babs nodded, her knuckles white. This confession must be torture for her, Marla surmised with a surge of sympathy. "I agreed to meet her where she lived in Orlando. She understood when I said it would destroy my marriage if Walter discovered her existence. He's missed out on having children; I haven't. Not to mention the fact

309

that he thought I was a virgin when we met each other." Her lips curled in a cynical smile. "Poor Walter, he was so naive."

"What's her name?" Of all the confidences Babs might have revealed, a secret baby wasn't on Marla's list.

"Jennifer. She's twenty-seven, single, and works as an office manager. Her adoptive parents are still alive, and she keeps in close communication with them. She hasn't told them about me, so our arrangement suits us both fine."

"Other than fearing Walter's reaction, how did you feel about meeting her?"

Babs lifted her gaze, and Marla noticed her lashes were tipped with moisture. "Wonderful. Amazed. Grateful. I'd never dreamed I would see her again."

"I won't give away your secret, but I'll bet Walter wouldn't be as upset as you'd think."

"Thanks, Marla. It's helped me just to talk to you about this. I didn't want you to think I was cheating on my husband when you found out I was sneaking off to Orlando."

"Did you hold a grudge against Ben because he was the one who brought you and Jennifer together?"

"Hell, yes. He should've contacted me privately first. But you can take that speculative gleam out of your eye. I didn't kill him. And in the long run, I'm extremely grateful. Anyway, I'm glad you know about this now. How are you doing with the fund-raiser? Everything okay with the chefs? I've sent the recipe booklet to the printers. I think our guests will love getting one for a table favor."

Marla sighed. "No one has resigned this week yet. I'm still wondering who was responsible for chasing away Max and the others. Either it was Alex Sheffield being spiteful, or whoever stands to inherit the mangrove preserve. I can't shake the feeling that Ben's murder is mixed up in all this."

"You may be right. It's all such a tangle. Probably what you need is a single clue to unmask the culprit. I gather you're no closer to identifying Popeye's heir."

"I did learn one piece of news that may interest you. Were you aware Darren gave a weapon from his knife collection to Ben in return for a favor? The killer used that weapon to murder the lawyer."

"Yes, I'd heard that tidbit."

Leaning forward, Marla lowered her voice. "I went to Darren's house, and I saw the long, curved knives that he owns. They're really heavy. Darren has muscles, too. He could easily lift one and swing it. A neighbor said Darren goes out every weekend without his wife. There's a lot of shouting coming from their house. Marital discord can be a source of hidden rage. Do you think Ben was involved in divorce proceedings between Darren and his wife?"

Babs waived a hand in dismissal. "Your imagination is running wild, dear. Darren has a perfectly good reason for possessing those knives. I couldn't believe it when he told me." Her lips curved in a sly smile. "You want to know where the man goes on weekends? Check out the show at the Polynesian Revue."

Marla puzzled over this remark, but she didn't have long to think about it. Errands kept her busy the rest of the morning until her stomach rumbled in protest. Her itinerary led her to Alex Sheffield's restaurant for lunch. After requesting to speak to the chef, she ordered a chicken Caesar salad. She'd just finished lunch when Sheffield came out to greet her.

"I'm Marla Shore," she said, rising.

Outfitted in a white chef's uniform, he accepted her brief handshake. His eyes, brown and hard as acorns, stared into hers. Irrelevantly, she thought his limp hair could use a bit of mousse and a shorter trim.

"I thought I made it clear during our

phone conversation that I want nothing to do with Ocean Guard," he stated coldly.

She smiled in what she hoped was an appeasing manner. "So I understand, but I have some concerns I'd like to share with you. Pierre Chevalier had an accident during his cooking class last month. Someone added a volatile substance to the bottle of rum he was using for a flambé dessert. Later, he told me that his assistant, Felipe, used to work for you. Pierre dropped out of Taste of the World, and so did Max from the Seafood Emporium. Someone's been scaring off our star chefs who've signed up for the fund-raiser. This has to stop."

His scornful gaze raked her. "And you think it's me?"

"The idea has crossed my mind."

"I wouldn't be so stupid. For your information, I learned Felipe was being paid to spy on me."

"Paid by whom, a rival chef who hoped to discover your secret recipes?" she joked.

"Someone wanted to make sure I stayed out of Ocean Guard's path," he said soberly. "Felipe was feeding me information about Jerry Caldwell, the organization's president."

Alex gestured for her to take a seat, then

he lowered his brawny body into a chair opposite her. "After you called me, I phoned Jerry Caldwell myself to clear the air. It's true that Ocean Guard supports legislation to regulate commercial fishing, but Jerry denied he'd been the one who ratted on my menu practices. I realized it must have been Felipe who'd substituted a cheaper product for mahimahi and then cast the blame on me."

"Did you find out who'd paid Felipe?"

"Nope. I've asked my colleagues about him, but no one's seen him recently. I'll bet he's skipped town."

Collecting her purse and the bill which the waitress had left on her table, Marla stood. "Well, thanks for the info. I'm sorry you won't be joining us for Taste of the World."

He rose agilely to his feet. "I've been a real *schmuck*. I realize it's short notice, but if you get an opening, give me a call. Otherwise, count on me for next year."

Her conversation with the chef reminded her of David's recent request for Mustafa's phone number. Tuesday morning, after checking supplies in the storeroom, she opened the drawer containing the envelope Ben had scribbled on. Grasping it in her hand, she checked her watch. Nine-thirty.

Maybe David would be in his office. Removing the business card he'd given her, she dialed his number.

"Hi, I'm Marla Shore, and I'd like to speak to David Newberg please," she said to the secretary who answered.

"Sorry, he's not in the office right now. May I take a message?"

"He requested some information from me, but I'd like to give it to him personally. Is Mr. Newberg still at home? I can call him there. We're friends," she explained.

"Oh, I don't know, miss. I'm new here, and he seems to come in at different hours each day depending on his appointments."

"I see." David hadn't mentioned hiring a new secretary, but then he never discussed his work with her, Marla realized. "Well, I'll try again later, thanks."

Hanging up, she stared at the envelope in her hand. Slit open at the top, it held a return address from Morton Riley. A letter from Popeye's trustee addressed to Ben?

She pried it open and her fingers had just grasped the folded paper inside when the phone rang. It was Cynthia. Dismissing the letter, she stuffed it into her purse for later examination.

"Where the hell have you been? I've been worried about you," Marla rasped.

Cynthia's voice sounded sleepy. "We went to a party last night and got in late. What's the matter?"

Marla expounded her theories concerning Shark. "Did you get the investigative report back about him yet?"

"No, but I'll give the man a call today. Did you want to stop by and pick up your clothes? My maid washed them, but they're still soiled. I'll reimburse you, Marla. Whoever attacked you is Ocean Guard's enemy, and you're working for us. Regarding the preserve, I have the photos you requested."

Marla did some rapid calculations. "I'm tied up all day. Will you be home around six? I can swing by after work."

"Okay. Bruce is hunting down a copy of Popeye's trust agreement. There must be one in Ben Kline's office. His legal assistant is still there helping to straighten things out. But if that's not successful, Bruce will go to Morton Riley's colleagues to plead his cause."

"Good, maybe we'll get some solid information for a change. I called Charlene earlier. Rebecca is home and doing well. Thank goodness, we averted a potential disaster."

"You did, Marla. I haven't forgotten about the pool fence. A man is coming to measure the patio tomorrow."

"Good move. Well, let's hope your photos shed some light on who's dumping medical waste on the preserve. In the meantime, please keep an eye on Annie."

Marla's first client walked in the door, and she pushed aside her worrisome thoughts to find comfort in routine. Her busy schedule didn't permit any further phone calls until a quick break in the afternoon.

"I have Mustafa's number if you need it," she said to David, who'd left a message earlier.

"Did you find Ben's envelope?" he replied in an oddly strained voice. "We could have dinner later, then I'll relieve you of the burden."

"Yes, the paper is here. I put it in my purse, so I won't forget it next time. Thanks for the dinner invitation, but I have to run over to Cynthia's house after work. She took some photos of the stuff that's being dumped, and I'm hoping that will help identify the culprit."

"Great, I'll meet you there."

"No, that won't be necessary. I've got some other things to do afterward."

"When can I see you then?"

"Probably this weekend. How about if I

call you later in the week and we can make plans?"

"Okay. Anything else new that I should know about?"

"I feel as though I'm getting closer to learning the identity of Popeye's heir," she confided. "I've spoken to Babs and have pretty much eliminated her from the list. It can't possibly be Cynthia, so that leaves the men. Remember, it was a man who assaulted me in the mangrove preserve."

She didn't mention Shark's role, because she couldn't be certain who'd hired him. Probably the attacker from the swamp, Ocean Guard's saboteur.

"That leaves Stefano Barletti, Darren Shapiro, Digby Raines, and Dr. Russ Taylor. Oh, and you," she added with a chuckle.

"Well, we know it's not me," he snapped. "What have you got on the others?"

"Besides the possibility that one of them is Popeye's heir and wants to hide his identity, Barletti, Raines, and Taylor all had reason to resent Ben Kline. Darren inadvertently provided the murder weapon."

"You mean, he knew it was there, hanging on the wall in Ben's office."

"Yes, I suppose so." Her brow wrinkled in thought. "Babs said I should go to the Poly-

318

nesian Revue if I wanted to learn more about Darren."

"Why is that?"

"I'm not really sure. Maybe we could check out the restaurant this weekend. It's a real cool place. I've been there once before, although I can't conceive of what Darren's connection might be."

She asked Cynthia when she stopped by her house later.

"I haven't any idea," Cynthia said, handing her the pack of photos. "But I do have some other news for you. I spoke with my private investigator. It took him some time to trace Shark's background, because the boy didn't give his real name. Shark is actually Angelo Barletti. Stefano's son."

18

Marla's stunned mind attempted to assimilate the news about Shark. Stefano's son! Did that mean Stefano was to blame for their mishaps? Could it be that he was Popeye's heir? *Perhaps so, but don't jump to conclusions,* she warned herself. A few loose ends needed to be tied off before she could target the man.

"Look what else I discovered," Cynthia said, gesturing for Marla to follow her inside the house. In a room designated as the library, she pointed to a faded photograph in a tarnished silver frame that sat on a dusty bookshelf. "It's a picture of Popeye Boodles."

"Who's that woman?" Marla peered at the youthful couple standing under a cluster of palms on a sandy beach. Barefooted, they wore carefree grins on their tanned faces. "I thought Popeye never married."

"That's his sister. I'd forgotten all about her."

"Really? What happened to the girl?" Here she'd been thinking Popeye's heir was some distant cousin, but he could be a closer relation.

"I believe she's deceased. Bruce's family lost touch with her, but I'll ask him if he can get more information. What should I do about Annie? Shark has been using her, and I don't want him around here anymore."

"Tell her the truth. Maybe it's time to assert some parental authority, cuz. He's a danger to us, especially if Stefano is behind everything."

She couldn't confront him until she eliminated certain other possibilities. The next day, she ran out on her lunch hour to waylay Dr. Taylor at his office. The surgeon strolled in looking his usual debonair self, hair fluffed with mousse, conservative navy suit with a striped tie. His glowering expression told her he wasn't pleased by her visit.

"What is it, Marla? You're disrupting my routine."

"You hate it when things get out of control, don't you?" she mused, surveying the neatly arrayed writing instruments on his desktop.

"Look, I have a busy schedule. Patients don't like to be kept waiting. Get to the point, will you?"

Whipping the photos from her purse, Marla shoved them at him. "See this? Someone's been dumping medical waste in our mangrove preserve. I was wondering if you might have any idea who's responsible. Your expertise could help us identify these items and perhaps the culprit."

He gave her a shrewd glance. "Is that why you were here the last time? You thought it was me?"

Pausing, she ran her fingers lightly across a bookshelf surface. No dust. He must have a meticulous housekeeping staff.

"The notion had crossed my mind," she replied, "especially when it was brought to my attention that your clinic was having financial difficulties."

He faced her directly, staring her down. "I don't see the connection."

"There was always the possibility you were dumping waste to avoid paying the disposal company. That would make sense if you're trying to save money. Let's say, for example, your clinic isn't doing well and you need funding for some private expense that your practice alone can't meet."

His brows drew together like angry thunderclouds. "Who's been talking to you?"

She smiled coyly. "I've spoken to lots of people, but I never believe gossip. Perhaps you'd care to enlighten me?"

Pacing the room, he threw her an annoyed glance. "I suppose you found out about Andrew. Well, I'm not ashamed of him. The institution can take better care of him than me and my wife. Our daughter requires our full attention if she's to be successful. There's no use wasting time on Andrew."

Marla hadn't been expecting this turn to the conversation. "Andrew is your son?"

Dr. Taylor stopped. "You'd never know it, would you? A blithering idiot, and there's nothing I can do. Of course, I tried. We consulted the best specialists, but their advice was the same. Put him away, unless you're willing to spend your life in his service."

Something in his expression, maybe the twinge of pain in his eyes, gave away the depth of his feelings. "You couldn't fix him, could you?" Marla asked, comprehending. "Broken bones, slipped discs you can repair, but you couldn't fix your own son. He remains a symbol of your own imperfections, which you'd rather deny. No wonder you're so obsessed with order. It must have really irked you when Ben screwed you on an investment prospect."

Dr. Taylor's gray eyes grew leaden. "Now I see where this is going." He jabbed a finger in the air. "I'm not polluting the mangrove preserve, nor am I a killer. You're wasting my time as well as your own if that's what you think."

"It's more logical that Popeye's heir is contaminating the land to void the provisions of Popeye's trust."

"Oh, so you think it's me?" His nostrils flared. "First you accuse me of polluting the preserve to save money. Now I'm fouling the land because I hope to inherit Popeye's estate. Which is it, Marla?"

"Neither. I'm just eliminating possibilities, but I really came to you for help." She pointed to the pictures. "Where else could this stuff be originating? If not a medical office or hospital, veterinarian or dentist, what other place would generate medical waste?"

The surgeon sent her a piercing gaze, as though deciding if he'd assist her. "Laboratories, nursing homes, diagnostic facilities. I don't see how you're going to track down the source."

"Thanks, you've opened up some other avenues even if I can't see how they're related. I'll show these to the guy at the biomedical waste company. It was his idea to get the photos."

"I'm sure Cynthia appreciates your efforts," Dr. Taylor said gruffly. "We all want Taste of the World to succeed."

Marla hesitated. She might have pushed him too far and didn't want to leave on a confrontational note. "I'm sorry if I offended you or brought up painful topics. Your patients and staff admire you greatly, so I wouldn't be concerned about what they'd think regarding Andrew. I believe you really do care about your son, and your anger is directed more at yourself than him. It makes you overly defensive. Now please forgive me if I've been too blunt."

He smiled wearily. "You've hit upon touchy subjects, but I understand your motivation. You're trying to do what's best for Ocean Guard. Just be careful whom you interview next. The cops seem to think Ben's killer is one of us."

His parting words lingered in her mind. Since she was driving by the vicinity, she decided to stop in at the police station to see Lieutenant Vail. It had been a while since they'd compared notes, and she wanted to tell him about Shark.

Vail, surrounded by paperwork, glanced up from his desk when Marla strolled into his office, a visitor's badge pinned to her camel blazer. Instead of the delighted grin she'd expected, a frown of annoyance crossed his brow.

"Hi, Marla. What's up?"

You look like hell, pal. Been keeping some late nights? "I was wondering how your case is progressing." Smiling coyly, she dropped into the seat opposite his desk and crossed her legs. "I miss your impromptu visits to the salon. When do you expect to snag Ben's killer? We'll have more time to be together after you wrap things up."

Giving a weary sigh, Vail leaned back in his swivel chair. "Why do I feel you've learned something I don't know? You've been interviewing murder suspects again, haven't you?" Her guilty flush made his frown deepen. "I don't have time for this, Marla. I told you not to interfere."

"I can help, Dalton. Listen to me."

"No, you listen," he said, pointing a finger at her. "I've assigned another detective to the case. We have accreditation this week, and I have too many other duties keeping me occupied." Scratching his jaw, he studied her a moment, evidently reaching a decision. "We're getting close to nailing the perp, but we still need final proof. What have you got?"

Marla glowed inwardly that he'd decided to trust her, however minutely. "Shark is Stefano Barletti's son. I think he's been spying on Cynthia and me. That makes his father my prime suspect as Popeye's heir.

Although," she muttered, "that would make Stefano the guy who attacked me in the swamp."

"What?" Vail's brows drew together. "Shit, Marla, didn't I warn you to be careful? What happened now?"

Marla described her adventure. "David saved me, despite what you think about him."

"You're not safe from anyone until the perp is behind bars."

"What's Darren Shapiro's connection? The murder weapon came from his collection. His neighbor is concerned that something fishy is going on at his house."

"Take my word for it, Shapiro isn't your man."

"Who is it, then? You must have a strong lead."

Shaking his head, Vail leveraged his large body from the chair. "My department doesn't leak information. Stay out of harm's way, Marla. We'll catch the guy soon enough. Now unless you have something more to add, you can go. I have a lot of work to do." He softened his words by rounding the corner of his desk, pulling her into his arms, and planting a light kiss on her mouth.

Marla finished the workday, her mind distracted by Vail's words of warning and the lingering taste of his lips on hers. She managed to get through conversations with friends while part of her processed what he'd said. Unable to deny her curiosity any longer, she drove to Darren's house after dinner.

Ringing the doorbell, she was dismayed when his wife answered the door. "He's not home," the woman said in response to her inquiry.

"Will I find him at the Polynesian Revue?"

A startled glance met her innocently wide gaze. "Perhaps. I don't think he'd be too happy if you showed up there."

I should've waited to eat dinner, Marla thought, giving her car to the valet at the popular restaurant in downtown Fort Lauderdale. Passing through the entrance, she admired the tropical decor enhanced by subdued lighting and lush greenery. Strains of Hawaiian music floated in the air.

"I'm looking for Darren Shapiro," she said when the hostess approached. "He works in a bank. Maybe he's a financial consultant?" She still didn't have a clue as to his association with the place.

"Oh, no." The sarong-skirted woman smiled. "He has a different, quite important, role here. I believe you'll see him best by being seated up front."

"But I didn't come here to eat. I —"

"This way, ma'am."

Helplessly, Marla followed the hostess to a long table perpendicular to the stage. She was seated alone and handed a menu while other diners filed into the room. Ordering a bushwacker and a pupu platter, she settled into her seat for what appeared to be the first show of the evening.

Marla was mesmerized by the swaying Hula dancers, energized by the hip-gyrating Tahitian girls, and stunned by the male Samoan fire knife dancers who twirled flaming batonlike knives to a ferocious drumbeat.

Hey, wait a minute. That dark-haired hunk was staring directly at her. It couldn't be.

Yes, it was. Darren Shapiro, dressed in a loincloth, his muscular body oiled, a grass crown on his head. A warrior cry tore from his throat as he flung the blazing knife high into the air, caught it, and daringly put the flames to his lips. Stretching his mouth into a menacing sneer, he sank to the floor, balancing the fiery knife on his bare feet while he spun like a break-dancer. Springing upright, he shrieked a war whoop while he tossed the knife, its blazing ends smoking the air. Transfixed, Marla couldn't move through his terrifying act, glad at last when he extinguished the flames and took his bows.

Right after the finale, a girl in a sarong with a hibiscus flower behind her ear approached Marla to invite her backstage.

"Bless my bones, I couldn't believe that was you!" Marla said, watching Darren rub down with a towel.

He mopped his forehead, then paused. "Why do you think I don't tell anyone? I'm afraid I'll lose my job at the bank if they find out. This is my passion, but it doesn't exactly fit the conservative image required during the day."

Fascinated, Marla watched the bustle of the other performers backstage. "How did you ever get interested in this?"

He shrugged his brawny shoulders, normally hidden beneath the sedate suits he wore. "When I was younger, my sister took hula lessons. I wanted to do something like that because it looked like fun, so my dad found a guy to teach me Samoan fire knife dancing. He gave me my stage name, Chief Pauahi. I love entertaining people, but I can't give up my day job. That's what puts bread on the table, you know?"

Picking up a shell lei, he hung it on his

thick neck. "Anyway, why are you here? Somehow I can't believe you wanted to see my act."

She blushed under his frank stare. "The murder weapon. It was one of these knives?" Their shapes were similar to the items she'd seen on his cocktail table at home.

He nodded at the objects laid out on the floor. "They're Samoan fire knives," he explained, lifting the two-foot-long handle wrapped in vinyl tape. "You can get them in different lengths. The Samoans used to hang skulls on this hook."

The knife was heavy, but she was able to heft it when he offered it to her. Its curved stainless-steel blade easily added another foot to the measurements. A good weapon with which to bash someone's head, Marla reasoned.

"Before my act, I bond asbestos to both ends, then soak the cloth in lighter fluid and ignite them so each side is flaming," Darren said, grinning with pride. "It's an impressive sight. Fire knife dancing is a modern interpretation of ancient warrior dances performed by Samoans. It's supposed to be very aggressive and warlike. I work on speed, twirling, and back tosses. My neighbors can probably hear me practicing at home in our fenced backyard."

"So that's what your yelling is all about. You're practicing war whoops."

The grin erased itself from his face. "Somebody used one of these for real. I'm not a detective, so you might want to tell your friend Lieutenant Vail that Stefano Barletti came in the bank today asking for a loan. His business is struggling, thanks to competition by the big chain funeral homes. But that's not the point. Stefano said he had collateral to back the loan. It's an inheritance he expects to gain early next year."

The final nails are being put in your coffin, Stefano, Marla thought during her drive home. She needed to make one more visit before confirming her opinion, however. Unfortunately, her work schedule didn't permit any deviations until Friday, when she ran out the door during lunch break.

The man at the biomedical waste facility was as cooperative as before. He took one look at the photos, and his expression brightened.

"You see all this stained clothing? Funeral homes are the most likely source. They dispose of bloody clothes from accidents. Sometimes you can tell from the formaldehyde smell, but I don't suppose being out in the swamp like this, you could sniff much."

Marla wrinkled her nose. "Don't nursing

homes throw out clothing as well?"

"Relatives would probably take those items home. Sometimes we'll get clothes from the sheriff's office, evidence that has been released."

"I see." Marla took back the photos from his proffered hand. "Well, you've been exceedingly helpful. Thanks so much."

Before beginning work on her next client at the salon, Marla ducked into the storeroom and put in a call to Stefano Barletti. "I'd like to make an appointment to see you," she said in a smooth tone. "I've been looking over the figures you gave me, and some of them seem a bit high for a Pre-Need plan."

"You realize we're an independent funeral home? We provide more personal service than the bigger conglomerates."

"Do you do price matching?" she asked bluntly.

"If necessary." Papers rustled in the background. "When did you want to stop in?"

"I get off work at six today. How late will you be there?"

"I can see you at eight o'clock. Do me a favor, and don't tell anyone you're coming. I wouldn't want word to get out that we're negotiable about costs." He chuckled, a false ring to the sound that alerted her like a warning bell. The man had something up his sleeve, no doubt about it.

After closing down the salon, Marla headed home. She wanted to change into comfortable clothes and contemplate her next move while she ate dinner. If Stefano truly was Popeye's heir, was she being wise to visit him alone? She couldn't call Vail to accompany her. He needed proof before bringing in Ben's killer, and besides, he'd already assigned another detective to the case. Prudence told her to get a backup, and Providence provided him.

David's car was parked alongside her curb when she arrived home. He wasn't anywhere in sight, though. She pulled into the garage, shut off the engine, and emerged from her car listening to Spooks's excited barking.

"You're home!" David exclaimed, rounding the corner from a side of her house. He must have finished work early, because he had on a polo shirt, slacks, and running shoes. Scratching his freshly shaven jaw, he regarded her with a curious gleam in his eyes. "You never called me back about this weekend, so I thought I'd pop over to see if you were free."

Marla gestured for him to follow her inside. Unlocking the door, she pushed into the kitchen, where Spooks attacked her ankles with affectionate yapping. As soon as David stepped over the threshold, the dog growled menacingly, prowling as though about to pounce on a squirrel.

"Come on, Spooks, I'll let you out. What's the matter?" The pooch was disturbingly reluctant to leave. She had to lift him bodily to get him beyond the patio door.

"Come with me," Marla said to David, striding toward the study. "I have to check my answering machine."

"So you've no plans for tonight?" His long stride kept pace with her.

"I'm going to meet Stefano." Noting the blinking message light, she pushed the play button.

"Marla, call me the minute you get in. I have news." It was Vail's voice, sounding unusually urgent.

"Oh God, what am I going to do now?" Cynthia wailed in the second message. "We had a fire in the laundry room last night. It got put out, but there's smoke damage in the house. Now we need to have the drapes cleaned, and everything smells. I can't possibly have a couple of hundred guests here in two weeks! Oh, and another thing. You won't believe what Bruce discovered at

Morton Riley's office. What fools we are. You've got to —"

"I'm so sorry, I hit the wrong button," David said in a low tone. "I meant to hit replay and got erase instead. You can call your cousin back later." Marla swallowed her retort when he grinned sheepishly. "How about if I take you to dinner to compensate?"

"I don't know —"

"That reminds me," he said, edging closer, his grin vanishing. "Do you have Ben's envelope with Mustafa's number? I can't find the chef's business card anywhere."

"It's in my purse. Wait, I've got to let Spooks in," she announced, hearing his frantic barking. The poodle wouldn't leave David alone, snapping at his ankles and attacking his pant leg while they stood in the kitchen. "I can't understand what's gotten into him. Look, do you want to come with me to Stefano's? I don't want to go there alone anyway."

"Why are you going to see Barletti?" Muttering a curse, David kicked at Spooks until Marla scooped the pet into her arms.

Dismayed by his behavior, she hesitated. Men who kicked dogs didn't belong on her list. Her hackles rose, and she couldn't prevent her gaze from narrowing.

"I believe Stefano is Popeye Boodles's heir," she said in a frosty tone. "The man at the biomedical waste facility looked at some photos Cynthia had taken of the stuff that's being dumped, and he said it most likely came from a funeral home. Shark is Stefano's son," she added, letting David weigh the implications of that statement. "Stefano recently applied for a loan at Darren's bank, claiming an upcoming inheritance as collateral. I gather Cynthia's message confirms all this."

She'd already forgotten about Vail. *I'll call him later,* she resolved, *after I get the evidence he needs.*

David gave her an appraising glance, his gaze shifting to her purse and back again to her animated face. "All right. It's early yet. We've got more than an hour before your appointment. Let's grab a bite to eat along the way."

Fortifying herself with a meal seemed a good idea. "Okay, but I need to get changed first."

"I'll wait here." As though realizing he needed to appease her, he scratched Spooks behind the ears. "Sorry, sport. Didn't mean to boot you in the butt, but you were being a pain. I'm just anxious to get this mess cleared up," he added with a lame smile.

So am I, pal. Nonetheless, she urged him to wait outside while she got ready. Having him in the house caused her unease for some reason she couldn't fathom. Maybe it was Spooks's hostile reaction to him.

"I think I'll go home while you're getting your act together," he said agreeably. "Would you mind picking me up on your way?"

"Oh. All right." It was strange that he couldn't wait a few minutes for her, but she didn't mind driving. Besides, his house wasn't far from where she lived.

At a quarter to eight, they approached the funeral home. The front lights blazed a friendly welcome, but the rest of the place seemed sheltered in darkness. Marla felt a moment's trepidation as she locked her car. Maybe she should've called Vail first, or at least phoned Cynthia to hear the rest of what her cousin had to say. Well, she'd made her decision.

She would face whatever Stefano had waiting for her.

19

When no one answered their summons at the funeral home's main entrance, Marla twisted the doorknob. It opened easily, and she slipped inside, with David at her heels. They faced an empty corridor, eerily silent. The lights were burning, and she sniffed the faint scent of men's cologne.

"Where is Stefano?" she whispered, hairs prickling on the nape of her neck.

"Barletti!" David yelled. "Where the hell are you?"

"His office is upstairs. Maybe he's waiting for me up there." Being in a funeral home at night gave her the willies. She wasn't eager to go exploring, visions of the living dead entering her consciousness. *I never did like horror movies.*

"Why don't you wait here? I'll look for him." David set his mouth in a grim line.

"Good idea." Remaining near the front door seemed a wise option. Just then she heard a sound like metal clanging against a hard surface. "What's that?" Her gaze darted about nervously.

"I'll check. Do you know what's beyond this corridor?"

She moistened her lips. "There are two chapels on either side, then the elevator. I don't know where those other doors lead." She wasn't so sure she wanted to find out, either. Why take risky chances? A *schnook,* she wasn't.

Watching David tiptoe down the corridor made her restless. If Stefano was lurking somewhere in the back, then it should be safe for her to go upstairs to search the man's office, right? Vail had claimed he needed proof. Now was her chance to get it for him. Besides, why let David have all the fun?

Tucking her handbag under an arm, Marla marched resolutely forward, glad she'd had the foresight to wear rubber-soled walking shoes. Too bad she hadn't thought to bring an umbrella from the car to use as a defensive weapon.

The elevator rose slowly, creaking as though announcing her presence to the world. Would the lights be on upstairs if no one was in the office? Momentary panic assailed her at the notion of being left in the dark, but when the door slid open, a row of overhead lights lit the spacious reception area.

Her heart pumping wildly, she stepped onto the carpeted floor and glanced around. Except for a small kitchen off to the left, mostly closed doors met her gaze. She couldn't remember which one Stefano had entered for their conference. They hadn't gone past the kitchen, so his office must be in that corridor straight ahead. Those looked like larger spaces anyway, more suitable for the owner and his administrative staff.

Hesitating while an attack of conscience held her in its grip, she cast her doubts aside. Stefano had no scruples, so why should she?

A crashing noise from below made her jump with fright. Heavy footfalls were followed by male curses and loud thuds that brought to mind unpleasant imaginings.

Now, girl. Stefano is occupied. Without stopping to consider how she'd escape if David's safety were compromised, she dashed across the reception area and entered a short corridor. On her right was the half-opened door to a darkened office. Wiping sweaty palms on her slacks, she took a deep, steadying breath. Beads of perspiration broke out on her forehead. Dalton needed evidence, and Cynthia was relying on her. If she hoped to put Stefano away and end the threat to Ocean Guard, she must get proof of the funeral director's misdeeds.

Mustering her courage, Marla pushed opened the door. Yawning blackness met her gaze. Her scalp prickled as she sensed another presence. Oh, God. She'd forgotten about Shark!

Before she lost her nerve, she fumbled for a light switch.

A hand clamped over hers, pinning her in place.

As she gasped in shock, something noxious sprayed her face just when she was inhaling. Her senses reeled, receded. Slowly, she sank to the floor.

She swam in a black void, a whirlpool sucking her into its depths. Struggling valiantly, she kicked toward the surface, her lungs expanding until they would burst. She couldn't take in a breath. Panic seized her when little Tammy floated by, her limp body pitching with the current. Marla tried to shove away the bloated corpse, but her arms felt leaden and wouldn't move. If she didn't breathe soon, she'd die. Rolling to her side, she felt something solid block her shoulder. Not hard. It had a soft feel, almost like a cushion.

Her eyes snapped open. As she drew in a labored breath, dry cloth stuck in her throat. She coughed, choking, her nostrils flaring. Air. It was possible to breathe through her nose. Carefully, she experimented, inhaling and trying to keep her throat closed to whatever was obstructing her mouth.

Fearful that she might gag and choke on her vomit, she concentrated on assessing her surroundings. At first, her vision seemed blurry, but then she realized she couldn't see because it was dark. Her arms wouldn't raise because she was bound at the wrists, hands in front. As she lay flat on her back, she ventured out a foot. Again, an obstruction limited her efforts. Outlines became palpable until she realized with horror where she was lying.

Inside a casket. Lined, no doubt, with one of the less-expensive crepe interiors.

Squeezing her eyes shut, she forced herself to wonder what had happened to David that he hadn't found her by now and freed her. Was it Shark who had attacked her, or had he been waiting below to waylay David? Supposedly, she'd been coming alone. Stefano must have been making sure she wouldn't escape. Two of them. She was trapped here, bound and gagged, lying in a coffin with an open lid. Was this to be her final resting place?

Desperate cries emerged from her throat as she struggled to sit up. She realized her purse had been set between her legs, presumably so no evidence of her arrival would be left behind. What would they do with her car?

Her grunts must have caught someone's attention, because she heard heavy footsteps approaching. *Uh-oh. Should I play dead? Whoops, I mean unconscious.* She couldn't close her frightened eyes, even though they burned from the substance used to gas her. Stefano might seal the lid, and she wanted to get in a last accusing stare if nothing else.

Bright lights clicked on, and she squinted instantly.

"So, my dear, you've decided to stay a while." Stefano chuckled. "Didn't I tell you to buy your funeral arrangements in advance?"

Muffled noises came from her attempt to speak. He stepped into her visual field, his narrow face looming overhead. Bulging dark eyes gloated at her helpless struggles.

"Allow me to make you more comfortable." Grinning, he yanked the cloth from her mouth. With his winged eyebrows and hollow cheeks, he looked like a Halloween death's-head. "Is that better?" he asked when she drew in a raspy breath.

Her throat felt like sandpaper, but at least her air passages were clear.

"What do you care?" she croaked, rotating her shoulders so she could push up on her elbows. "Aren't you planning to leave me in here permanently?"

He appeared horror-stricken. "Oh, no. You have a misconception. I only need to get you out of the way for a while. My inheritance, you know. Once I get Popeye's estate, I'll be home free. I already have a buyer for his property."

"You're going to sell the mangrove preserve?" While she was talking, she glanced around. Other coffins, lids raised, cluttered the room on display stands. Even if she were to somehow tumble over the edge of this casket and land on the floor, what then?

"The transfer papers are prepared. After signing, I'll cash in the money from the sale of Popeye's preserve and his estate, and I'll go on the long vacation I've always dreamed about." Folding his hands behind his back, he paced the room, seemingly eager to reveal his plans. "You're so smart. Did you figure out how I'm related to the old bugger?"

"Why don't you tell me." Testing her bonds, she noted with dismay that the duct tape tightened with her movements, making painful grooves on her wrists. Inspiration hit, but she had to guard her expression. Inside her purse were the shears she'd stashed to cut Annie's hair.

Stefano smirked. "Popeye was my uncle. His sister married into the Barletti family, much to the dismay of her snooty parents. Mother never ceased to remind me how much they'd hurt her and how she deserved better. When they didn't come to her funeral, I vowed to get what was due me. I should've been Popeye's direct heir, not Ocean Guard. I'm only taking what's rightfully mine."

"What about Shark? The rest of your family?"

"I'll leave enough money for them to bail out the funeral homes, which Shark will manage. They'll be okay. I'm tired of all this fuss and bother. It's time to live the rest of my life as I please."

No wonder Shark shirked responsibility. Look at his dad's example. "So you want me out of your way until Popeye's property passes to you, because after that it won't matter what I know?"

His expression darkened, and he jabbed a

finger at her. "You've been a nuisance. I told Shark to keep track of your movements. When he learned you were going to Nassau, I sent someone to the Bahamas after you, but the idiot didn't succeed in getting you out of the way. I had to think of something more drastic. Obviously, you weren't upset by that warning Shark left on your doorstep. Then you showed up on Thanksgiving night when I was making a dump. Oh, you're so clever. How did you figure the medical waste was coming from a funeral home?"

Marla dragged her handbag onto her stomach. "I asked Cynthia to take photos, then showed them to a man at the biomedical waste disposal company. He said bloody clothes often came from funeral homes."

He bared his teeth in an evil grin. "I thought I had you then, that night in the water, but you still escaped."

"What are you going to do with me now?" Wriggling her feet, she tried to loosen the tape around her ankles, but it didn't work. The tape twisted and strengthened.

"Don't worry, I'll put a breathing apparatus in the casket so you won't suffocate. Then I'll ship you up north. I have friends who will watch over you until this is over."

Dear Lord. He plans to seal me in this thing, alive.

Desperate to keep him talking until she could think of a plan, she went on: "What about Cynthia and Bruce? They've discovered your identity. They'll tell the authorities what you've done. You're responsible for the incidents with the chefs, aren't you?"

"I figured I might throw the fund-raiser off track. I'm sure your cousins will keep silent if I promise to produce you unharmed after I inherit the property. Otherwise, I can always take Annie for leverage. Stupid, gullible girl. She hangs on to Shark like he's the only man who will ever have eyes for her."

Please, no. Leave Annie out of this.

"Why did you trash my house? Was that another attempt to scare me, so I'd resign from my position with Taste of the World? Did you really think my absence would crash the fund-raiser?"

A puzzled frown creased his forehead. "I don't know what you're talking about."

"Didn't you send Shark to break into my place?" When he shook his head, she considered another possibility. "Well, maybe it was that other goon who followed David and me to Nassau. You know, the same one who broke into Morton Riley's house and killed him. I presume that same guy tried to shoot me at Crystal Cay on your orders, also."

"I'd heard Morton Riley was dead." He cocked his head, a glazed look in his eyes. "Same as Ben. Murdered."

"Ben knew your name was on the trust agreement, didn't he? Is that why you killed him, and later Morton Riley?"

"No, you don't understand." His gaze sharpened, swung to meet her inquisitive look. "It wasn't —"

David's large form lurched into the casket room. Taking in the situation at a glance, he launched himself at Stefano.

"Bastard!" David howled, punching Stefano straight in the midsection. Stefano doubled over, clutching his stomach.

"David, thank goodness!" Marla cried. "Get me out of here!" She glanced fearfully at the open doorway. "Where's Shark?"

"I beaned him with a lamp. Not as effective as a Samoan fire knife, but it'll keep him out while I deal with his villianous father." Growling, David gave Stefano a vicious chop on the back of his neck. The shorter man hit the ground.

Still conscious, Stefano yanked David's ankles, throwing him off balance. As David went down, Marla shrieked in terror. He was her only hope!

No, he wasn't. Prying open her purse, she turned it upside-down so the contents spilled onto her lap. She'd never had the chance to use the shears on Annie's hair. Lifting them with trembling fingers, she managed to turn them backward. With infinite difficulty, she cut the tape restraining her wrists. It didn't take long before she'd freed her ankles and leapt out of the casket. Two hundred-fifty dollars was a lot to pay for a pair of scissors, but they'd proved their mettle . . . er, metal.

A white paper caught her eye. While the two men grunted and fought in a deadly struggle, curiosity compelled Marla to withdraw the envelope. David had asked her a few times about Mustafa's phone number scrawled across it. Was that really what he'd been interested in? Come to think of it, how had David found out about the Samoan fire knife? Babs knew about it, she recalled. Maybe a news report had described the murder weapon. It could be common knowledge by now, but that didn't comfort her.

Oh, my God. What had David meant when he said the lamp wasn't as effective as a Samoan fire knife in clunking Shark on the head?

Springing to his feet, David dragged Stefano up by the collar and socked him on the jaw. Marla was barely aware of the punches David rained on his opponent. Instead of feeling relieved that he'd gained the upper hand, she felt a chill of foreboding.

Withdrawing the letter from inside the envelope, she unfolded it and scanned the contents. It was from the group to whom Ocean Guard was obligated every year to give a donation under the terms of Popeye's trust. Addressed to Morton Riley, it claimed the contribution had not been made for the past three years. The responsibility for sending in the money was that of Ocean Guard's accountant, David Newberg.

Apparently, Riley had sent this letter on to Ben Kline, expecting the attorney who was on Ocean Guard's board of directors to deal with the matter. When had Ben accused David of stealing the money, before or after the meeting she'd attended with Cynthia? She imagined that had it been before, Ben would've brought up the subject in front of the other board members. Instead, he'd absentmindedly passed the envelope along to her after scribbling Mustafa's name on top. It would've been easy for David to notice the return address.

Marla glanced up to see David's eyes resting on her. Stefano lay limp on the floor.

"I didn't mean to kill Ben," David said

quietly, a strange light in his eyes. "When he accused me of stealing sixty thousand dollars from Ocean Guard, I couldn't help myself. He wouldn't listen."

As she backed away, edging up against another coffin, David stepped closer. Feeling like a trapped animal, Marla glanced at the door. Unfortunately, David's massive body blocked the exit. His face had an oddly detached expression as he regarded her.

"Before you showed up at our board meeting, Ben said he was meeting with Riley that afternoon about an irregularity in Ocean Guard's records. Ben called me later and asked if we could meet. I made an appointment with him at seven o'clock. No one else was at his office since it was after hours."

Plowing his hand through his hair, David grimaced. "He accused me of stealing the money. I told Ben I knew nothing about it, but he didn't believe me. No one accuses me of dishonesty, Marla. You know that from our brief acquaintance. Honor means a lot to me. I got angry when Ben wouldn't listen, and figured I'd knock some sense into him. There was this weapon on the wall, and I grabbed it. I only meant to threaten him, but he fought against me. I cracked the fire knife against his skull. It's pretty heavy, you know, with a dull edge. Ben crumpled immediately."

Marla's hand flew to her mouth. Was David saying he wasn't a thief, but he was a murderer? Sashaying sideways, she advanced toward the door, but he put a hand out to grasp her arm.

"Listen," he ordered, squeezing. She clamped her lips, squelching a whimper of pain. Maybe she could appeal to his affection for her. Or maybe she should keep him talking. Her ears picked up faint sounds from below. Shark might have revived. *Better the devil you know than the one you don't,* she thought frantically, praying that the younger man would race upstairs to help his father.

"I cleaned things up and got out of there fast," David continued. "I bought a movie ticket for a show that had already started, so it appeared as though I'd been in the theater for a while. Later, I realized my secretary pretended to mail the donation every year. She diverted the funds so it looked as though I had stolen the money and then skipped town before I could confront her. I figured Popeye's heir had paid her to betray me."

"You didn't take the money. It wasn't your fault."

"I sent the proper funds right away to the organization to fulfill the terms of the trust, but I was afraid Riley would still believe I was guilty."

Her mouth dropped open. "You killed him!"

He bared his teeth in a nasty grin. "It was easy to run downtown while you were relaxing in your room. I hoped to convince you to let me deal with the trustee, but you were so damned persistent. Then I feared that you wouldn't believe me, either, if you read that letter."

"Of course I would. . . . I do. You're an honest man, David. Please let go of my arm."

His eyes glazed. "My father accused me of stealing. He'd always favored my younger brother. I thought Dean had taken the hundred dollars, but found out it was my mother. She'd been putting away money for her retirement because Dad couldn't save anything. She'd told Dean, and both of them were afraid to confess the truth. So I took the blame. Dad never had any respect for me after that."

"Is that why you became an accountant? To prove you could handle people's money and be trusted?"

He looked at her in an odd manner that

chilled her blood. "You trusted me, didn't you? I became friendly with you to get that letter back before you read it. I searched your house, but the envelope wasn't there. Now you know what it says, and I can't have you telling anyone else. It impinges upon my honor. Besides, you know too much. It's a shame, because you and I could've been a number."

"We still can, David. I thought you liked me. We can go away together." She tried to give a coaxing smile, but her mouth wouldn't cooperate. Her veins felt like ice, but she steeled herself for action, putting one foot slightly in front of the other to maintain her balance.

"Shut up, liar. You're too friendly with that cop not to tell him the truth." He lunged forward, grabbing her by the shoulders. Marla shrieked and brought her hand up to scratch his face. He swept a leg behind her ankles to trip her. When she buckled, he tossed her like a sack of flour into the open coffin.

"Good-bye, darling. Stefano had the right idea for you, except I'll do it without the breathing apparatus. Looks like you'll save on the cost of a funeral, after all."

"Wait!"

He'd reached his hands to the rim, about

to slam down the lid when Shark staggered into the room. Congealed blood coated his cheek. David, spying this new threat, crashed down the lid. Marla saw him wheeling away before blackness engulfed her.

"Help!" she screamed, battling the wood surrounding her. How long before she'd suffocate in here without oxygen? Her fingers pushed at the solid cover, but it wouldn't budge. Too heavy, or David had locked it somehow.

A heavy weight crashed against her casket, barely rocking it. That gave her an idea. Maybe she could pound her body against the side until the thing toppled over. The lid might fall open when it fell to the floor. But try as she might, she couldn't even turn sideways, let alone move such a heavy object.

Despair threatened to overwhelm her, but she refused to give up. Her breathing, already rapid, grew more labored. Sweaty fingers tried to find a hold on the lid and slipped.

Holy highlights, what's that cold object against her leg?

The metal shears!

Grasping the tool by its blades, she banged the handle against the solid surface.

"Help, let me out!" she screamed.

Bright lights flooded her as the lid was flung open. "Marla!" exclaimed Cynthia, gazing down at her in shock. "What are you doing here? And why is Stefano lying on the ground?"

Marla toppled over the edge and landed with shaky legs on the carpeted floor. "He was knocked out. Where's David?"

Cynthia gazed at her with wide, blue eyes. "David? I came here to see Stefano, but it looks like you already dealt with him. What happened?"

"I'll tell you later. Let's get out of here."

Grabbing Cynthia by the elbow, she hustled her elegantly clad cousin into the hallway and around a corner past the kitchen. "There's got to be a staircase somewhere," she mumbled, glancing at a row of closed doors.

A crash sounded, and Marla nearly jumped out of her skin. It came from below. "David must be fighting Shark. We have to get to the front door."

"Oh dear. I hadn't counted on Shark being here, too."

"Move, cuz!" Opening one door after another, Marla sought the stairs in vain. It was only after they'd entered the corridor past Stefano's office that she found an exit.

Never mind finding any evidence, now. Saving their lives was more important.

They emerged onto the first landing and were nearly bowled over by Shark barreling into David. Both men were bruised and bleeding, and they ignored the women. Seeing that the way to the front was blocked and the side entrance was out of range, Marla urged her cousin to retreat.

Pushing open a door, she charged into some kind of laboratory at the rear of the funeral home. Metal instruments glistened on sterile countertops, while three examining tables took up space in the middle of the room.

Cynthia stumbled after her. "Will you tell me what's going on? I came here to ask Stefano to call off Shark after learning that he is Popeye's heir. Now that the game is over, he'll have to quit polluting the preserve, and I don't want his son bothering my daughter. But what are you doing here with David?"

"I added things up and came here to confront Stefano, also." Marla wheeled on her cousin, eyes blazing. "David invited himself along. He's the one who killed Ben Kline and Morton Riley."

"Who? Stefano?"

"No, David. Quick, we don't have much

time." Curses mixed with loud thuds from outside in the corridor. Marla couldn't guess who would win the battle, but it didn't matter. They needed an escape route regardless of the outcome. Her glance scanned the laboratory, resting on a steel door at the far end.

Striding forward, she yanked on the handle and flung open the door, receiving a blast of ice-cold air. Catching a quick glimpse of what lay inside, she hastily shut the insulated cooler door. Vomit rose in her throat, and she swallowed hard. This wasn't the time to be sick. Realizing the function of the room they were in didn't change her plan.

"Listen, do you remember 'Hansel and Gretel'?" Marla said. "I have an idea."

Cynthia's manicured fingers plucked at her silk dress. Her eyes, wide and frightened, snared Marla's. "Are you nuts? What does a fairy tale have to do with our getting away from a killer? I don't get it. How could David have murdered those people, and why?" Knowledge dawned in her expression. "He was going to kill you, too. That's why you were in that horrible coffin. Oh, no!"

Seeing that her cousin was about to have hysterics, Marla held out a steadying hand to grasp Cynthia's shoulder. "Listen to me. David may not have seen you. We can use the element of surprise in our favor. If he comes to get me, I'll lure him closer while you crouch between those tables. I've got to open this cooler door. If you're wise, you won't look inside."

Cynthia had just scurried into cover when David staggered through the doorway. Blood oozed from a cut on his lip, while a purplish bruise darkened one cheekbone. He loped forward like a wolf with a gloating grin on his face.

"Now that I've put those two down, I can take care of you. Let's finish what we started upstairs." At one of the counters, he grabbed a long metal needle and started toward her.

Marla calculated the distance between them. "You told me once that we make good teammates," she said, hoping he wouldn't notice the quaking in her voice. "We can still be partners."

"That's not an option." The murderous gleam in his eyes told her just what he intended. He advanced, holding the needle aloft. On his face was a grin which belied sanity.

Marla backed away until her buttocks tapped the open door of the refrigeration unit, which hinged to the side. David neared, snarling as he moved in for the kill.

"Now!" screamed Marla.

She hadn't known her cousin could move that fast. In a blur of speed, Cynthia shoved David from behind. At the same time, Marla began closing the heavy door. It clanged shut, and together they sealed the latches.

David was trapped inside like the fairy-tale witch in the oven.

20

"You wouldn't believe how calmly Marla faced David when he approached her in that funeral home," Cynthia confided to Eloise Zelman, a wealthy mortgage broker, at Taste of the World. "I hid behind one of those tables they use for, ugh, preparing bodies. If it were me, I'd have been screaming my head off, but Marla kept her cool the whole time."

"You helped put him on ice," Marla added, clinging to the arm of Lieutenant Vail, who looked smashingly handsome in a rented tuxedo. "Now David is in the deep freeze, where he belongs."

Despite what he'd done, she had a hard time picturing Newberg in prison. He'd believed what he was doing was right, but for all the wrong reasons. To preserve his sense of honor, he'd killed people. David couldn't have done a greater dishonor to himself, and yet he didn't realize it.

Twisted minds were beyond her comprehension, more in the sphere of things Vail was accustomed to dealing with in his routine. She didn't envy him his work.

"Marla is a hairdresser," Cynthia said to her friend. "I love how she did my hair, and she gave Annie a great cut, too. You should make an appointment," she urged. "Marla owns the Cut 'N Dye Beauty Salon in Palm Haven."

"Really?" Eloise, a fiftysomething woman who kept her hair an attractive shade of auburn, turned an interested eye on Marla. "How did you come to be involved with Ben Kline's killer?"

"It's a long story." Marla gave her escort a pleading gaze. She didn't want to discuss her recent troubles all night, but people were curious and drawn to lurid details like spectators at an accident.

Vail caught her cue. "Let's go for a drink. Can I get you ladies anything?" he asked the others politely.

"No, thanks," Eloise replied. "My husband Sam is at the bar getting me a strawberry daiquiri. I swear, I'm going to need to work out extra hard after the holidays this year. Cynthia, you should join me."

Her cousin chuckled, and Marla was glad to see her in such a gay mood. "I'm not into group exercise, darling. Besides, Perfect Fit

Sports Club is too far west for me to drive. It's closer to where Marla lives."

"What is?" Tally's voice called from behind.

Letting go of Vail's arm, Marla whirled around. A smile split her face as she regarded Tally and Ken spiffed up for the occasion. Tally, her blond hair in an upsweep, looked great in a black-chiffon creation.

"We're talking about a sports club," Marla explained. "Eloise was saying she'd have to exercise more to wear off the extra calories after all these parties."

"So will I!" Tally exclaimed. "After that big bash you threw at your salon, you might think about it, too." Her eyes sparkled mischievously. "Not that you're ever concerned about your weight. Maybe you should work on muscle power in case you confront any more murderers."

"God forbid!" Vail cried, rolling his eyes. "Come on, Marla, I need a drink." Taking her firmly by the elbow, he steered her away from Tally's bemused glance.

Marla glowed inwardly with satisfaction. All that she'd hoped for had come to pass. Earning her cousin's respect was worth everything she'd suffered. Their fund-raiser was a rousing success, even if it had to be held in tents on Cynthia's extensive estate.

Bruce had even convinced the new trustee that Ocean Guard still met the terms of the agreement.

"It's a good thing Bruce was able to get the preserve cleaned up before tonight," she confided to Vail, as they strolled toward the bar set up on the lawn. Colorful lanterns strung among the trees lit the way, while a jazz band provided musical accompaniment for the festivities. Laughter and a steady hum of chatter sounded through the cool night air. Marla shivered in her skimpy cocktail dress. It had cost a bundle, but she couldn't resist when she'd seen it in Tally's boutique. *Better watch what you eat, or you won't fit into it after tonight,* she warned herself.

Talk about snug outfits. Annie loomed in sight, showing off her youthful figure in a short black skirt and a low-cut top that revealed more cleavage than Marla would ever permit had she a daughter. The girl's textured haircut set off her high cheekbones to advantage. She wore too much makeup, but instead of distracting from her looks, it enhanced them.

"Marla, have you met Cash Halliday? He's a new friend of mine." Annie's heavily mascaraed eyes exuded warmth.

Marla eyed the youth at her side, a gangly

guy wearing baggy pants, a shirt that wasn't tucked in, and an earring stud in his nose. Quite a difference from Shark's conservative image, she thought. At least this fellow's scruffy appearance was more in line with teen culture.

Marla exchanged a few more words after introducing Vail, then watched as the couple strolled away holding hands. "Annie didn't waste any time getting a new boyfriend," she remarked.

"How about you?" Vail said quietly. His dark eyes gleamed as he peered down at her. He seemed taller in the moonlight, sturdy like the trunk of a live oak. Silver highlights glinted in his ebony hair, slicked off his forehead.

How could I ever have been attracted to David? Marla wondered, thrilling to the pure physicality of Vail's presence. The angles of his face sharpened as he turned partly into the shadows. Just being near him made her pulse race. David had never produced that effect. She'd been snowed by his presumed interest in her, just as Annie had been bowled over by Shark. At least both of them knew better by now.

"You're not still jealous over David, are you?" she asked perceptively.

"Huh." Aware that other couples passing

by were giving them curious glances, he indicated they should move on.

"What did you say?" Her heels sank into the soft soil as they headed toward the catering tent.

A flush crept up his face. "I thought you were interested in, uh, seeing me, you know."

"I can see you very clearly right now." A betraying twitch curved her lips.

"Hell, you know what I mean."

"Yeah, you want my exclusive attention. It surprised you when I started going out with David. I have other friends, too, Dalton, and I won't restrict myself to dating just one person. That doesn't mean I'm not interested in finding out where our relationship can go."

Vail's face closed like a curtain. "I see."

"No, you don't." Her voice gentled. "Please understand. I'm afraid of getting burned like I was before, so I can't rush into any commitments. And you're overbearingly protective sometimes; even you have to admit it. I don't like being told what to do."

"Unlike Stan, I respect your abilities, Marla. I'm only concerned for your well-being. You put yourself at risk to catch a murderer twice now."

Didn't things happen in threes? "I know. Next time, I'll swallow my tongue before I volunteer for anything again."

"Impossible." His expression softened, and his mouth quirked into a smile. "Guess I want too much too soon."

"Go on," she teased Vail, "you're just upset because I solved Ben's murder."

"With Newberg's prints and DNA, we've got our case. I have to confess, I was leaning toward Barletti. We knew he was Popeye's heir a while ago, but I couldn't tell you."

She stepped back. "After all I've done, you still don't trust me?"

He grimaced. "When you stick your nose into police business, you can get badly hurt. Most people never see in a lifetime what I do in my line of work. You don't belong there, and I can't help it if I want to protect you from that world. I've lost someone I cared about once already. I don't know how I'd take it if anything happened to you."

His words brought tears to her eyes. Did he really feel so deeply about her? She wasn't ready for this, not now, maybe never. "Your life is in jeopardy every day when you're out in the field. I'm willing to accept that risk, if you can give me the same consideration. Let me find my own way, Dalton."

He plowed a hand through his hair. "All

right, but level with me. Is there a chance that you and I might —"

"Yes . . . no. I don't know." The heat from his body radiated toward her like the rod of a curling iron. Her insides quivered in response. Thinking of rods brought to mind certain male body parts, and that mental picture played havoc with her hormones.

"Did I tell you how much I like that dress?" he rasped, raking her with his dark glance.

"No, but you can tell me now." Moistening her lips, she resisted the urge to move closer.

"We have unfinished business, remember? I promised you something when we said good night after the show with Brianna, but circumstances weren't right when we met again."

He put his hands on her shoulders, and his warmth spiraled through her like a torch. "I'd like to fulfill that promise tonight," he said in a husky tone. "Every time I'm with you, I feel so . . . restless. Don't you feel that way, too?"

"Yes," she whispered. A delicious weakness swept her when his dark gaze lowered to her mouth.

"Maybe that's why I come down so hard

on you about your activities. I'd really rather be coming —"

"What's that?" Anita chimed, moving in with a crowd of relatives. "Marla, why are you lingering here? Go get something to eat. You're too thin."

"Yes, Ma." What lousy timing! Reluctantly, Marla disengaged herself from Vail's overpowering presence. Gads, that man had the power to raise her to a level of tension that cried for release. *Okay, Marla, chill out. You're in a public place here.*

"Nice to see you again, Lieutenant. How are things down at the station? Marla told me you passed accreditation."

"Yes, ma'am."

"So have you cut back on your hours?"

"Well, not quite." He threw Marla a panicked glance, but she ignored him and marched toward the bar. Not that a drink would help. At this rate, she'd need to jump in the pool to cool off before the night was over.

Poor Ma. She'd been disappointed about David. So what if the guy had murdered a few people? He was a nice, Jewish man who happened to be a wealthy accountant. *Too bad, Ma, he'll need his bankroll to pay the lawyers. So will Stefano, who's being charged with illegally dumping medical waste on private property.*

She detoured to a food station offering freshly prepared crepes. "Hey, Pierre. Glad you decided to join us at the last minute."

The stout French chef blustered at her approval, his white toque wobbling on his head. "Once you found out Barletti paid zat son-of-a-gun assistant to tamper with my expensive rum, I realized what a fool I was. *Mon dieu!* Who would have thought a funeral home owner was behind all our troubles?" He shifted the sauté pan in his hand. "I see you brought Alex Sheffield back to Taste of the World. You've got *chutzpah*, no?"

Helping herself to a plateful of mushroom crepes, Marla laughed. "I just don't let anything, or anyone, get in my way."

Author's Note

Dear Reader:

HAIR RAISER was fun to write because I could talk about one of my favorite subjects: food. With all the chefs signed up for Taste of the World and Marla's trip to the Bahamas, I delighted in describing the different meals she encountered. Her adventure in Nassau followed my own journey where I diligently scribbled notes and sampled the cuisine. Similarly, Marla's feast with David takes place in a fictional Moroccan restaurant that bears a strong resemblance to a Fort Lauderdale dining establishment. Another area attraction turned into cousin Cynthia's estate in the story. If you visit Fort Lauderdale during the balmy winter season, be sure to tour Bonnet House. Lush tropical gardens at the beachfront mansion are a tribute to the region.

If you thought Marla's troubles were over after she stopped dating David by the end of HAIR RAISER, wait until you see what happens between her and Dalton Vail in the next book, MURDER BY MANICURE. Vail's jealousy over David pales in comparison to the mess Marla lands herself in next. And if you haven't yet read PERMED TO DEATH, the first book in *The Bad Hair Day Mysteries*, I hope you'll run right out and get it!

I love to hear from readers, so please write to me, P. O. Box 17756, Plantation, FL 33318, or e-mail me at *ncane@worldnet.att.net* or *http://nancyjcohen.com* and I'll answer you personally.

Nancy J. Cohen

About the Author

Nancy J. Cohen earned a bachelor's degree in nursing from the University of Rochester and a master's degree from University of California in San Francisco. After working for several years as a clinical nurse specialist, she retired to assume writing as a full-time career. HAIR RAISER is her second mystery novel and the first book in The Bad Hair Day mystery series. Nancy J. Cohen lives in Florida with her husband and two teenage children.

The employees of Thorndike Press hope you have enjoyed this Large Print book. All our Thorndike and Wheeler Large Print titles are designed for easy reading, and all our books are made to last. Other Thorndike Press Large Print books are available at your library, through selected bookstores, or directly from us.

For information about titles, please call:

(800) 223-1244

or visit our Web site at:

www.gale.com/thorndike
www.gale.com/wheeler

To share your comments, please write:

Publisher
Thorndike Press
295 Kennedy Memorial Drive
Waterville, ME 04901